*That's how you _____ _____?
he thought. You ____ ___ ___ world Francis
Kincaid first and the rest of us be damned. You
were always that way and combat hasn't
changed you.*

"How was everyone when you left the States?"
Francis asked. *Eileen?* he wanted to ask. *How is
Eileen? Why doesn't she write?*

Jerry's working full-time with Henry at Kurkin.
Business is booming, what with the war. Henry's still
spending money as though it grew on trees. Bought
a new touring car for himself and a pony for the kids."
*You want to know about Eileen, don't you? You'll have
to ask.*

"And Eileen?"

"Better. Still in New York. In her last letter she
said she was working part time in a hospital there.
Presbyterian, I think."

"Better? Was she sick?"

"Didn't you know?"

"She never said a word about it to me. What was
wrong? She's all right, isn't she?"

You bastard; Martin thought. *You were what was
wrong.* He clenched his fists and glanced across the
room. Why didn't that fool stop playing the same
record over and over? "Ah! Sweet Mystery of Life."
He'd never liked the song anyway. Francis did seem
surprised about Eileen. He might be telling the truth.
Maybe he didn't know.

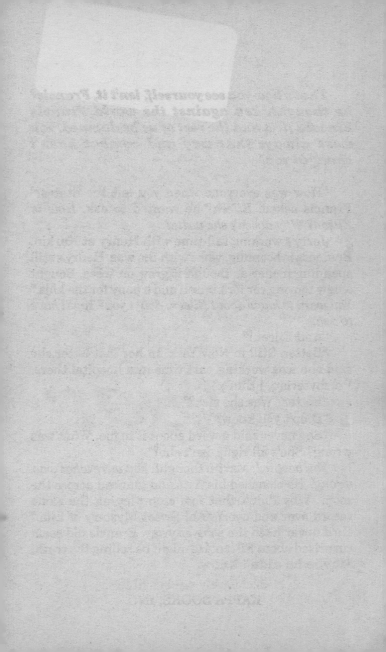

Birds of War

JANE TOOMBS

Exclusively published by
KAPPA BOOKS, INC.

© 1997 by Jane Toombs

Published by: Kappa Books, Inc.
Fort Washington, PA 19034

Manufactured in the United States of America.
ISBN: 1-56682-038-3

1

FRANCIS Kincaid pulled back on the stick and the nose of his Kurkin Plymouth pointed skyward, rising higher and higher until the biplane seemed to pause for a moment on its tail before it dropped over so Francis hung upside down, suspended from the straps holding him in the open cockpit. The plane dived toward the ground, down, down, down, the green of the Massachusetts countryside rushing up to meet him until he again pulled back and, with a shudder, the biplane righted itself.

Francis grinned. He hadn't lost his touch despite his three weeks on the ground since Deborah came down with intermittent fever. Thank God she was getting better. And thank God Eileen had decided to stay on at the house to help. He closed his eyes, recalling Eileen's long jet-black hair, the challenge in her brown eyes.

He began to climb toward the nearest of the scattered cumulus clouds, plunging inside the gray moistness, pushing his goggles up onto his helmet when he felt the cool damp on his face. He was free! Here in the sky he was his own man, accountable to no one.

Suddenly his biplane burst from the top of the cloud into the warmth of the everlasting sun where the blue sky stretched endlessly around him, to the far horizons, up to the heavens themselves. His heart leaped with awe and wonder.

You're too old to still feel this way, he told himself. For an aviator, you're an old man. Thirty. Married for more than ten years. A father for almost as long.

"Time you were thinking of settling down," his brother Henry had told him the week before. "You should stop ramming around, pay more attention to the business."

"Go to hell," he'd told his brother, joking yet meaning what he said.

They could all go to hell, his brother Henry and the Kurmans, too. Except for Eileen. He smiled, remembering coming on Eileen the day before in the dimness of the walnut-panelled library.

With an impatient shake of his head he pushed the memory to one side. That had been there, down on the earth he now glimpsed between the clouds. Just as the roads, the ponds, the villages and the farms seemed diminished, so did Henry and the Kurmans. So, too, did the war spreading across Europe. Even Deborah, her fever broken at last. Even his son, nine-year-old Bill, worried about his mother, though he tried not to show it.

Francis climbed, leveling off at 6,000 feet with the August sun warm on his face, the Plymouth hundred-horsepower engine roaring steadily, the pungent odors of castor oil and gas mingling with the foulness of the exhaust fumes. He breathed them in with pleasure. If only he could fly on and on forever.

Knowing he couldn't, Francis glanced at his wristwatch. Damn! Two-thirty already. That meant he had enough fuel in the tank beneath his seat for only another fifteen minutes. A damn-fool place to put the fuel tank, he thought for perhaps the hundredth time. But then Martin Kurman was something of a fool. A stubborn fool.

Reluctantly he climbed, banked to the left and headed back toward the Kurkin field. Looking over the side of his cockpit he saw the humped top of a cloud rising slowly to meet him.

Too slowly.

He yanked down his goggles, pushed the stick ahead and the plane's nose pointed earthward. He dived into the cloud, plunging down and down, breaking out under the cloud, wings and struts straining as his dive steepened, the air stinging his face, his heart racing as he relived Arch Hoxsey's Dive of Death, the stunt Hoxsey repeated once too often, crashing, the final time, to his death in front of the grandstand in Los Angeles. In 1910. He could hardly believe it had been four years ago.

Below him Francis saw a field, trees, a road. Rushing up at him. Drawing his plane to them. For an awful, exhilarating instant he froze, unable to move, his heart thudding in his chest. And then he pulled back. The plane responded, shuddering and groaning. He swooped over the tops of the trees, hearing himself laugh, feeling the sweat under his arms.

He laughed too shrilly, he thought. It frightened him sometimes. Not the dive. Not the danger. He was frightened by his own feelings. Someday he wouldn't pull out.

Shit!

He'd die when his time came, no sooner. Once you threw the dice your life was out of your hands. The only way to avoid the inevitable was to quit the game. He'd never do that. Life was to live.

He circled to the west so he'd land heading into the wind off the Atlantic. On the ground ahead of him, in the sunlight between the racing shadows of the clouds, he saw a long trail of dust from an auto speeding toward the Kurkin airfield three miles away. The shadow of his plane followed the car, neither gaining nor losing. That car's going like hell, he decided. A mile a minute at least.

Looking more closely he recognized the auto's yellow hood and fenders. The Mercer Raceabout, Eileen's car. He smiled, opening the throttle, trying to overtake her, but the steady breeze held him back. The Plymouth's top speed was 64 miles an hour.

He wigwagged his wings, trying to attract Eileen's attention, all the while realizing it was no use. She was coming to the field to drive him home. He breathed deeply, anticipating being with her, and he sang softly to himself:

> You're a pretty baby
> That's why I'm in love with you.

Pretty baby.
Pretty baby.

Again he remembered going into the library and watching Eileen as she stretched to reach a book on a high shelf, her full breasts straining against the green silk of her dress. He stepped behind her, breathing in the scent of lilies-of-the-valley.

"Let me help," he said.

When he reached over her head his arm brushed her shoulder and she turned to look at him, her brown eyes glistening, her mouth slightly open, her black hair framing her pale face. He drew in his breath.

"You startled me," she said.

She wants me to kiss her, Francis thought. He lowered his hand to touch the ruffled cloth of her sleeve.

Eileen stepped back. "Deborah's better," she said, her voice almost a whisper.

He let out his breath, watching her, their eyes meeting. What did her eyes promise? She looked away as though confused and walked quickly from the library without a backward glance. She was almost running. You'd think she was a schoolgirl, Francis thought, not a twenty-three-year-old woman who'd only laid aside her widow's black the year before . . .

Francis circled the field once, cut off his motor, and set the Kurkin Plymouth down easily. As he unstrapped himself, he was conscious of Eileen standing near the hangar, her hands clasped in front of her. God, she was lovely. He leaped to the ground, pulled his helmet from his blond hair, and strode across the field.

"Francis," she said urgently when he was still twenty feet from her.

He smiled but she didn't smile back. Her brown eyes seemed to be trying to tell him something. To warn him. Of what? He stopped, frowning.

"Deborah's taken a turn for the worse." He could tell she was trying to keep her voice calm and matter-of-fact. "Dr. Thompson's with her now. He sent me to get you. To bring you home."

He stared at her, not fully understanding. "How is she?" he asked.

"She's dying, Francis." Tears glistened in her eyes. "Deborah's dying."

2

Eileen had left the Raceabout's motor running.

"I'll drive," Francis told her.

She started to object, then nodded and climbed into the bucket seat beside him. He shifted and the auto, purring throatily, bounced over the rutted track beside the hangar and onto the dirt road leading to Plymouth.

"What happened?" he asked.

"It was just after you left on your motorcycle." Eileen reached under her seat, found a pair of goggles and fitted the straps over her black hair under her hat. The monocle windshield on the Mercer Raceabout's steering column protected only the driver.

"All at once her fever grew worse," Eileen went on. "When it got to a hundred and two, I called Dr.

Thompson. Deborah was unconscious by the time he arrived."

"And I thought she was getting better. I could have sworn she was."

"We all thought so. Now Dr. Thompson's calling what she has a relapsing fever. That's the way of the disease, he says, it comes back when you least expect it. When you think the patient's recovering."

"Relapsing fever doesn't *sound* serious."

"It's not just the fever. The disease affects the kidneys, too, or the liver, I forget which he said. The doctor told me, but I forget."

Francis stared ahead at the road. He held the Raceabout at sixty and dust streamed behind the car in a billowing wake. Eileen put her hand on his sleeve.

"Oh, Francis," she said, "I hate to see you hurt again. After what happened to Curt last year." She paused. "And I'm very fond of Deborah. That goes without saying."

He slowed imperceptibly for the turn at Reynolds' Woods. Swinging left, he pumped the brake and the car skidded. He turned into the skid and the Raceabout straightened and sprang forward. They were silent, awkwardly so.

Francis saw a trail of dust from a car jouncing slowly in front of them.

"A damn Model T," he muttered.

He squeezed the bulb at his side, the horn honking, "*Augh-wah, augh-wah*," as he swung wide and passed. He glanced at Eileen who sat grimacing from the dust, her mouth tight.

"This is one hell of a car," he told her.

"The auto salesman who drove it here from their

factory in New Jersey guaranteed me it would go seventy-five miles an hour."

Seeing Eileen settle back in her seat now that he'd given her a safe subject to talk about, Francis pressed down on the accelerator and the speedometer edged to sixty-five. To seventy.

"He was right," Eileen said. "I've gone seventy-five. Not here, on South Pond Road."

"No complaints? The Raceabout's all you thought she'd be?"

"I love her. I hate getting stuck in the mud, though. A farmer had to pull me out with his team last week. And the tires have a way of blowing out at the worst times."

He slowed as they passed Forest Hill Cemetery. After turning right and driving along Warren Avenue, he entered Chiltonville. At his house, a large white Victorian with elaborate scrollwork around the edges of the roof, he eased the car into the semi-circular drive past the ancient dying elm and stopped in front of the porch.

Francis jumped out and was at the bottom of the steps before he looked back at Eileen.

"Don't wait for me," she told him.

He climbed the steps two at a time and hurried inside, leaving the door open behind him. The front hall was dim and cool. He started up the curving stairs but stopped halfway to the top when he saw Dr. Thompson watching him from the upper hall. The two men stared at one another.

"How—?" Francis began.

The balding, heavy-set physician shook his head. "She's a very sick young woman," he said.

As Francis climbed to the upper hall, the doctor

held out his hand and, after an awkward moment, Francis realized he wanted to shake his hand. They clasped hands and, as they walked down the dim hall, the older man put a fatherly arm on Francis' shoulder.

Benny Stouffer, Eileen's three-year-old son, peered at them from around a door. Anne, the hired girl, appeared in the doorway, saw the two men approaching and, taking Benny's hand, hurried him back into the room.

The door to the sickroom was open. Dr. Thompson stood aside, nodding to Francis, motioning him to go in. Francis paused in the doorway. Deborah's face was yellow against the white pillows and her cheeks and forehead glistened with perspiration. Her hands were clasped on top of the white coverlet. Her eyes were closed.

Francis crossed the room and knelt at her side. "Debbie," he said. He heard the door close behind him and, looking around, saw that he was alone. He felt lost. Abandoned. "Debbie," he said again, louder this time.

Her eyes didn't open. She didn't seem to be breathing. He started to call to the doctor when all at once she took a breath, a long, shuddering gasp of air, and was still again.

Francis stared at his wife in fascinated horror. Tears stung his eyes and he felt his throat tighten. Gingerly, he touched her bare shoulder. Her skin was warm. Again she drew in a shuddering breath. A lock of her brown hair had fallen across her forehead.

Francis glanced around the room, looking for a pair of scissors. He wanted to cut off the lock of hair and save it. He didn't see a scissors. He shook his head, ashamed to be thinking of himself instead of Debbie, thinking of her as already dead when she wasn't.

He leaned forward and kissed her gently on the cheek. "Debbie," he said softly. "What am I going to do without you?"

Francis stood at his bedroom window looking across the moon-silvered lawn. In the distance he heard the bell of the Plymouth Congregational Church toll eleven. The tree frogs in the field across the street stilled as though they, too, were listening, and then resumed their rhythmic croaking louder than before.

He crossed the room and walked quickly along the hall past the locked gun case and down the front stairs. Though the sleeping house was dark, he found his way easily. Stopping in the hall, he paused in front of the closed door to the parlor. Taking a deep breath and letting it out with a sigh, he opened the door and stepped into the room.

Two candles burned on each side of the coffin. Flowers were banked along the sides of the room and around the head of the closed casket. The Stowes, Deborah's parents, had wanted to have an open coffin, but Francis had refused.

"I want to remember her the way I knew her," he'd said. "Alive."

"We respect your wishes, Francis," Mother Stowe told him, "though it does seem a shame. She had so many friends who'll want to see her for the last time. To pay their respects." Mother Stowe dabbed at her eyes with a handkerchief.

Why not just say I'm selfish? Francis wanted to

ask. You have often enough in the past. Why not now?

He brushed the memory aside as he walked across the parlor and approached the coffin. He knelt on the thick pile of the carpet and stared at the whorls carved on the side of the dark mahogany. Bowing his head, he repeated the Lord's Prayer, skipping the parts he couldn't recall.

After murmuring, "Amen," he shook his head angrily. Why am I kneeling here like this? he asked himself. She's not here. Debbie's not here. Her body will be buried at Forest Hill tomorrow but she's gone. She's been dead for two days. Once you're dead, that's the end of it. Funerals were a barbaric custom.

Francis stood up. All at once he felt dizzy and he reached out and put his hand on the top of his wife's coffin to steady himself. He felt stunned by his loss; he still couldn't really believe Debbie was dead. He was angry at her for leaving him with a nine-year-old son to raise even while realizing his anger was foolish.

And he was angry at himself—ashamed of himself—because of the many times he could have been with her and wasn't. Because of the flying. Because of the business, Kurkin Flight Research. He'd meant to make it up to her somehow, someday, but now he never could. As far as Debbie was concerned, it was too late for everything except regret.

He needed her. He'd always thought of himself as erratic, never able or wanting to follow a straight course, veering off in this direction or that. He'd depended on Debbie to be his rudder, to be there when he needed her to remind him of his responsibilities. Now he had no one to help him, to guide him.

And he wanted her, wanted her physically. Shocked by the knowledge of his need, he still had to admit its truth. In his frustration he pounded his fist on the top of the coffin. His blows echoed in the room. Dully, hollowly.

He sensed that someone was behind him, watching him. He stood, letting his hands fall to his sides, and turned slowly toward the door where he saw a figure silhouetted against the lesser darkness of the hall. A woman wearing a long flowing white robe.

"Eileen," he said.

"I heard a noise. I was afraid. I thought—I don't know what I thought."

As he walked to her, he breathed in the scent of lilies-of-the-valley. Eileen always smelled of flowers.

"I couldn't sleep," he said. "I was restless. Kept listening for the church bells and counting the chimes. So I got dressed and came down here."

"I'll make you some coffee."

"Coffee will only keep me awake."

"A glass of milk then."

"All right."

He followed her through the dining room into the kitchen, switching on the overhead light before sitting at the oilcloth covered table. He watched her go into the pantry where he heard her open and close the icebox. She returned with a bottle of milk, removed the cardboard cap, poured two glassfuls and sat across from him.

"I'm so very sorry." Her brown eyes glistened and he knew she'd been crying. "If there's anything I can do, tell me. What with Marty and Jerry driving down and father flying in from Boston, I haven't had a chance to tell you how terrible I feel."

"Do you know what your brother Martin told me this morning?" he asked.

"No."

"He said he'd always liked Debbie. Not everything about her, he said, but he'd always been fond of her even though there were things he didn't especially like about her. I wanted to punch him in the mouth."

"He was just trying to tell the truth. He doesn't believe in glossing things over. He's like father that way, like Leon. Jerome's more of a diplomat. He always wants everybody to get along."

He found himself staring at her. She'd unfastened her black hair so it cascaded around her shoulders. Her white robe, wrapped tightly about her and tied with a sash in the front, emphasized the narrowness of her waist and the swell of her breasts. He put his empty glass on the oilcloth harder than he'd intended. Eileen jumped.

"Sorry," he said.

"Some more milk?"

He shook his head and got up, waiting while she put the bottle in the icebox. When she came back and was about to walk past him he switched off the light and she brushed against him in the darkness. He followed her to the hall where he paused a moment to glance into the dark parlor before going up the stairs behind her. They were almost to the top when a voice cried out.

Eileen drew in her breath and stopped, grasping the rail.

Francis glanced behind him in the direction of the parlor and then looked past Eileen into the darkness of the upper hall.

"It's someone up here," he said.

She walked swiftly and quietly ahead of him along the hall. When she stopped near the locked sickroom to listen, he almost ran into her. The scent of lilies-of-the-valley was all around him. He heard sobs.

"Billy," she whispered.

They stopped in front of his son's closed door. The sobs came from inside.

"I'll wait here," she said.

He eased past her into the small room. In the moonlight slanting through the window he saw Billy sitting up in bed. The boy, his hands to his face, cried softly.

"It's all right, Billy." Francis sat on the edge of the bed and drew the boy into his arms. "Don't cry, son," he said. "I'm here."

Billy pressed his head to his father's chest and after a few moments his sobs lessened.

"I thought—" Billy drew in a choked breath. "I thought I heard someone out there." He nodded toward the window.

"I'll take a look." From the window Francis saw the great oaks looming darkly against the moonlit sky.

"There's no one outside," he said. "You had a dream. A nightmare."

"I heard someone. At the window. Like they were trying to get in."

"It must have been a tree limb brushing against the side of the house. I'll cut it off in the morning."

"I thought it was her." Francis knew the boy meant his mother. Pain stabbed through him. What can I tell him? he wondered. How can I explain any better about death than I already have?

"This weekend," he said, "if the good weather holds, I'll take you up in the Plymouth. We'll fly to Boston and I'll buy you a soda at Crain's."

"You will?" Billy's voice was eager. "You won't forget?"

As I've forgotten so many things so many times before, Francis thought.

"Cross my heart and hope—" Francis stopped abruptly. "Cross my heart. We'll fly up Sunday afternoon if the weather's good." He sat on the bed. "Lie back," he said. "Aviators need all the sleep they can get. You can't be flying along at a thousand feet and start dozing off."

"Tell me about how they flew across the English Channel." Billy settled back.

"The London *Daily Mail* offered a prize, a thousand pounds I think it was, for the first aviator to fly from France to England. That was five years ago, in 1909. Two men were ready to make the attempt, an Englishman named Hubert Latham and Louis Blériot, a Frenchman. Your uncle Henry and I were with Blériot, of course, because Henry's wife, your Aunt Marie, is his niece . . ."

As he related the now-familiar tale, he heard Billy's breathing deepen and knew the boy had fallen asleep. Francis pulled the sheet up over his son, leaned over and kissed him, then quietly left the room.

The hall was empty. Eileen's door was slightly ajar and a light burned inside, the soft glow of a candle rather than the harsh yellow of the electric ceiling light. Francis paused, looking first to his left toward his own room and then right at the rectangle of light on the hall floor.

He tapped almost soundlessly on her door.

"Come in." Her voice was a whisper.

When he pushed the door open, he saw the flame of a single candle on top of the secretary against the opposite wall. Eileen stood beside the desk, one hand resting on its high top, staring at him, her brown eyes sparkling in the candlelight. She wore a white, diaphanous nightgown; her robe lay folded over the back of a chair.

He didn't know what to do or say.

She picked up the candleholder, raised it and leaned forward and blew out the flame. The room was suddenly dark and he realized the shades had been pulled down. He stood, unmoving, with the scent of lilies-of-the-valley enveloping him. Her hand touched his wrist.

He drew her into his arms and, as he kissed her, her mouth opened to his and he tensed in surprise. Their tongues met and he kissed her hungrily as her hands went around his neck. She pressed herself against him so he felt the length of her body touching his, her breasts on his chest, her thighs against his.

He led her to the bed She took her hand from his and slipped beneath the covers. He drew the covers down and lay beside her, reaching down to pull up her nightgown. Her hands stopped him.

He felt her sit up in the bed and heard her pull the nightgown over her head and let it fall on the far side of the bed. He rolled from the bed, stood up and removed his clothes. When he slid in beside Eileen he took her in his arms, kissing her. Feeling her warm flesh against his, he began to tremble. She cradled him in her arms, crooning to him as she might to a baby.

"You don't have to do anything," she said. "Just let me hold you."

He let himself relax in the circle of her arms, savoring the comforting warmth of her body. Desire left him. He lay with his cheek nestled in her hair, letting himself be soothed by her voice, by the softness of her, by the gentle caress of her hand on his hair.

After a time her hand stilled. The house was quiet; far away the churchbell tolled one. Francis closed his eyes and slept. He woke in the dark of night with his arm thrown across a woman's breast and for an instant he wondered where he was, thinking that Deborah had come to him during the night.

Then he remembered and sat up and tried to make out the features of the woman lying on her back next to him. Her breathing told him she slept. Suddenly he was aroused, knew a desire greater than any he could remember. When he touched her bare shoulder with the tips of his fingers, she moaned in her sleep and turned to him.

"Eileen," he whispered.

She murmured words he couldn't make out.

"Eileen," he said, louder this time.

She drew in her breath and he knew she was awake. Leaning to her, he touched her cheek with his lips, seeking her mouth. When he kissed her he found her mouth closed to him. She turned her head away but he pursued her with his lips, his tongue probing into her mouth as his hands slid down her bare body to her hips, to her thighs, and finally between her legs. She twisted away, closing herself to him, but he thrust his hand savagely between her legs and, with a gasp, she opened them to him.

He entered her quickly. She clutched him to her, crying out and then, as though she had, these last two years, held her emotions, her love, in check until her need passed all endurance, she hurled herself at Francis, biting and clawing him, kissing him, nipping his lips with her teeth, arching to meet him, her body wild and demanding. He thrust within her, feeling his passion mount until, with a half-suppressed cry of release he throbbed within her, feeling her rise to join his passion.

"Oh, God," she said a few minutes later. Her breath still came in short, quick gasps. He expected her to accuse him but instead she sighed. "It's been so long," she said. "So very long."

He left the bed and went to the window where he pulled up the shade and stared out over the silvered lawn to the road and the fields beyond. The moon was low over the trees in the west.

"Are you all right?" she asked from the bed.

"I'm fine," he said. "I don't feel guilty, if that's what you mean."

"That's not what I meant. But I don't either. Feel guilty, I mean. Not yet, anyway."

"I'll never feel guilty again," Francis said, "about anything. After all, what difference does it make? Whatever we do, however we act, whether we're saints or sinners, we all end up the same. When our time comes we die and that's the end of it."

"I don't believe that," she said quietly. "We're all here for a purpose. We're meant to help others, not hurt them. I've hurt people in my life, Francis.

No more. Never again. If I thought that what we did tonight could possibly hurt anyone . . ."

"You were wonderful, Eileen." As soon as he spoke he realized his words were wrong, yet he didn't know what else to say to her.

She left the bed and came to stand beside him at the open window, her naked body shimmering palely in the first light of early morning.

"I don't want you to think," she said, "because of what happened between us tonight . . . Don't think this will happen again."

He turned and gently touched the black hair curling across her shoulder and falling to cover the top of her breast. "I've only just now found you," he said.

"I'll have to leave tomorrow. I couldn't stay longer. Not after tonight."

He leaned to her, kissing her, feeling her nipples brush against his chest. She returned his kiss, her hands on his face, and then she slipped away from him and drew on her robe.

"I have to see you again," he said.

"You will. In Boston. At Father's. At the Kurkin directors' meetings. Perhaps at the next air meet. If I have a chance at the next meet, I'll come to you."

He grasped her arm. "There must be another way."

He said the first thing that entered his mind. "Do you want to learn to fly?" he asked. "I could teach you."

"My father won't approve. Leon's dead set against my flying. Because of what happened to Curt. He doesn't even like Martin and Jerome flying anymore, though there's nothing he can do about it."

"We won't tell Leon. Your father need never know."

"He'd find out. Sooner or later he finds out everything that Jerome and Martin and I do. He makes it his business to know what his children do. His family means more to him than anything else in the world."

"But you want to learn to fly?" Something told him not to press her but, perversely, he did anyway.

"Yes, I always have. And I want to be with you. Though I don't think I should. Do either one, I mean."

He kissed her. When he drew away almost at once, she gasped, clinging to him.

"But you will?"

"Damn it, you know I will. Now get out of my room and let me get some sleep before it's time . . . before I have to get up."

After dressing hurriedly, Francis carried his shoes in his hand as he padded along the hall to his room. Once inside, he leaned back against the door.

"Before it's time for the funeral," Eileen had been going to say. He didn't usually believe in omens, but still he shivered with apprehension.

3

JEROME Kurman nosed his Kurkin X down toward the fog bank laying offshore over Plymouth Bay.

All right so far, he told himself. He glanced at his compass and saw the needle indicating that north lay to his left. No problem there. Not yet, anyway. He listened to the throb of the Kurkin water-cooled radial engine. Did he detect a missed beat? He leaned forward, listening more intently. He frowned. The rhythm seemed wrong.

Jerome debated whether or not to return to the Kurkin airfield. Don't be an ass, he told himself, it's your imagination. Hadn't he checked the plane meticulously before taking off? As he always did? He cursed his uneasiness as he headed for the gray-white bank of fog just off Gurnet Point.

Jerome Kurman flew with a constant companion. Fear.

He'd always been cautious. Ever since he learned to fly.

"By the time you finish checking the damn plane," Francis had told him once years before, "it'll be too dark to go up."

Jerome had laughed. He could laugh at himself then. Since his brother Curt's death the year before, though, his natural caution had turned to fear. A fear that became an enemy to be fought but, it seemed, never defeated. An enemy lurking in the thunderheads over the mountains in summer, in the autumn rain squalls sweeping in off the Atlantic, in the air pockets that caused his plane to plunge earthward for frightening seconds on the clearest days, lurking in the plane itself, in the engine, the fragile linen wings, the erratic instruments.

Though unable to conquer his fear, he hadn't let it conquer him. Jerome smiled grimly. He hadn't quit. He'd considered grounding himself, giving up flying for once and all, but he'd rejected the idea. Kurmans weren't quitters. Not his father Leon, not his brother Marty, not his sister Eileen.

Quite the opposite. Wasn't Eileen learning to fly? He shook his head unhappily.

"Whatever you do, Jerry," Eileen said to him, *don't tell Father.*"

"Why in God's name would I do that?"

"Because you know Francis is teaching me. You and Marty have always had it in for Francis."

"That's not true. You're imagining things."

"Marty envies him," she said, "because Francis is a better flyer than he can ever hope to be. And both of you still blame Francis for what happened to Curt."

"Nobody made Curt go up. Nobody forced him to try an inside loop. Francis didn't put a gun to Curt's head and tell him to perform aerobatics that had never been done before."

"Oh, Jerry." Eileen put her arms around her brother and buried her face against his chest. "I miss Curt so."

They held one another, remembering Curt's Kurkin climbing, looping over, diving. They waited for Curt to pull out. Diving. He had to pull out. Now. Diving, diving. The upper wing crumpled and tore free, twirling from side to side like a leaf above the crippled aircraft, the Kurkin spinning earthward, the other wing shredding, Curt pushing himself from the cockpit as though intending to leap from the plane, the Kurkin crashing on the far side of the field. Men running, calling out. Julia, Curt's wife, sobbing. The plane burning, exploding, leaving a pitiful smoldering jumble of wood and canvas. Curt's body charred, unrecognizable.

Jerome hated Francis Kincaid. Not because of Curt. Every aviator flew with death, it was part of the game. When you couldn't take it anymore, you quit. If you didn't quit you paid the price and had no one to blame but yourself.

He didn't hate Francis because of the other man's skill; he envied him that. Francis was a great pilot, one of the best. If he ever learned to hold his rashness in check, he'd be the best there was. Francis had a God-given gift. His every instinct was right. Once in the air, Francis didn't have to think, to plan, he met every emergency with the right countermove. He was a gifted pilot. And lucky. The chances that man took! And walked away afterwards with that cocky lopsided grin on his face.

Nor did he hate Francis because of Eileen.

"I hope you know what you're doing," Jerome told his sister, realizing he sounded like a prig.

"Don't lecture me, Jerry. Two people in the family telling me what to do are enough." They were sitting facing one another in the swing on the front porch of the Kurman house in Plymouth.

"I only want you to be happy," Jerome said. *God, you're a stuffy bastard,* he thought.

"And I am happy, Jerry. As long as I can lead my own life I'll be happy. Sometimes I wonder why all Kurman men think they know better than I do what's right for me. It's not as though I was planning to *marry* Francis."

"Good God, I hope not." The idea had never occurred to him before.

"After all, I've already been married to a *goy.* My next attempt will probably be with a nice Jewish boy from New York City. I think Father would approve of a doctor or a dentist, don't you? In fact, he probably has one all picked out and waiting in the wings."

When he saw her smile, he realized she was teasing him.

"You know I don't have much of a sense of humor," Jerome said.

"A Kurman curse. No sense of humor, I mean."

"Are there others?"

"Curses? Gosh, yes. Worrying so much about the family is one. The business is another. First the department store and now Kurkin Flight Research. Ever since I can remember it's been the family this, the business that. Damn Father. Damn the family. Damn the business!"

"You shouldn't talk like that, Eileen, even if you're joking. It's bad luck."

"Do you think Jehovah or Satan actually bothers to listen to me? Other men don't seem to, so why should they?"

"You should want the business to succeed," Jerome said. "And want the family to stick together. You should be proud of what Father has made of Kurkin. Look at all he's done and he's only forty-four."

"Yet he's not the oldest of the Kurmans. You are. I think you were born sixty-years-old."

"I can't help it if I'm serious. Life's a serious business."

"Is it? Is it really, Jerry? Life's so short. You have to live all you can while you can."

"You've been listening to Francis Kincaid again. The voice is the voice of Eileen Kurman, but the words are the words of Francis."

"That's from the Bible, isn't it? You're becoming the family scholar."

"At least one of us should take our heritage seriously."

"Oh, Jerry, you're so exasperating." She took his hand and pulled him from the swing, leading him down the porch steps. "Get your bike, Jerry. Let's pedal to the lake and go swimming."

"You'll make sandwiches?"

She nodded.

"And bring Benny?"

"You really like Benny, don't you?" she asked.

"I love him."

"I suppose that's why I can forgive you being sixty years old," she said, "when you're really only twenty-four. Because you love my son."

"He's a Kurman. His last name may be Stouffer, but he's a Kurman."

"All right, you win." Eileen raised her right hand. "I'll swear an oath. The Kurman family comes first. The Kurman business comes second. No sense of humor is third." She smiled fondly up at him. "You bring the bikes from the garage while I pack our lunch. What'll it be? Strawberry jam? Cream cheese? Salmon salad?"

Jerome smiled, remembering. No, he told himself, he didn't hate Francis because of Eileen. She'd soon get over her infatuation. He didn't blame her. Francis, blond, blue-eyed, slender, was good-looking and had a certain *sang-froid*, that was all. After a few years she'd marry again and he wouldn't be at all surprised if her new husband turned out to be a dentist or a doctor.

The reason he hated Francis was because Francis knew. Jerome had no idea how Francis had discovered his secret. Yet Francis knew. Jerome could see it in the other man's eyes, hear it when he talked, could tell by the way he acted. Francis had always been impatient with him, had accused him of being as cautious as an old maid, but now Francis' irritation was laced with disdain.

Francis knew he was afraid. Yellow, Francis would have said.

Damn Francis Kincaid.

Jerome flew above the fog bank at a thousand feet with wisps of moisture drifting past his open cockpit. The October sky over his head was a deep

deep blue, autumn-hued woods rolled inland to his right while below the fog lay the gray waters of Plymouth Bay and the Atlantic.

He nosed his plane down into the fog, drawing in his breath, waiting. He felt nothing. Hope rose in him. Perhaps today would be different. Perhaps—

He glanced at the compass but couldn't read it. He lifted his fog-beaded goggles onto his helmet. The compass needle wavered erratically. Damn. Instruments only worked right when you didn't need them. The altimeter read eight hundred feet. Fog eddied and swirled around him. The plane was falling, he could sense it.

Without thinking, he looked for the horizon and saw only the dense, enveloping fog. Fear gripped him and he tasted bile at the back of his throat. Pulling the stick, he felt the plane rise. He had to get out of this damn fog. He rose higher and higher until the Kurkin emerged from the top of the fog bank into sunlight. His climb, he realized now that he could see the horizon, was too steep. He eased forward on the stick. Too late. The motor coughed, stalled, and the aircraft hung suspended in space, nose up.

The plane fell, slowly at first, then faster and faster. Plunged into the fog once more. Panic gripped him. Oh my God, he thought, oh my God. The plane twisted earthward in a tailspin like a falling leaf. He switched the motor on. Nothing. He switched off and on again. Still nothing, the engine refused to catch.

The fog pressed in around him. The waters of the Bay were a scant three hundred feet below. The plane twirled downward. Jerome grasped the straps holding him in the cockpit. Should he unsnap the buckle and leap from the falling plane before it was too late?

He remembered Curt, again pictured his brother trying to climb from his cockpit as the wings tore off. Down, down, down he plummeted. Death waited in the water below. Jerome screamed in terror. Frantic, he switched the motor on again. It coughed once and caught. His pulse thundered. Drawing slowly back on the stick while centering the rudder, he felt his body being pressed against the seat.

The plane leveled. The mist thinned and looking over the side he saw, twenty feet below him, the dark waters of the Bay punctuated by an occasional white-cap. The Kurkin sped over the surface of the water before climbing into the fog once more. Higher and higher he rose, the engine roaring throatily.

The plane burst from the fog into the sun. A beach stretched ahead of him with cottages beyond. A man stood on the sand looking up and waving at him. Jerome glanced right and left. The fabric covering the wings looked intact. He pulled a handkerchief from his pocket and mopped fog and sweat from his face.

Jerome cursed himself. He'd panicked just as he'd feared he would. Like a greenhorn. He'd never lick it, he told himself. Why had the motor started when it did? he wondered. Had the steep dive spun the propeller and primed the engine? He'd ask Francis what he thought. No, not Francis, if he asked him he'd have to admit what had happened. Maybe Marty would have an idea. He filed the incident in a corner of his mind.

As he neared the field he saw another plane below his horizon. When he flew closer, he recognized his father's Kurkin. Leon must be flying down to the Plymouth house after a meeting in Boston. Yes, he was heading in for a landing at the Kurkin field.

Jerome circled above the other plane, intending to follow his father down. When he glanced casually below him he drew in his breath, jerking erect. His father was in the final stage of his approach, a few yards from touch-down. That other plane off to the side of the field. Was it moving? By God, it was! The plane on the ground taxied ahead, gathering speed.

The two planes were on a collision course.

Eileen stood beside the Curtiss trainer, her eyes closed. Francis leaned forward with one hand on the fuselage on either side of her and kissed her, his hands leaving the plane to slide up her sides until they cupped her breasts.

"You haven't answered my question," he said as he drew his head away. He had to speak loudly to be heard above the roar of the engine being tested in the Kurkin shop behind the hangar.

Her breathing was rapid. She opened her eyes. "How can I? You don't give me time to think."

He stepped back. "Is that better?"

"No. Worse. Kiss me again."

"First tell me what you've learned."

"About what?" She smiled, teasing him.

"The plane."

"The wings support the aircraft in flight," Eileen said. "They're slightly tilted so the air flows below them and collects there. The speed of the plane has to be great enough to skim over the air before it's gone. All right?"

"Go on."

"First I want a reward."

He kissed her quickly. God, she was a desirable woman. His senses quickened in anticipation.

"You push the wheel away from you to go down," she said.

"Why?"

"Pushing the wheel lowers the elevators on the tail. You pull the wheel toward you to go up. Turning the wheel right or left steers the plane. Because of the rudder on the tail. Like a boat."

"What about planes that don't have a wheel? The Kurkins, for instance."

"They have a stick," she said. "It works the same as the wheel."

"And to keep the Curtiss level?"

"I use the harness on my shoulders. If the plane tips to the left I lean the other way to lower the aileron on one side and raise it on the other." She put her hand to the nape of Francis' neck and drew him to her. "You said I could taxi by myself today." When she saw him frown, she said, "Don't scowl at me like that. You promised."

"And will I get a reward if I let you?"

"I really haven't the slightest idea what you're talking about, Mr. Kincaid."

"I think you do." His fingers found her nipple beneath the cloth of her green dress. She gripped his wrist and pushed his hand away.

"Your feet?" Francis asked.

She looked down. "My feet? Oh, you mean when I'm in the plane. My right foot operates the brake and my left's on the throttle. Faster. Slower."

"All right. I'll help you climb aboard."

He held her around the waist and lifted her onto the lower wing. As she swung her leg over the side of the cockpit he glimpsed her knee and thigh beneath the hem of her skirt. He climbed to the wing and helped her adjust the harness. He leaned over to kiss her again, a lingering kiss.

"Gosh," she said when his lips left hers. "I think I'm ready."

"To taxi?"

"No, silly, to give you your reward for letting me."

He smiled, dropped to the ground and walked around to the front of the plane where he spun the propeller. The engine sputtered into life and he stood nodding at the sound of its steady roar as she revved the motor.

Kneeling in front of the lower wing, he grasped the ropes attached to the chocks and pulled them from in front of the wheels. He stepped clear of the wing and waved her forward. Eileen's hand went to her forehead in a mock salute as the plane rolled slowly across the field away from him.

Francis ran his hands down over his thighs. He'd never wanted a woman as much as he wanted this one. The thought of her was a fever in his blood, a burning ache in his loins. He'd have her today, she'd as much as promised him that. It would be the first time since he'd come to her on the night before the funeral.

He watched the four-cylinder Curtiss trainer taxi away from him. Eileen had gathered her black hair at the back of her head. He should have made her wear a helmet. Well, what the hell, she wasn't taking the Curtiss up, didn't know how, except in theory. He'd be in the cockpit behind her when she did. She learned quickly, though. Might make a good aviator some day. Good for a woman.

She should be starting her turn now. He looked beyond the Curtiss and froze in horror.

Another plane was landing, the two planes approaching each other at right angles. He saw the "LK" on the fuselage of the other plane. LK—Leon Kurman. Didn't he see Eileen? Yes, now he did. Kurman's plane lifted away from the ground, rising slowly. Too slowly? No, he'd make it. Francis sighed with relief.

All Eileen had to do was taxi under her father's plane. Or brake the Curtiss. What in the hell was she doing? Her plane accelerated and began to climb. Good God, no. She'd panicked.

The planes met twenty feet above the ground in a grinding crash, the right wing of the Curtiss hooking the left wing of Leon's Kurkin. The Curtiss swung about in mid-air and smashed headlong into the nose of Leon's plane. The Kurkin flipped upside down and, still locked in a death-grip with the Curtiss, smashed to the ground and burst into flames.

Francis, fifty yards away, stared at the planes, too startled to move. He recovered and dashed to the splintered wreck. A mechanic ran after him. Francis reached the Curtiss. Eileen was in the cockpit trying to unbuckle and pull off her twisted harness. He climbed onto the shattered wing and yanked her free. He held out his arms and she fell into them. Holding her to him, Francis leaped to the ground and ran with her in his arms away from the burning wreckage. He laid her on the grass. She moaned; blood trickled from the corner of her mouth.

Eileen's lips moved. What was she saying?

He leaned close. "Father," she murmured. "Father."

She knew, then, whose plane she'd hit. Francis put his hand on her cheek. "You'll be all right," he told her.

He ran back to the blazing wreck. The mechanic, one arm raised to shield his face, was trying to reach the other plane but the flames and heat drove him back. The Kurkin lay upside down and was burning fiercely. The collision, Francis realized, had ruptured the gas tank.

He raced around to the other side of the plane. He caught his breath. Leon Kurman had been thrown or had climbed from the cockpit. His feet were caught in the fabric of the bottom of the upper wing and his ankles were bent as though they were broken. His arms, tangled in the support wires, held him erect.

The propeller of the Curtiss had struck Leon's face and sheared off most of his jaw. His head, though, was supported by a strut and his short stocky figure stood on the burning plane with his open eyes staring at Francis as though he were still alive.

He had been caught between the wings in the middle of the fire. The whole plane blazed, sending a black cloud of smoke drifting across the field. As Francis watched, the fuselage of the other plane, the Curtiss, caught fire. Francis ran forward to try to reach Leon only to be stopped and then forced back by the furnace-like heat. He stood helpless amidst the crackle of the fire, smelling burnt flesh. His throat was seared from the smoke and heat.

As he staggered away from the wreckage, he couldn't take his eyes off Leon Kurman. The older man seemed to stare accusingly at him from the midst of the flames. Kurman's arms were outstretched and all Francis could think of was a man impaled on a cross being burned alive.

Francis turned his back to the fire. He stumbled a few feet away, leaned forward and vomited onto the brown grass of the airfield.

4

BRITISH, FRENCH COUNTERATTACK ALONG MARNE
CASUALTIES REPORTED HEAVY ON BOTH SIDES
PRESIDENT WILSON REAFFIRMS U.S. NEUTRALITY

When he heard the front door open, Francis laid the morning Boston *Globe* on the table and stood up, straightening his suit coat.

Henry Kincaid walked into the room holding his black homburg in his hand. He nodded when he saw his brother's dark suit.

"So you decided to attend after all," Henry said.

"I thought I'd better."

"It's up to you." Henry brushed the flossy felt of his hat. His red hair, Francis noticed, had been freshly cut. "I want to see you tomorrow morning," he said. "At the office."

"Business?"

"You might say so. Yes, it's business." He sighed. "Well, let's get it over with. Marie and Alicia are waiting for us in the car."

They drove in Henry's new black Packard to the Kurman house where they sat inconspicuously in the last of the rows of chairs that had been brought into the parlor. They stared at the plain walnut casket in front of the fireplace. There were no flowers.

Henry leaned to Francis. "I'm told they drill holes in the bottom of the coffin."

When Francis said nothing, Henry added, "They take the dust unto dust rigmarole seriously."

Francis shrugged, watching the room fill with mourners from Plymouth, Boston and New York. Some he recognized as associates of Leon Kurman from his years in retailing. Most, though, were strangers to him.

He glanced at Henry. His older brother sat stiffly erect, his hat on his lap, gazing straight ahead, his eyes glazed with boredom. Beside him his wife, Marie, sobbed softly into a lace handkerchief. To Marie's left, Alicia Kincaid sat with bowed head, her face taut, her mouth a thin line of grief. Her sixteen-year-old son, Sam, sat silently beside her. For the first time, Francis noticed gray tinging Alicia's blonde hair where it showed beneath her hat. He wondered again if there had ever been anything between his sister-in-law and Leon Kurman. Probably he'd never know.

The Kurmans filed to their places in the front row, Julia Feldman Kurman, Curt's widow, leading her twin sons, Brent and Joel, Jerome, his black curly hair precisely combed, his face expressionless, his older brother Martin, who had just flown in from California, where he'd been temporarily supervising the Kurkin Flight School, not bothering to hide his agitation as his eyes darted about the parlor. When he saw Francis Kincaid he scowled and looked quickly away.

Eileen, though out of danger, was still a patient in Plymouth Hospital.

Rabbi Samuel Silverman walked to the front of the room and nodded to Martin Kurman. When Martin stepped forward, his brother Jerome rose to stand a short distance behind him. Francis leaned to one side so he could see. Martin was holding a knife whose curved blade glinted in the light from the candles on a table near the casket.

"What the devil's going on?" Henry muttered.

Martin held his black tie away from his shirt with one hand and nicked its edge with the knife. Placing the knife on the table, he grasped the tie in both hands and ripped it in two.

Jerome stepped past his older brother, picked up the knife and cut a small incision on the right side of his vest. He tore the fabric with his hands until the gash was several inches long.

The two Kurman brothers, Martin and Jerome, faced one another and embraced. The only sounds in the parlor were Marie's muffled sobs.

When Leon's sons returned to their seats, Rabbi Silverman began speaking in a quiet, conversational voice. "The Lord is my Shepherd," he said, "I shall not want." When he finished the Psalm, he asked, "What is man?"

After a pause, he went on:

"O Lord, what is man that You regard him, or the son of man that You take account of him? Man is like a breath, his days are like a passing shadow. You sweep men away. They are like a dream: like grass which is renewed in the morning. In the morning it flourishes and grows, but in the evening it fades and withers."

Francis nodded in agreement as he tried to concentrate on the rabbi's words while pushing all else from his mind. Leon Kurman was dead. He couldn't accept the fact of Leon's death any more than he could accept his wife's death. His memory of the last few months was as blurred as an imperfectly remembered dream.

I shouldn't have come here, he told himself. You had to, he answered, you had to show them. Show them what? That he felt no guilt? That he wasn't afraid? He didn't know for sure.

"The Lord redeems the souls of His servants," the rabbi was saying. "None of those who take refuge in Him will be condemned. The dust returns to the earth as it was, but the spirit returns to God who gave it."

A memorial prayer was followed by the rabbi's eulogy of the dead man.

"The death of Leon Kurman marks the end of an era," he said. "A generation has passed away, never to come again. Much was given to Leon Kurman and he, in his turn, gave much to others. He was an honest man, a humane man, and a tolerant man. Not the least of his achievements was raising decent God-fearing children in this world of troubles.

These children, Martin, Jerome and Eileen, are Leon Kurman's legacy to the future.

"Some men strive to be somebody. Others, and Leon Kurman was one, seek to accomplish something. He has helped mankind attain the blessings of the miracle of flight. More important, he has helped those who knew him best to bring meaning to an even greater miracle, the miracle of life."

"That doesn't sound like the Leon Kurman I knew," Henry whispered to Francis.

"Shut up," Francis told him.

Henry's brown eyes glowered at him, then he shrugged and subsided.

At the cemetery, Francis stood apart, watching the pallbearers lower the casket into the grave. The day was overcast with a steady wind off the Bay. Rabbi Silverman prayed. "The Lord gave, and the Lord hath taken away . . ." When the prayer ended, Martin Kurman grasped a shovel, thrust it into the mound piled beside the grave, and threw earth down onto the casket. The dirt thudded on the wood.

Francis heard a short, sharp cry. Glancing to his right, he saw Alicia's hand go to her mouth. Her cheeks were stained with tears. Francis felt his own throat tighten.

A second shovelful of earth thudded on the casket. The other mourners followed the two Kurmans, each taking a turn with the shovel until the newly spaded earth rose in a mound above the remains of Leon Kurman.

The mourners formed a double row leading away from the grave.

"May the Lord comfort you," the black-garbed men and women prayed as the Kurmans walked between the rows, "among the other mourners of Zion and Jerusalem."

Francis turned from the grave and started down the hill to his brother's touring car. As he walked he idly read the names on the headstones while at the same time avoiding stepping on the graves.

"Francis!"

He stopped. When he looked over his shoulder he saw Martin Kurman striding toward him.

Martin faced him. "You bastard," he said. "You killed my father, you Goddamned bastard."

Francis stared at him. Martin balled his fist and swung wildly, striking Francis' shoulder. Francis stumbled back, tripped over a gravestone and sprawled on the ground.

Jerome Kurman ran up, grabbed his brother's arm and pulled him away.

"You dishonor the dead," Jerome said fiercely. "You dishonor our father." He held Martin by both arms.

Martin shook his head. "No!" he cried. "No!" Suddenly he slumped forward, sagging against his brother. Talking softly, Jerome led him away.

Francis stood and brushed dried grass from his coat and trousers. He glanced after the Kurman brothers.

Martin looked back. "You'll pay," he shouted at Francis. "You'll burn, just like my father did. And afterwards you'll roast in hell through all eternity."

Francis arrived at the Kurkin factory for his meeting with Henry a few minutes before nine the next morning. On any other day he would have stopped to talk to the workmen, to compare notes, perhaps, or discuss the latest news of the war in Europe, but today he passed the brazing room, the paint and woodworking shops, and the motor testing room without turning his head.

He caught a glimpse of Martin in the laboratory sitting at a drafting board, his instruments idle as he stared out of a window across the room. Francis walked quickly on. Behind him he heard a motor roar to life as one of the lab men measured its horsepower by a brake test.

He entered Henry's office without knocking. His brother glanced up from a sheaf of invoices, nodded Francis to a chair, and returned to his calculations. After several minutes he looked up, tossed his pencil on the papers on his desk and leaned back in his chair.

"Latham stopped by to see me last night," Henry said. Kurkin Flight Research had hired Oliver Latham to represent the company in Washington. "He says Woodrow Wilson expects the war will be over by Christmas."

"I don't believe it will be over inside of a year."

"Latham claims the losses on both sides are monstrous. Greater than anyone in this country can imagine. The French had 140,000 casualties in just four days at the end of August. Both sides are bleeding themselves white. It can't go on at this rate."

"I've thought about signing up with the French," Francis said. "After all, we're half French."

"Don't be a fool. We're Americans. It's not our fight."

"The trouble is I'd lose my U.S. citizenship. Unless I joined the Foreign Legion. But I don't want to spend the rest of the war up to my ass in the mud of a trench."

"It's the air service or nothing, I suppose."

"I can't imagine not flying. There's talk of an American air squadron attached to the French Army. An *escadrille*. But nothing's come of it."

"I still think Latham's right when he says the war will be over by Christmas," Henry said. "The French and English and Russians aren't idiots. Neither are the Boche. There's nothing to be gained from trench warfare except misery. Our Civil War should have taught them that."

"The French shot down their first Hun plane the other day. Near Reims. An Aviatik. There was a piece about it in the *Globe*."

"Oh? What were they flying?"

"A rear-engined Voisin 3. The observer made the kill with a machine gun fitted to his cockpit in the nose." Francis shook his head. "But you didn't ask me here to talk about the war."

"You're right, I didn't." Henry leaned forward, his elbows on the desk. "Leon Kurman's twenty-five percent of Kurkin Flight Research went to Martin."

"I expected it would. Martin's the older son."

"I didn't appreciate that scene between you and Martin at the cemetery yesterday. You shouldn't have gone to the funeral in the first place."

"Get to the point."

"Martin talked to me a couple of days ago. The day after the accident. I won't beat around the bush, Francis. He wants you out. O-u-t, out."

"I know how to spell it."

Henry stood up so suddenly his chair thudded against the wall behind him.

"Listen to me," he said, his blue eyes cold. "I'm trying to run a business, not ride herd on a flying carnival. Just when I thought we'd have fair sailing now that the Wright suit's been thrown out of court, this had to happen. I'm not getting much help from you."

"Simmer down, Henry. Do you think I'm proud of what's happened? What do you want to do, sentence me to thirty-nine lashes?"

Henry groped behind him for his chair and sat down. "Leon Kurman could be a curmudgeon sometimes," he said, "but . . ."

"What's a curmudgeon?"

"An avaricious, grasping gentleman. Yet he was smart, you can't take that away from him. Now I'm doing his work and mine, too."

"You're breaking my heart."

"I've had enough."

"All right." Francis' voice rose. "What are you going to do? Can me? You and Marty Kurman will make a great pair. The lovable president of Kurkin and his protégé, Martin Kurman, the boy wonder."

"Marty's a good designer. He's come up with some great ideas."

"My nine-year-old son has great ideas, too. But I wouldn't want to risk my neck in any plane he built."

"You're selling Martin short. Right now he's working on a stabilizer that promises to . . ."

"Sperry's five years ahead of him."

"Give Marty some credit. You've seen his plans for the new Kurkin for the Army Air Service. Latham's enthusiastic."

"We pay Latham to be enthusiastic." Francis slid a silver cigarette case from his pocket, snapped it open and offered his brother a cigarette. Henry shook his head. Francis lit up and, leaning back, blew a smoke ring into the air.

"If a pilot could fly a plane across a sheet of drafting paper," Francis said, "Marty would be the greatest aviation designer in the world. But you can't, you have to fly in three dimensions, not two. And when it comes to real flying, Marty Kurman doesn't know his ass from a hole in the ground."

"You're being unfair to the boy."

"Unfair, hell. If Marty didn't have the Kurman money behind him, he'd be an apprentice draftsman in a machine shop, not a designer." He reached across Henry's desk and stubbed out his half-smoked cigarette. "Well," he said, "what's the decision? Am I out? O-u-t?"

"No, you're not," Henry said. "I stood up for you, Francis. You don't think I ever do, but that's where you're wrong. Blood's still a lot thicker than water. The Kincaids have to stick together."

"I've heard too many sermons lately, don't make me listen to another one. I'd rather take off my shirt right here and now."

"I haven't the slightest idea what you're talking about."

"So you can give me those thirty-nine lashes, Henry."

"This isn't a joking matter."

Francis slammed his fist down on Henry's desk. "Don't you think I know that? What do you think I am, a, a—" He couldn't find the right word.

"Here's what I suggest we do," Henry said. "The Air Service has asked me to send one of our pilots to San Diego to train Army and Navy officers."

"I thought Glenn Curtiss would be doing that now that our North Island lease is running out."

"He will be. They've got some of his Jennies and a Curtiss hydroplane there. The Service is buying a Kurkin and wants one of our pilots to go along with it. You'll like going back to San Diego, Francis."

"Like hell I will."

Francis sat back and ran his hand through his blond hair. Maybe he should get away for a while. He'd never admit it to Henry, but he'd had a hard time sleeping since the accident. When he'd sought out Eileen, visiting her at the hospital, she'd refused either to speak or look at him.

"I've talked it all over with Martin," Henry said. "He agrees not to disturb the status quo if you take the San Diego job."

"That's big of him."

"I agree with him, Francis. It's best for everyone."

"I'll go." Francis prided himself on making quick decisions. "And I'll be taking Billy with me." He frowned for he'd spoken without thinking. Until that moment he hadn't considered what to do about his son.

"Billy? He's living with his grandparents on Newbury Street, isn't he? I guess I assumed he'd be staying on in Boston with the Stowes."

"The boy's *my* son, not theirs. Billy goes where I go. It's time he got to know his father a little better. And vice versa."

"I didn't think you—" Henry shrugged. "Never

mind. I'm sure the boy will want to go. You'll be selling the house?"

"I expect the Stowes will. I'm giving it back to them. After all, George Stowe lent me the money to buy it."

"Can you be ready to leave on Monday?" Henry asked. "I'll reserve two Pullman berths."

"Here's your hat, what's your hurry. Is that it?"

"Once a decision's been made I don't believe in procrastinating." Henry held out his hand. Francis stared at it for a moment before shaking hands with his brother. Damn it, blood *was* thicker than water. When Francis left the office, he closed the door quietly behind him.

Henry stared after his younger brother. The interview had gone better than he'd expected. Damn! Two company planes destroyed. And Leon dead. Henry shook his head. So Francis was taking his son with him to San Diego. He hadn't thought his brother cared about the boy, not that much. It just went to show you.

Francis stood in the hospital room doorway. Eileen, pale, her long black hair cut short, sat propped up in bed reading a magazine. God, she was beautiful. Through the window on the far side of the room he saw rain slanting down.

Eileen looked up, saw him, and turned her face away.

"Look at me," he said.

Eileen shook her head.

Francis crossed the room to the bed. "Look at me!" he shouted at her. "Damn it, look at me!"

"If you don't go," she told him, "I'll have to call the nurse."

"You're not going to call any nurse. If you do, I'll kick her out of here. You're going to listen to what I have to say." She closed her eyes. "It was my fault," he said. "Leon getting killed was my fault. It had nothing to do with you. I was the one who killed him."

Tears ran from beneath her eyelids and made wavering lines on her cheeks.

"I should have looked," he said. "I should have been paying attention. It was a beginner's mistake."

"I panicked," Eileen whispered. "I couldn't remember what you'd told me to do."

He took her hand in his. "Billy and I are taking the train to San Diego on Monday," he told her. "I'll be teaching flying at North Island. I'll be the Goddamnedest carefullest pilot they ever saw. No more stunts, no more aerobatics, no more taking chances."

"Francis," she said, "you know you'll never change."

"Like hell I won't."

She looked up at him with glistening brown eyes. "I don't want to talk now," she said.

"You don't have to. I just want you to listen." He drew in his breath. "This is what I came here to say. I love you, Eileen. I know you don't want to have anything to do with me after what happened, because of your father, and I don't blame you. I know how you feel and I respect that. Give me time to prove myself, Eileen."

"Don't say any more, Francis. Please don't."

"When I come back from San Diego, I'll find you, no matter where you are. And I am coming back.

It might be a year from now or it might be two, or more, but I'm coming. I have to, as long as you're here. Don't say anything. I don't expect you to say anything now. I just wanted you to know how I felt. About you."

Francis leaned over the bed, kissed her cheek, then turned on his heel and left the room.

Eileen stared after him. Her *Ladies' Home Journal* slid from the bed to the floor.

"Are you all right, dear?" A nurse was looking into the room.

"No. Yes. Yes, I'm fine."

"You'll be going home tomorrow, you know," the nurse said. "You're a lucky young lady." She smiled cheerily before walking on.

Why did you have to come here, Francis? Eileen asked under her breath. Why couldn't you have left me alone? All I want is to be left alone.

On a cold November morning two weeks later, Jerome Kurman was in the hangar at the Kurkin field when he heard footsteps, looked up and saw Eileen walking toward him.

"You look wonderful, sis," he told her. "I like your hair that way."

"Dr. Thompson says I'm one hundred percent okay."

"Why don't we take a spin in your Raceaway after lunch? I've got some free time this afternoon. We could drive over to the Cape."

"I want you to teach me to fly," Eileen said.

"To fly?" He stared at her. "You want me to teach you to fly?" he repeated.

"I can begin today if that's all right with you."

"Why, Eileen? Why?"

"I don't know why, Jerry. It's something I have to do. Don't ask me to explain. I don't even know myself."

"And if I won't teach you?"

"I'll find someone who will."

He nodded. "I thought you'd say that. All right, I'll teach you. I'll probably regret it, but I will. We'll start next week."

As he watched Eileen drive away, Jerome shook his head. If he lived to be a hundred, he decided, he'd never understand women.

Hans Reinhardt looked apprehensively from his instructor to the Albatross BII with the black Maltese crosses painted on its yellow wings, fuselage, and tail.

What am I doing here? he asked himself. He wanted to save lives, not destroy them. That had been the reason he'd studied so diligently all year to prepare for the entrance examinations to the *Fachbereich Medizin Technische*, the university medical school at Munich.

And now, even before he had a chance to compete in the examinations, he was a recruit in the German *wehrmacht*.

He could never bring himself to kill another human being, he was sure of that, so he'd avoided service in the infantry. Would the Army's air service be any better? He eyed the newly-mounted machine gun on the top of the Albatros' upper wing. Had he made the right decision?

Captain Adolph Bettenge, his instructor, motioned Hans to the rear cockpit of the Albatros while he climbed in the front and settled himself at the controls.

"We're off!" the captain shouted over his shoulder.

The incredible din of the Mercedes six-cylinder engine obliterated all thought. The vibration of the aircraft alarmed Hans and he shouted to the captain to ask him if something was wrong. Bettenge couldn't hear him above the noise. Hans hastily buckled himself into his harness and gripped the sides of the cockpit.

The Albatros lifted from the field and, at the plane's full speed of 104 kilometers an hour, they climbed into the cold sky, turning now to the right, now to the left.

Hans gazed out over the countryside and slowly his apprehension gave way to curiosity as he tried to identify landmarks. How like a map the fields and forests around the aerodrome at Esslingen seemed. His curiosity turned to interest, his interest to joy. To excitement. Elation. He was flying! Soaring! He flew like a hawk, a falcon!

Captain Bettenge flew into the wind, cut the Albatros' motor and landed. As the aircraft taxied to the hangar, Hans realized with a shock of surprise that they'd been aloft for almost an hour. It had seemed like mere minutes.

As soon as he had a chance he'd ask the captain when he could fly again. He smiled. He, Hans Reinhardt, had made the right decision.

5

"DAD."

Francis, unheeding, his hands in his pockets, walked on ahead of Bill across the brown stubble of the Fort Sill parade ground.

"Dad?" Bill said again.

"Sorry." Francis tousled his son's blond hair. "I was five thousand miles away."

"Five thousand miles? In France?"

"Right. We're going to have to get into that scrap over there sooner or later. No question about it. Not after the Huns sank the *Lusitania*."

"They agreed to pay us."

"How can you pay for the loss of a hundred lives? What's even one life worth? The Germans can't afford to stop sinking ships and Wilson won't put up with it much longer. He can't if he wants to be re-elected. War's on the way. Wait and see if I'm not right."

They walked in silence with the brisk November wind in their faces.

"We're really going back to Plymouth?" Bill asked. "You and me? We're leaving Oklahoma?"

"The day after tomorrow."

"Is that what Captain Foulois wants to see you about?"

"I haven't the foggiest notion what the captain wants. After I talk to him we'll stay at the field to watch his planes take off for Texas. Like I promised you."

"I don't remember much about Plymouth," Bill said. "I remember Grandma and Grandpa Stowe's in Boston better."

"You'll like Plymouth. Maybe as much as you liked San Diego. I know I did when I was a boy. We'll find a house near Kurkin Research and get you started in school again. I expect we'll be back in Massachusetts in time for you to play football before the snow starts."

Francis stopped and tilted Bill's face up. The boy's blue eyes and blond hair reminded him of pictures of himself at the same age, eleven. Bill's taller and better looking, though, he thought.

"How's that eye?" he asked.

"Better." Bill lowered his head as soon as he could.

"Don't be ashamed of getting banged up in a football game. Bruises are like badges of honor. Your eye looks good, there's just a little of the yellow left."

Bill walked on with his head down. Francis

shrugged. Sometimes he didn't understand the boy. When I was a kid, he told himself, I was proud when I twisted my knee sliding into a base during my first summer in America. Proud when it swelled up so I had to hobble to school using my grandfather's cane. Hurt like hell, too.

"It's time I was getting back to Plymouth," Francis said. "These planes they sent us are . . ." He paused, not wanting to use barracks' language to the boy. "I've a thing or two to settle with Martin Kurman."

"Our Kurkins didn't crash like the Jennies did," Bill said.

"Thank God for that. At least we don't have three lives on our consciences. It's luck, though, not because the planes are any better." He shook his head. "When they first uncrated the Jennies and Kurkins here at the Fort I knew they weren't right. All the pilots could tell as soon as they saw them."

They climbed the outside steps to a drab one-story wooden building identified by a sign as "Headquarters—First Aero Squadron." When the flimsy door banged shut behind them, the sergeant in the orderly room looked up from his desk.

"The captain wanted to see me," Francis told him.

Sergeant Jennings nodded. "He's going over the San Antonio flight plans with Lieutenant Bragg. They should be through any minute now."

Bill sat on a chair against the wall. Francis snapped open his silver case, offering a cigarette to the sergeant, but Jennings shook his head. Francis lit up, sat down and stretched his legs.

"What *is* wrong with them?" Bill asked. "The new Jennies and Kurkins."

"They're unstable. They fly fine in calm weather at low elevations. As soon as you try a maneuver that's out of the ordinary there's no telling what they'll do. The pilots call them flying coffins. I didn't blame the artillery spotters for refusing to go up in them."

A door opened, they heard voices, and Lieutenant Bragg walked out of the captain's office. He stopped at the sergeant's desk, pulled a pack of Pall Malls from his pocket and offered one to Jennings. The sergeant took the cigarette and lit up.

When the lieutenant passed Francis, he said, "Kincaid," and Francis nodded.

"Just go on in," Sergeant Jennings told Francis.

Butting his cigarette, Francis knocked on the door to the inner office and entered. Captain Benjamin Foulois, trim in his olive drab Army uniform and Sam Browne belt, waved him to a chair as he leaned back in his. Through the window behind the captain, Francis saw six planes, four Jennies and two Kurkins, being rolled by mechanics from the hangars onto the airfield.

"Did you know, Kincaid," Foulois asked as he went through the ritual of filling and lighting his pipe, "that for two years I was the Army's only heavier-than-air pilot?"

"I'd heard that, sir." Francis, though a civilian, always called the captain "sir." He admired Foulois. The man was stubborn and at times wrongheaded but, by God, he could fly.

"Not quite two years, actually," Foulois said. "More like eighteen months. From late 1909 to early 1911. Let's see, that's more than four years ago. The Army Air Service was a laughing stock then." He smiled. "It's a worse one today."

Francis, knowing Foulois was right, said nothing.

"We have a grand total of fifty-three aircraft." Foulois blew smoke over his head. "How many of them are fit to fly is anybody's guess. My squadron has six planes. Six planes! God knows how many will reach San Antonio in one piece."

"Yet you intend to fly them there."

Foulois eyed Francis narrowly. "Do you object, Kincaid? Do you suggest we crate the planes and ship them by rail like we did the two Jennies we sent to Brownsville last summer? Good God, we're an air service that travels by train!"

"I'm sure you have good reasons to fly."

"The best. I'm an aviator and aviators fly. Besides, my orders are to do whatever I can to restore public confidence in our air arm. If I had my way we'd show the public the truth. The United States ranks fourteenth in air power. Fourteenth! Fifty-three planes! Good God, Kincaid, what will it take to wake up the Congress."

"I'm inclined to think nothing will," Francis said.

"Inclined? Damn it, Kincaid, do you always have to be so cautious? A cautious aviator is a contradiction in terms."

"I realize you and the other pilots want me to fly with more flare. Take more chances."

"I suspected you were aware of how they felt. You're not insensitive."

"They think I'm yellow. That's the size of it, isn't it, sir?"

"Those are your words, not mine."

Francis shrugged. The hell with them. He didn't give a damn what the pilots of the First Aero

Squadron thought. He'd taught most of them to fly the Kurkins and Jennies, hadn't he? They were as good pilots as he could make them. What they thought of him was beside the point.

"I did a little checking on you," Foulois told him. "In Boston and Plymouth."

"Boston and Plymouth are none of your damned business." Francis felt his anger rise.

"That's where you're wrong. It is my business. Aren't you curious why I wanted to see you today before the squadron flies to Texas? Before you leave for Massachusetts?"

"I'm curious," Francis admitted.

"I have an offer to make you, Kincaid, and I want you to consider it carefully. I'm empowered to offer you a commission as a second lieutenant in the Air Service of the U.S. Army. As a pilot."

"After telling me I'm a coward?"

"Damn it, Kincaid, get that chip off your shoulder. I'm giving you a chance to prove them wrong, the ones who've been bitching. Isn't that worth something to you? I'm offering you more. You're a flyer and a good one. I'm giving you the chance to fly for your country."

"One question, sir. Do *you* want me in the squadron?"

Francis sensed a slight hesitation before Foulois said, "I wouldn't be talking to you like this if I didn't."

"Thanks for the offer, captain. If it had come at another time . . ."

"War's in the offing, Kincaid. If not with Mexico, then with the Central Powers. We'll be in it up to our necks within a year. You know it and I know it. If you accept a commission now, you'll be an officer, a pilot, when war comes."

Francis looked away from the captain, picturing Bristol Scouts roaring from a British airfield in France, climbing as they headed east over the trenches, imagined three Fokker EI's swooping down on them out of the sun at eighty miles an hour, guns chattering, the British and German planes whirling across the sky in a ballet of death. He'd give his right eye to be there.

Francis took a deep breath and let it out before shaking his head. "Sorry, captain," he said, "but I can't take you up on your offer. Not that I don't appreciate it."

"You're a flyer," Foulois said, "and a better one than you've shown us. I haven't forgotten you're the same pilot who flew inside the Machinery Palace in San Francisco." He laid his pipe on an ashtray on his desk. Behind him, Francis saw the Jennies and Kurkins aligned in pairs on the field.

"Is it the boy?" Foulois asked.

Francis nodded. "I've only gotten to know him this past year. Since . . ." He paused. "Since we went to San Diego. His mother died last year."

"I know. A tragedy."

"It wouldn't be fair to the boy if I left him. I'd have trouble accepting it myself. I've grown fond of him this last year. He's going to make something of himself and that's not just a father talking."

"Bill's a fine lad. I'd be proud to have him for a son. But you're right, taking him to Texas won't work. We'll be in San Antonio for a while and then

we'll be God knows where. I wouldn't be surprised
if the powers that be in Washington have Mexico in
mind, that they're looking for an excuse to send in
troops. And our planes as well, such as they are."

"As a rehearsal? To prepare for the big fight
that's coming in France?"

"Remember, you said it, I didn't." Foulois gestured toward the airfield outside his window. "Are
you sure you won't reconsider, Kincaid? I've cursed
the Air Service twenty times a day since I joined,
yet I've never regretted making it my career. From
now on a large part of the history of the world will
be written in the air."

"The boy would never forgive me."

Francis' anger had drained from him, leaving
him with a sense of loss. He felt as he had years
before when, a boy no older than Bill, he stood on
a dark small town railroad platform watching the
express speed by, the windows lighted, the whistle
calling to him.

Foulois stood. "Thanks for all you've done for
us, Kincaid," he said. "Perhaps we'll meet again. In
fact, I have a hunch we will."

Francis controlled his impulse to salute, nodding
instead. "Good luck, captain," he said. With those
planes you'll need it, he added under his breath.

As Bill followed him from the headquarters building and along the edge of the field, John Shackleford
looked across at them, frowned, seemed to hesitate,
then left his Jenny to walk toward them.

"Kincaid!" he called.

Francis nodded. He'd never particularly liked
John Shackleford though his son, Dale, was one of

Bill's best friends. Dale, he'd heard, was leaving Fort Sill with his mother to go to their home in Washington State.

Shackleford stopped a few feet away and clasped his hands behind his back. Francis noticed that Bill had lagged several paces behind him.

"My apologies, Kincaid," Lieutenant Shackleford said stiffly. "I guess we both know what kids are like."

Francis frowned, wondering what in hell the man was talking about.

"I don't follow you," he said.

"If Bill was my boy, I'd have wanted him to do the same." Shackleford held out his hand. "No hard feelings?" he asked.

Shackleford's grip was strong. Francis knew the lieutenant worked out daily with barbells, shunned liquor and called cigarettes "coffin nails."

"No hard feelings," Francis said.

"Great." Shackleford began walking back to his plane.

"Have a good flight," Francis called after him.

Shackleford waved without turning.

"What was that all about?" Francis asked his son as soon as the pilot was out of earshot.

"Oh, nothing."

"It was more than nothing. If you don't want me to go out there and ask the lieutenant, you'd better tell me here and now."

"We had a fight, me and Dale and a couple of other kids at school." Bill looked up at his father. "That's all it was, a fight."

"I'm waiting." All at once Francis snapped his

fingers. "Your black eye," he said. "You didn't get it playing football. You got it in a fight."

Bill hung his head, then nodded sheepishly.

"And you didn't tell me about it. The other fights you've been in, you've always told me." He drew in his breath. "It was about me, wasn't it? You were fighting because of what Dale or one of the other kids said."

"Those kids," Bill blurted, "they don't know what they're talking about. I told them to take it all back and when they wouldn't I lit into them. It was a pack of lies." He turned away, his voice breaking.

Francis put his hand on his son's shoulder.

"My dad's the greatest flyer in the whole world," Bill said. "That's what I told them."

"Once I thought I could be," Francis said quietly. "Now I don't know. This last year's been hell. I can't tell you the times I've wanted to fly the way I used to. But after Leon Kurman was killed in that accident, I promised myself I wouldn't."

They stopped beside a low fence at the end of the field and looked back.

"They're almost ready to take off," Bill said.

The November sun glistened on the newly painted silver wings of the Jennies and Kurkins. A red streamer fluttered from the rudder of Captain Foulois' plane.

The pilots and the artillery officers assigned to the squadron as spotters climbed from the planes after completing their last-minute inspections. They gathered around Captain Foulois, bundled in leather coats and wearing snug sheepskin boots, holding their maps steady in the breeze as the captain gave them their final orders. As the pilots walked to their planes, they pulled on their helmets and wrapped scarves around their necks before clambering into the cockpits and strapping themselves in.

The mechanics spun the propellers and one by one the planes roared into life. The pilots ran up their engines, letting them warm for three minutes before throttling down. They were ready, the engines throbbing, a deep thrumming from the vibrating struts and wires filling the air.

The captain raised his arm. A mechanic pulled away his Jenny's chocks and Foulois opened his engine up, turned, and taxied down the field with the other planes following in single file. Francis watched entranced as the lead Jenny headed into the wind, Foulois pushed his throttle all the way open, and the plane, swaying in the ground gusts, sailed toward the fence where he and Bill stood.

He felt the pounding of his heart as he listened to the beat of the engines and smelled the tang of burnt oil. His breath caught in his throat as the planes hurtled at him, one by one, the goggled pilots and spotters leaning from their cockpits, scarves streaming in the wind, to wave a last farewell to comrades on the ground.

On and on they came, one after the other, a drumroll roar as the planes gathered speed, a crash of sound as they passed directly over his head, a rapid fading of sound as they gained altitude. Francis thought his heart would break. These men were flying beyond the horizon into the unknown, leaving him behind. They challenged the limitless skies while he watched from the ground.

At last all six planes were airborne. They circled, formed into V's of three planes each and began climbing like two arrowheads pointing southward toward Lawton, the Red River Valley, and Texas.

"It's O.K. with me."

Francis drew in his breath and looked around him. For a moment he'd forgotten where he was. Then he realized his son had spoken to him so he looked down at Bill who, he saw, had been staring up at him. For how long, he didn't know.

"What?"

"It's all right, Dad," Bill said, "if you go with them. I like Grandma and Grandpa Stowe just fine. I won't mind if you send me to live with them in Boston."

"I don't know what you're talking about," Francis said.

"What's it like?" Bill asked. "Being a pilot."

"It's like nothing else in this world. Because you leave the world behind, that must be the reason. You're free up there, like men were meant to be. You'll see what I mean when I teach you to fly."

"You promise you will?"

"I promise."

"Don't worry about me when I'm in Boston," Bill said. "I'll get along just fine."

As Francis looked down at his son, he felt tears gather in his eyes. For a moment he wondered if he were the boy and his son had become the man.

"Look," Bill said, "there they are."

Francis followed the boy's pointing finger and saw the planes climbing into the sun, growing smaller and smaller as they flew southeast, the roar of their engines diminishing to a murmur, the murmur dying into silence.

Finally, when they could no longer see the planes,

he put his arm around his son's shoulder and they walked, man and boy, from the field, the man talking and the boy nodding, the man lifting his arm from the boy's shoulder to point to the sky, the boy looking up, his eyes narrowing against the light from the sun.

Bill smiled as though he glimpsed something of the future in the clear sky. His future.

6

AT 4:15 A.M. on March 9, 1916, Pancho Villa, angered by American support of his rival, Venustiano Carranza, led a band of a thousand horsemen in a surprise raid on the New Mexico town of Columbus.

When Villa's trumpets sounded retreat at dawn, the streets of Columbus were littered with dead and the center of the town was a gutted ruin. The more than two hundred Mexican corpses were stacked in a huge pile on the desert, soaked with oil, and burned. Seven American soldiers had been killed in the fighting and eight wounded; eight civilians died and five were wounded.

The next day the Secretary of War telegraphed President Woodrow Wilson's orders to the commanding general of the Army's Southern Department:

"President has directed that an armed force be sent into Mexico with the sole object of capturing Villa and preventing any further raids by his bands, and with scrupulous regard for sovereignty of Mexico."

"Who should command the punitive expedition?" the Secretary of War asked the Army chief of staff and his deputy.

Without hesitation, they both answered, "Pershing."

On March 11, Captain Foulois and his men were attached to General John J. Pershing's command for the duration of the campaign. The commanding general decided to ship the squadron's planes to Columbus rather than risk an overland flight. The Jennies and Kurkins were disassembled and crated and, the following day, Foulois boarded a Southern Pacific train with ten pilots, including newly-commissioned Second Lieutenant Francis Kincaid, and eighty-five support personnel.

On Sunday afternoon, March 19, Captain Foulois assembled his pilots on their improvised airfield outside Columbus. He took a telegram from his jacket pocket and unfolded the yellow sheet of paper.

"Gentlemen," he said, "I've just received this wire from General Pershing at Casas Grandes in Mexico. We're ordered to proceed there at once for immediate service with the expedition."

It's about time, Francis thought. Seeing the pilots' nods of approval he realized they were as eager as he was to head south in pursuit of Villa. The week in Columbus, with little to do except gripe about the poor shape of the planes and the absence of machine guns and bombs, had been frustrating. Now, going into action, they'd be forced to make the best of what they had.

"We'll prepare the planes and leave at once," Foulois said.

The pilots looked at one another in surprise.

"Do you mean we'll take off tomorrow morning?" Lieutenant Shackleford asked.

"No, that's not what I mean," Foulois said. "General Pershing has ordered us to proceed south at once. We'll fly to Casas Grandes today."

The pilots' surprise turned to dismay.

"The planes can't possibly be ready before five," Shackleford said.

"I'm well aware of that, lieutenant."

Glancing from face to face, Francis saw consternation mingled with a reluctance to speak out.

"Any questions?" Foulois looked at each man in turn. The pilots stood silent.

"Sir." Francis stepped forward.

"Kincaid."

"Casas Grandes is ninety miles from here," Francis said. "That's a two-hour flight. If we're lucky."

Foulois, his face expressionless, stared at him without commenting.

"As far as I know, sir," Francis went on, "only two of us have flown at night. None of us have been to Casas Grandes. We'll be flying into hostile, rugged country without reliable maps."

"Any other objections, Kincaid?"

"The planes have no lights. As soon as it's dark we won't be able to see our instruments."

"Thank you for your critique, lieutenant," Foulois said caustically. He glanced at the others before going on. "I'll lead the flight south," he said, "and the rest of the squadron will follow in single file to Casas Grandes. Are there any more questions?"

There were none.

The planes were ready for takeoff a few minutes after five. Foulois' Jenny led the way with the other seven aircraft following. Lieutenant Kilner, his motor dropping revs, barely cleared the wire fence at the end of the field so he returned to change engines. The remaining seven Jennies and Kurkins flew into Mexico in a straggling, bobbing formation. When dusk fell the pilots followed the dim silhouettes and the exhaust flames of the planes ahead of them.

A little after six Foulois changed his mind and landed at Ascension, halfway to Casas Grandes. Francis and three others followed him safely to the ground but the remaining three pilots, who had climbed above the leaders to avoid the possibility of a midair collision, flew on south, unaware of the sudden change of plans.

Lieutenant Kilner, his plane equipped with a new engine, left Columbus the next day and was the first to arrive at Casas Grandes. A few minutes later Lieutenant Carberry flew down the wide valley and landed. He had missed the landing at Ascension the night before, flown on ten miles to Janos where he'd brought his plane down on a road and spent the night guarding it. A short time later Foulois, Francis, Shackleford and the other four who had spent the night in Ascension, arrived at Casas Grandes.

The remaining two men, Willis and Gorrell, were unaccounted for.

Pershing ordered Foulois to make a reconnaissance flight south toward Cumbre Pass to locate the American cavalry heading for Babicora.

"You're my eyes," he told the captain. "Without you, I'm blind."

With Foulois acting as observer, the Jenny climbed toward the Sierra Madre Mountains. Less than an hour later the plane was back at Casas Grandes.

"We couldn't get her over the foothills," Foulois reported with disgust. "These planes have the trajectory of a brick."

"Let me have a go at the mountains without an observer," Shackleford suggested. "I might get enough lift without all that weight."

Francis, feeling the freshening breeze tug at his cap, started to object but bit his lip and was silent.

The pilots watched as Shackleford ran up his engine and started down the field into the strong gusts of wind. The Jenny rose unsteadily, climbed to fifty feet and then slipped off on one wing and plunged to the ground.

The pilots ran to the wreckage and pulled Shackleford from the cockpit. Blood streamed from his nose and his face was bruised but as soon as he was on his feet he pushed free and walked dazedly away from his smashed plane.

The first air mission in support of Pershing's punitive expedition was over.

The next day Lieutenant Willis walked into camp. He'd run out of fuel, he reported, was forced to land in rugged terrain and damaged his landing gear. When, later, an American cavalry patrol found the plane it had been hacked to pieces. The soldiers left the Jenny to rot in the desert.

One man, Gorrell, was still missing from the flight across the border to Casas Grandes.

Pershing's cavalry pushed south, vainly seeking the elusive Villa. The Mexicans, though still fighting one another, were united in their distrust and growing hatred of the *gringos* invading their country.

A week after the air squadron's arrival in Mexico, Gorrell returned to Casas Grandes. He'd been forced to land in high desert country, became lost, and used his last eight silver dollars and his cocked .45 to hire a Mexican guide. He was finally surrounded by a troop of U.S. cavalry and, ragged, dirty and bearded, had to show his West Point ring to convince the horsemen he wasn't a bandit.

The American advance south continued as Pershing deployed two columns, one to the east and the other to the west as he sought to catch Villa between the jaws of a mobile pincers. The Signal Corps strung telegraph wires from the rear to the advance command posts but the lines were often cut and so Foulois' planes, without enough horsepower to cross the high mountains to perform far-flung reconnaissance, were used more and more as couriers between Pershing and his troops to the south and his bases of supply in the north.

Captain Foulois sent for Francis and Shackleford.

"Pershing's at Satevo," the captain told them when they reported to his tent beside an airstrip twenty miles west of the Mexican city of Chihuahua. "You're both to fly there and report to the general."

They headed south, Shackleford in his Jenny, Francis in the Kurkin. When they landed at Satevo they found that Pershing had left the camp on an inspection tour but would return within the hour.

Francis walked back to his plane where he found a sergeant standing on the lower wing examining the instruments in the pilot's cockpit.

"Sergeant Mike Ritchey, sir," the man said, jumping to the ground and saluting. "This is the first airplane I ever had a chance to get close to. Never even saw one of the buggers till two years ago and then I had to ride fifty miles on a train to see it. That was a Wright Model B."

"Like to go up?" Francis asked.

"You mean it?" Ritchey asked. "Would I!"

Francis motioned the sergeant into the front observer's cockpit and climbed aboard behind him. Bareheaded, he flew into the rising wind and circled the field. A trail of dust approached the camp from the south. When Francis flew low and saw that the dust was being thrown up by a black car with a flag on each side of its hood, he came in for a landing.

"Thanks, lieutenant," Ritchey called as Francis hurried to the parked staff car.

General Pershing and three aides stood beside the black Dodge and the chauffeur sat stiffly erect at the wheel as they posed for a newspaper photographer. The wind snapped the general's one-star flag and the small Stars and Stripes.

As soon as the picture-taking was over, Francis approached Pershing and saluted. "Lieutenant Kincaid reporting as ordered, sir," he said. "Lieutenant Shackleford's with his aircraft."

"Damn newspapers," Pershing muttered as he returned the salute. The general's face was lined and weary, his moustache and hair were white. Despite his drive in the Dodge in the desert heat, his olive drab uniform, black tie, and campaign hat were immaculate. His high-laced boots shone as though they'd been polished only minutes before.

Francis said nothing.

"I've messages for Letcher in Chihuahua," Pershing told him. "Important enough to send two sets, one with each of you. Can you both leave in an hour?"

"Sooner, sir. We just have to refuel."

"The copies aren't ready. An hour. Sergeant Ritchey will give you the details."

Pershing turned on his heel and left Francis saluting his retreating back. Well, Francis thought, at least he'd be able to write Bill and tell him he'd met Pershing.

As he returned to his plane, he saw Ritchey smiling at him. He walked over to the sergeant.

"I'm going to learn to fly those crates." Ritchey nodded at the planes.

Francis winced at the word. They *were* crates, he told himself. Certainly not fit for campaigning in Mexico. If he ever got back to Plymouth, Martin Kurman would have a lot to answer for.

"I'll take you up again when I get the chance," he promised.

Ritchey lowered his voice. "Never met Black Jack before, did you?" he asked.

"Never."

"He's a real soldier's soldier."

"Seems all business," Francis said cautiously.

"He's changed, these last eight months. Since last August. I was with him when the telegram came."

"The telegram?"

"About his wife and kids. You don't know about them?"

Francis shook his head.

"We were in El Paso. An orderly came in with a yellow slip of paper in his hand. He'd read it, of course. Pershing looked up from his desk and saw the telegram. 'Read it to me,' he said. The orderly hesitated. 'Go ahead,' Pershing told him. The orderly read the telegram, trying to keep his voice steady. It was from Army headquarters at the Presidio in San Francisco. A few hours before fire had broken out in the old wooden house where Pershing's wife and four children were living until they could leave to join him in El Paso. His wife had been killed in the fire. His nine-year-old daughter Helen was dead, his seven-year-old daughter Anne was dead and his three-year-old daughter Margaret was dead. Only his son, Warren, was saved.

"The orderly stopped reading. There was a long silence and then Pershing asked, 'Is that all? Is that everything?' 'Yes, sir,' the orderly told him. Pershing didn't say another word. I'll swear his face didn't even twitch. He's been a changed man ever since."

Francis sighed, thinking of Billy, thinking of Debbie, picturing her smiling up at him, remembering the look of her, the touch of her. His throat tightened and he stared across the camp at the barren mountains. He heard the thud of hooves and, to his right, saw a cloud of dust. A horseman galloped into camp, leaped his black stallion over a stack of ammunition cases and reined up beside the general's car.

The horse reared. The rider, a young lieutenant, held the reins with one hand, took off his campaign hat with the other and waved it over his head, all the while shouting like a red Indian. Francis smiled, reminded of his younger self, of Teddy Roosevelt and Cuba.

When the rider dismounted, he handed off the reins to a corporal and, flicking his riding crop against the side of his cavalry breeches, strode to the general's tent.

"What was all that?" Francis asked.

"That's the general's aide," Ritchey said. "He's sure one wild son-of-a-bitch." He used the words approvingly. "Plays polo whenever he gets the chance. He's crazy about horses. Crazy, period, some claim. Can't say I agree with that."

"Cavalry officers are a dying breed. The war in France is proving that."

"He'd be lost without a horse to ride. Trench warfare would drive him out of his mind. But like you say, he's in a dead end."

"What's his name?" Francis asked.

"Lieutenant Patton. George S. Patton."

The two biplanes fought headwinds as they flew north through the mountain pass and over monotonous desert country toward Chihuahua. At times the winds were so strong that Francis, in the lead plane, thought his Kurkin was making no headway at all, though he knew that wasn't literally true.

Ahead of him he saw Chihuahua shimmering in the heat of the early afternoon, a large city of adobe houses and tree-bordered avenues. Below him a troop of horses raised dust as they loped along a dirt road and, flying lower, he recognized the uniforms of a U.S. cavalry patrol.

He followed the white ribbon of the road as he'd been ordered to do, saw the tell-tale double row of trees with the field beyond. He circled once, the Kurkin shuddering in the wind, and set his plane down. The Kurkin jounced across the field and rolled to a stop. Shackleford waved from his cockpit as the Jenny droned overhead on its way to a landing on the far side of the city.

Francis had his finger on the engine switch when he saw the Mexicans. At least a hundred men ran toward him along the road, some waving rifles and swords, others armed with clubs and pitchforks.

What in the hell?

The mob left the road, scrambled in and out of a ditch and onto the field. He couldn't hear them above the din of his plane but he could tell they were shouting at him while they brandished their weapons. A rifle cracked and he heard a plunk as the bullet struck the fabric of his fuselage.

I'll be Goddamned, he muttered. He didn't know why they were attacking him but he wasn't about to wait to ask. He settled back in his seat and pulled the throttle. The engine roared. He brought the plane about in a wide U and, gathering speed, headed directly at the mob. His pulses raced with excitement.

One white-garbed Mexican knelt on the ground and raised his rifle to his shoulder. The plane bore down on him. At the last second he threw the rifle aside and flung himself face down in the dirt. The Mexicans scattered to both sides of the oncoming plane. Francis heard a thud and guessed a rock had hit the wing.

Then he was beyond the shouting Mexicans, the Kurkin still gathering speed, its tail coming up. Elated, he pulled slowly back on the stick and felt the plane rise with the wind behind him, fighting for altitude as the wires hummed and the motor's roar sang in his ears.

He banked to his right and glanced down at the men scattered on the field below. Some shook their fists at the plane while others raised their rifles and fired. Unscathed, he flew on toward Chihuahua. Ahead of him he saw the ancient cathedral with its twin bell towers.

What reception had Shackleford received? he wondered. Francis flew low over the adobe houses on the fringes of the city, looking for Shackleford's landing field. There, that was it to the right of the star made by the intersection of three roads. The field was empty. Shackleford was nowhere to be seen.

Was this the wrong field? Puzzled, Francis shook his head. He circled lower. There. About a mile away he spotted the Jenny on the ground in another barren field. Three roads met a short distance away. The terrain where Shackleford had landed looked rocky and uninviting.

Francis came down below five hundred feet. At this height he had no leeway for error. He saw white-jacketed Mexicans running past the Jenny. A short distance ahead of them a man wearing an aviator's helmet sprinted toward a road. Shackleford's reception at Chihuahua had been as hostile as his own. Worse yet, they'd caught him away from his plane.

Francis swung the Kurkin into the wind. His wings groaned in protest. He put the plane's nose down and, though slowed by the wind, roared over the field with the Mexicans fifty feet below him scattering as Shackleford turned, looked up, and waved.

He climbed over a row of trees at the edge of the field. His brief glimpse of the boulders below had told him he'd be a fool to try to land. Even if he was lucky enough to set his plane down safely the mob would tear it to pieces before he had a chance to become airborne again.

He slammed his fist against the side of the cockpit. Shackleford didn't have a chance and there was nothing he could do to help him.

Wait. There was one chance. He remembered Shackleford's routine with the barbells. No, it wouldn't work, couldn't possibly succeed. He smiled. What the hell, he told himself, let's give it a try. You only live once. He circled and flew at the mob once more, fighting to make headway against the wind.

The caution he'd imposed on himself for so many months fell away as though it had never existed. Like a mask worn for a few hours and then discarded. His heart thudded as he felt the excitement rise, driving him on.

He throttled down as he passed over the mob a second time. Shackleford, twenty yards ahead of the Kurkin, stared up at the plane. Francis slowed to near stall speed, the wind holding the plane. Lower and lower he dropped. Now he was only twenty feet above the ground. Now ten. The mob was behind him, Shackleford just ahead. He brought the Kurkin still lower.

Would Shackleford understand what he wanted him to do? The plane wobbled but Francis fought the controls to bring it back to level flight. He couldn't hold her steady much longer. He felt a sudden tug on the plane and knew that Shackleford had reached up to grab the axle connecting the wheels.

Slowly, ever so slowly, he brought the Kurkin's nose up. Bullets thudded into the plane, he hadn't heard the sound of the shots over the engine's roar. The plane gained altitude and cleared a row of trees. When he was fifty feet above the ground he leveled off and glanced back. The Mexicans shook their fists and weapons. He couldn't see Shackleford below him but he felt the drag of his weight on the plane.

Ahead of him dust rose behind a column of horse-men on a dirt road leading into the city. The same cavalry troop he'd spotted earlier. He couldn't land, not with Shackleford clinging to the undercarriage. How much longer could Shackleford hold on?

Again Francis headed into the wind and nosed down toward the road a half mile in front of the horse-men. When he was ten feet from the ground, the plane bobbed up. He sighed with relief. Shackleford had dropped to safety. He climbed and banked to the right.

A gust of wind caught the Kurkin as it turned and the right wing lurched down. Francis fought for con-trol but the plane plunged earthward. Not now, he thought. Great boulders came at him. Eileen. I'll never see her again, he thought. He heard a splintering crash and pain sliced across the right side of his forehead and down his cheek.

The rest was darkness.

7

FRANCIS came groggily awake. He heard an irregular click-click and he tensed. There was a muffled explosion. The blast of a distant shell?

He jerked erect, his heart racing, and opened his eyes. Footsteps pattered across a hardwood floor below him. Looking around he saw a desk, a chest of drawers, a bookcase, and two doors. Though the light in the bedroom was muted by the drawn yellow shades he knew it must be late morning. Cursing his spasm of fear, he pulled the ring of the cord and let the shade flap up and around the roller.

He blinked as sunlight flooded the room. From the window he saw the green of a maple with blue sky visible through the leaves. Another click of wood on wood was followed by a boy's exultant shout.

When he looked down at the lawn behind the house he saw Bill and two young girls, one black-haired, the other a brunette.

As he watched, Bill bent over, swung a mallet between his legs and slammed a red-striped croquet ball through two wickets to click against a post. Triumphant, Bill looked at the girls and Francis saw one of them, the brunette, drop her mallet and put her hands on her hips as she spoke to his son. Bill walked to her, grinning, and when he spoke the girl nodded and laughed up at him.

A sharp, sudden bang in the distance was followed by three more explosions in quick succession. Firecrackers, he realized. He'd done the same when he was a kid; he never could wait till the Fourth.

Francis threw aside the single sheet and got up. He had no time to waste. He had a debt to settle with Martin Kurman and he meant to settle it today.

He swore under his breath when, shaving in the Stowe bathroom, he nicked his chin time and again. He held the straight razor in front of him and saw the red stain of his blood mixed with the leather. His hand shook. Damn, he muttered, angered by his lack of control.

He shaved carefully around the puckered pink wound running from the corner of his right eye across his cheek to his jaw. At least he didn't have to worry about whiskers growing there. Nature's silver lining, he told himself.

When he was dressed he walked downstairs and saw that a place had been set for him at the kitchen table. Mother Stowe bustled into the room, smiling, her eyes going to his wound, holding there for a second and then moving quickly away. She wiped her hands on her apron while Francis stood awkwardly in the doorway, not knowing whether she expected him to kiss her. He never seemed to know what to do where his mother-in-law was concerned.

"Sit down, Francis, sit down," Amy Stowe told him and he pulled out a chair while she poured his coffee.

"Is my cycle still stored in your garage?" he asked.

"Your motorcycle?" She put a plate of rolls on the table and opened a jar of strawberry jam. "I suppose it is. You're not going to ride that motorcycle, are you, Francis? Those machines are so dangerous."

"I have to go down to Plymouth after breakfast," he said.

"Must you? So soon? After all, you only got here last night. George and I hoped you'd have a good rest while you get acquainted with Billy again. There's no reason to become involved with those Kurmans." She turned to the stove. "The eggs and bacon will be ready in a minute. I didn't know what time you were getting up."

"You didn't have to go to all this trouble."

"It's no trouble at all. I told Annie she was to stay away from the kitchen this morning. I'm still a pretty good cook, Francis, even if I do say so myself."

She ladled three sunnyside up eggs and four crisp bacon strips onto his plate.

"I have to go to Plymouth today," he said again.

"They're so pushy." For a moment he didn't know who she meant but then realized it was the Kurmans. "Imagine," she went on, "her and her boy coming here to see Billy the way they did. What kind of woman is she? Learning to fly after what happened? The night after she came here I said to George, 'Some people don't know when they're not welcome. Or else they do know but they don't care.'"

Francis, who'd lost the thread of what Amy Stowe was saying, looked up with his fork halfway to his mouth. "Who came to see Billy, Mother Stowe?"

"Why, that Eileen Kurman Stouffer, of course. She brought her son. What's his name? Benny?"

Eileen. Francis felt his pulses quicken as he nodded.

"She drove here as bold as brass and wanted to take Billy with her on the cars into the city to stuff him with ice cream and goodness knows what else at Crain's. I would have told her no, but by that time she'd made sure Billy knew what she had in mind and I could see how disappointed he'd be if I didn't let him go, so I said yes. Mind you, it was against my better judgment."

Eileen had come to Newbury Street to see his son. Francis stifled his elation. Eileen would have to wait. He had other things to attend to first.

"I'm sure Bill likes Eileen Stouffer," Francis said, trying to sound unconcerned.

"Of course he does. Billy likes everybody. Yet do you know what she did? After I let her take the boy to the city the one time, she started coming for him every other week. That's the way they are. Give them an inch and they'll take a mile."

Francis bit back a protest. He'd learned years before that it was useless to argue with Amy Stowe.

She refilled his cup with coffee. "Would you like a piece of apple pie, Francis?" she asked.

"I've never been known to refuse your apple pie."

She disappeared into the pantry, returning a few minutes later to set the pie in front of him.

A girl's shout of laughter came from the yard outside. Mrs. Stowe walked to the sink and, with her back to Francis, looked through the screen on the open window. "Do you remember," she asked, "how Debbie always said you married her so you could have all of my apple pie you wanted?"

"I remember," Francis said quietly.

Amy Stowe sighed and when she turned Francis saw tears glistening in her brown eyes. For an instant, he saw Debbie mirrored in this middle-aged woman, in her eyes, in the tilt of her nose, in the curve of her lips. He stood and went to her.

"Oh, Francis," she said.

He opened his arms, embracing her awkwardly, and she buried her face against his chest. After a moment she backed away. Taking a handkerchief from her apron pocket, she dabbed at her eyes.

"I'm just a silly old woman," she said.

"We both miss Debbie."

"I'm sorry about what I said just now. I know it's wrong to speak ill of people you don't really know, but sometimes I can't help myself. Both George and I love Billy and we don't want to lose him. That's why I said what I did. I was jealous."

"Of Eileen Stouffer?"

"Of course, who else? On the day I first saw her waiting for me in the parlor I said to myself, 'She's come to take Billy away from me.' And I didn't mean just for a day's outing in Boston."

"Did you really think that Eileen . . ? That we . . ?"

"I've always liked you, Francis."

He frowned, not understanding what she meant.

"Don't look at me like that. How could I help liking you?"

"You didn't want me to marry Debbie."

"Of course I didn't. Liking you has nothing to do with your marrying my daughter. Francis, I've said it before and I'll say it again, you have your head in the clouds in more ways than one. You don't understand women, not in the least, and you never did. You don't know what we women want. You're what we used to call fiddle-footed. Here today, gone tomorrow. You'll break the heart of every woman unlucky enough to fall in love with you."

"I only do what I have to do."

"Oh, you mean well enough, Francis Kincaid. You're full of good intentions. That only makes it worse." She walked past him to the hall door. "If you'll excuse me," she said, "I have to freshen up."

When he started to rise from the table she shook her head. "Finish your apple pie," she told him.

Francis drove the Indian Hendee Special at a steady forty-five. Despite the wind on his face, he felt the heat of the July sun burning down on him from a blue sky fringed with white clouds. There was no breeze off the bay.

In Quincy he stopped at an intersection as a trolley rattled by in front of him. He heard the cry of a boy hawking papers, bought one and glanced at the headlines:

BRITISH ATTACK ALONG WIDE SOMME FRONT
ADVANCE FOLLOWS WEEK-LONG
BOMBARDMENT

BOMBERS DESTROY
TWO GERMAN MUNITION TRAINS

Francis thrust the paper in the rack on the back of his cycle and rode on through Hingham, Cohasset, and Greenbush, Marshfield and Kingston to Plymouth.

Heat rose from the dusty main street, the leaves of the trees in the yards were white with dust and the July flags hung limply from their staffs on the porches. A shadow flitted over him and Francis looked up above the trees to see a new-model Kurkin circling in the west.

He gunned the cycle to sixty, exulting in the throb of the motor and the lash of the wind on his face. Suddenly the bike jounced in a hole, the handle-bars wobbled in his hands and he felt the sickening start of a skid. Easing the gas, he skirted the top of a ditch as he steadied the machine. He sped on, smiling. He hadn't lost his touch.

Two American flags fluttered beside the entrance to the road leading to Kurkin Flight Research. Francis looked to the northwest and saw the massive white arcs of thunderheads. Another flag unfurled lazily atop the main building and still others flew from the roofs of the hangars.

He dismounted and left his Indian cycle beside the first of the hangars. In a newly-built grandstand on the far side of the field men in dark suits and women wearing large, broad-brimmed hats looked up to watch the Kurkin approach the field for a landing. Francis saw his brother Henry in the center of the first row sitting next to Oliver Latham. There was no sign of Martin or Jerome Kurman. Or of Eileen.

Francis watched the Kurkin, its engine off, glide

gently to the ground, bounce once and then touch down again and roll slowly toward him. He heard a smattering of applause from the grandstand. What in the hell were they clapping for? he wondered.

The pilot unstrapped his harness, climbed from the cockpit and leaped to the ground. Francis drew in his breath as he recognized him despite his blue jacket, Sam Browne belt, red pants and high leather boots. It was Martin Kurman. I'll be Goddamned, Francis thought, he's got himself up to look like a French aviator.

As Francis strode across the field toward him, Martin glanced up, then stared at him, his gaze lingering on the wound on the side of his face.

"Francis." Martin forced a weak smile. "I didn't know you were out of the hospital."

"Get back in the plane. In the front this time."

"Now, Francis." Martin held up both hands, palms out, in a placating gesture. "I have to talk to Latham and the delegation from Washington. They're interested in the Kurkin XV." He patted the fuselage of the plane. "In fact, I wouldn't be surprised if . . ."

"Fuck the new Kurkin."

"We've ironed out the bugs," Martin went on as though he hadn't heard him. "I admit the planes we shipped west to Foulois weren't perfect. We've been working on the lift and the fabric of the wings. We put in an engine with more horsepower and . . ."

Francis gathered the front of Martin's jacket in his fist and pulled the other man to him. "Get in the Goddamn plane," he shouted.

"All right," Martin said, "all right."

When Francis released him Martin straightened his jacket and glanced around as though looking for help. A mechanic was walking slowly across the field from one of the hangars.

"Are you going to get in or do I have to lift you up and stuff you in?" Francis demanded.

"I'll get in. I know you were hurt in Mexico, Francis. I know the Army gave you a medical discharge. It wasn't my fault, Francis, you shouldn't blame me."

Francis took a step toward him and Martin backed away.

"Just don't made a scene, Francis. We'll lose the contract to Glenn Curtiss if you're not careful. You wouldn't want that, would you?"

"I don't give a damn about the contract."

"You should, Francis." Martin climbed to the wing and stood looking down at him. "It's not my company, it's Henry's and yours, too. Look, your brother's over there waiting for us. Why don't we discuss this later? Over a drink."

"Stop talking to me as though I'm some kind of an idiot."

"You don't know what you're doing, Francis. Not that I blame you. I've read about what happens to flyers when they get hurt in the war."

Francis stepped toward him, hands clenched into fists, and Martin climbed into the observer's cockpit.

The mechanic walked up to them and looked questioningly at Martin. Francis waved him to the front of the aircraft. "Spin the prop," he told him as he lowered himself into the pilot's cockpit.

When he switched on, the engine roared to life. He saw Martin rise and turn in the cockpit ahead of him, saw him shout at him but he couldn't make out what he was saying. Francis taxied in a U-turn and, gathering speed, raced past the grandstand. He glimpsed Henry staring at him. Martin sank back in his seat.

"We'll see what this new plane of yours will do," Francis shouted, knowing Martin couldn't hear him above the throb of the engine.

Twenty minutes later, at five thousand feet, Francis put the wind behind him and opened the throttle. At eighty-miles-an-hour the Kurkin began to vibrate. The wires hummed and the planes of the wings shook. Ninety. Even with the tailwind he couldn't coax any more speed out of her.

He pulled back on the stick and the plane soared higher, slowed, rising reluctantly until she stood on her tail. The engine stalled and the Kurkin XV fell into a spin. He saw Martin shouting at him, his face contorted with rage and fear, but his words were swept away in the whine of the wind.

The plane fell, gathering speed as it twirled down and down. Four thousand feet, thirty-five hundred, three thousand. Francis put his head back and laughed. A ripping sound to his front right sobered him. The linen fabric was shredding from the upper wing.

He switched on. The motor spluttered into life. Died again. The plane plummeted earthward. He saw green fields contoured around tree-topped hills. South Pond, the sun glittering from the glass roof of a greenhouse off toward Manomet, the Kurkin hangars, the grandstand, all spinning around and around him.

The motor caught on his second try, roaring into life. He pushed the nose down and the Kurkin dived at the ground. Fabric from the upper right wing streamed behind the plane like a battle-shredded flag.

He pulled back the stick and shouted in triumph as the plane leveled and zoomed out of the dive.

A crack louder than a pistol shot startled him. He glanced right and left, saw nothing amiss other than the rent fabric. A wire lashed across his forehead, making him grimace in pain. He brought the plane around, sighted the field and, struggling to control the lurching Kurkin, came down with the wind on his tail.

He switched off as the ground rushed up at him. Too fast an approach, he knew, yet he didn't have time to circle. At the last moment the Kurkin slipped sideways and the right wheel struck the ground hard, buckled, and the plane bounced across the field. Ahead, in the grandstand, men and women leaped to their feet and ran.

The Kurkin skidded on its smashed right wheel, the undercarriage collapsed and, in a swirl of dust, the plane spun in a circle, tilted up on its nose, wavered in midair for a moment before settling back on its bruised belly.

Francis unbuckled, hoisted himself from the cockpit and dropped to the ground. His fury had left him and he was calm, almost listless. Through the settling dust he saw two Kurkin mechanics running toward the plane. The grandstand, some twenty feet in front of the plane's splintered propeller, was empty. Men and women huddled in small groups nearby staring in shock and horror at the wrecked aircraft. Francis saw a woman brushing the dust from her dress, saw Henry hurrying toward the plane.

A hand grabbed his arm and spun him around. Martin Kurman, his face flushed, his eyes bloodshot, shook his fist in Francis' face.

"You bastard," Martin shouted. "You Goddamned fucking bastard. You've spoiled everything."

"Junk this plane, too," Francis told him. "Before it kills somebody."

"It's not the plane, it's you. You don't know how to fly a plane, you never did. You talk about killing somebody. You're the one who killed my father and almost killed my sister. They shouldn't have let you out of that hospital, you're not safe to have walking around. You ought to be grounded for life."

"You saw what happened to the wing," Francis said. He glanced at Henry who was standing to one side, watching them.

"I don't design planes for fools to fly," Martin said.

"You think you're a flyer because you can get a plane off the ground and land it. You fly with your mind when a real flyer flies with his guts."

"You're not a flyer," Martin screamed. "You're a damned maniac."

"Oh, shit."

Francis started to walk away. Martin yanked his arm and lashed out with his fist. Francis stepped back. Martin threw himself at him, swinging wildly. The two mechanics seized Martin's arms and pulled him away.

Henry, his face as red as his hair, stared at his brother. "Good God, Francis," he said.

Francis turned on his heel and walked away from the Kurkin to his motorcycle.

"I'll kill you," Martin shouted after him. "I swear to God I'll kill you."

Francis glanced back. Beyond Martin and beyond the disabled plane he saw the flash of a red dress and caught a glimpse of bobbed black hair. Eileen. Her eyes met his for a moment, she glanced at her brother Martin, and then, as though wishing she could call down a plague to strike them both, she raised her parasol and walked away.

As Francis watched, a tall dark-haired young man raised his hat to her and Eileen stopped, twirling her parasol on her shoulder. After a moment she linked her arm in his and together they walked to his waiting auto.

What was wrong with Hans Reinhardt?

His fellow pilots agreed that he was a competent aviator. He had, in fact, the makings of a great pilot, one of Germany's finest. Yet they looked at him from the corners of their eyes and shook their heads.

Why wouldn't he fight?

Hans had been flying missions over the western front for six weeks. Every time he encountered an enemy plane he avoided combat, seemed to find an excuse for not fighting. His guns jammed. His fuel ran out. He was totally unlike the other pilots in his six-plane unit who, after disabling a French fighter, were apt to riddle its fuselage for good measure. It made sense. A dead Frenchman couldn't fly and fight again.

Hans was on the verge of being transferred from the air service when a call came from a frontline observation post. Three French Morane Saulnier fighters had been spotted flying into German territory. Hans, the only pilot available, climbed into his Fokker EI monoplane and left the aerodrome at Rethel to intercept. He climbed until he reached the cloud cover at 11,000 feet, slightly below his plane's ceiling.

He found the French aircraft almost at once. In the wake of the three fighters a thousand feet below him were ten pusher-type Voison 5's, obviously laden with bombs, on their way to attack a German aerodrome, probably Hans' own field at Rethel on the Aisne.

Hans, as yet unseen, hesitated. Common sense told him to turn back. Yet he knew that at this very moment his unit's patrol of five Fokkers must be returning to their field, low on fuel and helpless to defend against the French attack.

He had two advantages. One was surprise, he was still undetected. His second advantage was what the English called the Fokker mystique. Since the year before the Fokker Scrouge had kept Germany supreme in the air over France. For one reason: the Fokker monoplane was the first fighter to have a machine gun synchronized to fire through its propeller.

"The greatest technical advance of the war," his mechanic had told Hans. "The mechanism is simplicity itself. A cam is attached to the crankshaft of the engine in line with each propeller blade. When the blade reaches a position in which it might be struck by bullets from the machine gun, a cam is activated by a pushrod, and this, by means of a series of linkages, stops the gun from firing. When the blade is clear, the linkages retract again and the gun can fire."

"I see," Hans said.

He wondered if he'd ever understand exactly how the damn thing worked. It sounded like the closing of the epiglottis when a man swallowed. So food wouldn't enter his lungs.

The synchronized machine gun worked just as efficiently.

Despite his better judgment, Hans flew directly above the unsuspecting French fighter escort and dived to come up beneath the lead Voisin. When he was a hundred yards from the bomber he opened fire, sending a rain of bullets into the plane's belly. He saw a flash of orange flame. Smoke trailed from the Voisin's fuselage as it plunged heavily earthward.

When he attacked a second bomber, the French planes, knowing a lone fighter wouldn't attempt such a foolhardy attack, suspecting he was the harbinger of a flight of Fokkers, scattered to the south and east. Hans smiled grimly. He had killed and, surprisingly, had felt no revulsion, no guilt. He'd hardly glimpsed the two-man crew of the bomber he'd sent down in flames.

He'd fought to save his comrades at Rethel. But weren't all Germans his comrades, whether they were pilots in his unit, soldiers in the trenches, or workers in the factories behind the front? His duty as a German aviator was to protect them all. To kill two men or a hundred, what did it matter? The next would be easier and the one after that easier still.

When he returned to Rethel and his victory was confirmed, he asked Max Graab, the aerodrome artist, to paint a black falcon on his Fokker's fuselage.

8

Eileen drove the Mercer Raceabout east to the Cape in the half-light of early evening. On both sides of the road were dark and shadowed cranberry bogs. Beside her, in the passenger seat on the left side of the auto, Francis whistled a British marching song as he stared ahead into the gloom.

After a time Eileen began to sing the words:

> It's a long way to Tipperary;
> It's a long way to go;
> It's a long way to Tipperary,
> To the sweetest girl I know!

As he listened, Francis turned in his seat to look at her. She was lovely, he thought. A thunderstorm earlier in the afternoon had muddied the roads so Eileen had left her linen duster, automobile bonnet and chiffon veils home. She wore a black and white checked jacket fastened with a sash and a white skirt that came to her lower calves. Bareheaded, her bobbed black hair was tousled by the wind.

"Are you really going?" she asked.

"I have to be in New York the day after tomorrow. We're supposed to sail the next day on the *Orduna*, but with the war you never know for sure."

"Every time I see you," she said, "it seems to be the wrong time." When he saw her hands clench the wheel, he knew she must be reliving the horror of seeing her father trapped in the burning plane.

"I almost wish—" she began, a catch in her voice.

"—that you'd never met me?"

"Something like that." She sighed. "And here I am supposed to be cheering up the warrior as he leaves for the battlefield. A fine cheerer-upper I turned out to be."

"And a fine warrior I am. Invalided home from Mexico after less than a month. Sometimes I wonder if the French will take me."

"They'll welcome you with open arms and a kiss on both cheeks. Francis Kincaid, *aviateur extraordinaire*. Guynemer and Fonck and all their other aces had better look to their laurels."

Though she was smiling there were tears in her eyes. When she saw him looking at her, she said, "I'm not crying, it's this damn wind. Light me a cigarette, will you, Francis?"

She slowed the Raceabout while he took his silver case from his pocket and, bending low behind the dash, lit two cigarettes. He reached over and put one in her mouth.

"I see you're still smoking Fatimas." She sighed. "I suppose if I can't be a cheerer-upper, I can play the flirt, though it's not my style." She glanced at him, deliberately coquettish, but he was staring straight ahead and didn't seem to notice. "This conversation is like a Model T," she said, "all fits and starts."

"Sorry, I was miles away."

She made one of her intuitive leaps that always surprised him. "Debbie?" she asked.

"Yes, Debbie. I was thinking how she always wanted me to give up smoking. Claimed cigarettes were bad for my lungs."

Eileen covered his hand with hers.

"I'm not very good company," he said.

"You don't have to be. Not when you're with me."

"I suppose Charley is, though." Henry had told him the name of the handsome black-haired young man who'd escorted Eileen from the disastrous demonstration at the Kurkin field.

"Charley? Why, Francis, I do believe you're jealous. Now you're the one who's cheering me up. I always wanted to have two good-looking men fighting over me."

He touched his scarred face with his fingertips. Suddenly he leaned over and kissed her cheek.

"Francis," she said, "if you don't stop you'll have us in the ditch."

"Pull over then."

She swung the Raceabout to the sandy shoulder

and stopped, leaving the motor running. The car vibrated gently. He put his fingers beneath her chin and turned her face to his. For a moment he looked into her eyes as he breathed in the faint scent of lilies-of-the-valley.

He kissed her, finding her lips warm and clinging. Excitement flared through him and he pulled her close. Her arms went around his neck and her lips parted and their tongues touched. Her eyes were closed and he could feel the beating of her heart through the thin fabric of her dress.

Eileen pulled away. He followed, kissing her cheek, her eyelids, his lips going beneath her hair to nip the lobe of her ear. She put her hands on his chest and held him from her, shaking her head.

"You do have a way with women, don't you, Francis?" she said lightly.

"I love you, Eileen."

"You love all women. It's your nature, you can't help yourself. Gosh, I'll bet you said the same thing to all the Mexican *señoritas*. In a few weeks you'll be saying it to the *mademoiselles*."

"There's been no one since you." He sat back in his seat, switched on the single headlamp on the hood and stared along its beam at the weeds growing along the road. "We'd better go. We'll be late."

She eased the Raceabout from the shoulder. He wanted to touch her, put his hand on her thigh, feel her body against his. He glanced at Eileen. She was staring straight ahead. A horse and wagon approaching them in the middle of the road loomed up in their headlight and she swerved around it. The farmer waved as they passed and Eileen waved back.

"He probably thinks I'm a daring adventuress," she said, "when all I am is a nice Jewish girl who wants a home where she can raise a family."

"You're teasing but I know you're serious, too."

"You're Goddamned right I am."

"I wish you wouldn't talk like that. Women shouldn't talk that way."

"Don't be such a prig, Francis." She paused. "Why don't we talk to one another like other people do? Sometimes I wish we could. Talk about the war in Europe and the stock market and Henry Ford's peace ship. Talk small talk to me, Francis. Please."

"I had to laugh at something George Stowe said the other day."

"Tell me. Cheer me up. Make me laugh, too."

"He has a sailboat up at Nahant, you know. George thinks flying is for birds and madmen. He was . . ."

There was an explosion and the car wobbled to a halt. "Damn," Eileen said.

Francis got out and walked to the back. "It's the right rear tire," he told her. He jacked up the car, took the spare from the case on the rear of the Raceabout, and put it on while Eileen watched. Brushing off his hands, he returned to sit beside her. "If I can't get the tire repaired in Yarmouth," he said, "I'll patch it myself."

"You were telling me about George Stowe," she said as they drove on.

"He's never liked planes, has always been afraid they'd stall in midair and crash. 'Airplanes are as safe as your boats,' I told him. 'Boats sink all the time, you know,' I said. 'My boat might sink,' he said, 'but I can swim.' "

She glanced at him, grimacing. He didn't seem to notice.

"I thought it was pretty funny," he said. "What he meant was that he could swim but I can't fly."

"For God's sake, Francis, you don't have to explain it to me."

When she looked at him again, the car swerved and he turned to her and put his hand over hers to steady the wheel.

"And cars can crash," he said.

He expected a biting reply but, frowning, she said nothing. A short while later she slowed as they entered Yarmouth, driving past buggies and wagons in town for Saturday night. She turned onto Mayfair Road and stopped.

"The inn's two miles farther on," he said.

"Look at me, Francis."

He turned, leaning to her, intending to kiss her, but she shook her head and, reaching to him, put her palm over his left eye. "Now read that sign in front of the store behind me."

He twisted his head free of her hand.

"It says 'Groceries.' "

"Can you see out of your right eye at all?" she asked.

"Not much. A little. Light and shadow. It's like looking through frosted glass."

"Oh, Francis." She put her hand on his arm. "I'm so sorry." She looked up at him. "Is there a chance it'll get better?"

"None. The Army doc said the damage was permanent and the specialist I went to in New York last month agreed."

"And you didn't say a word to anyone."

"I don't want a fuss. I'll never forgive you, Eileen, if you mention it. To anyone. Ever."

"And yet you expect to join the French Army? The air service?"

"Actually the Foreign Legion. The French are desperate to find flyers for their new American *Escadrille*. If I can fly, and I can, a bad eye won't matter."

"But can you fly? Safely?"

"You forget I took your brother Martin up for a little spin over Plymouth only last week. Come to think of it, though, he didn't act too pleased when I brought him down. Seemed to think my flying left something to be desired. At least that's what I got from his remarks."

"I could have killed both of you," Eileen said. "You behaved like a couple of schoolboys."

"I think you have to have a bit of the schoolboy still in you to be a flyer. More than a bit. A sensible person wouldn't risk his neck in one of these wired-together assemblies of ash and steel tubes. At least not one designed by Martin."

"Don't take Martin lightly," she said. "He was still livid the day after the demonstration. I think he'd actually kill you if he got the chance."

Francis shrugged. They left Yarmouth behind and a few minutes later saw the lights of the inn.

"I'm so afraid for you," she said. "Not because of Martin, because of the flying. Especially since you came back from Mexico. When you were in the Kurkin with Martin it was almost as though you wanted to crash to prove your point. As though you didn't care what happened to you. Or to anyone else for that matter."

"Sometimes I don't care, not since Debbie died. My moods soar up and down and around as though my mind was doing the aerobatics. You're right, at times I don't give a damn what happens to me."

She parked the car beside the inn. As they walked up the gravel path, she took his arm and he felt the warmth of her body against his side.

"You have so much to live for," she said. "There's Bill, and the flying, and the company. And there's—" He thought she was about to say "me" but instead she added, "so much more."

They ate by candlelight in a dining room overlooking Bass River. Later, singing, lightheaded from the champagne, they drove farther out on the Cape with the tang of salt in the air and the sea breeze cool on their faces. They saw, in the distance, the flash of the beacon from Nauset Beach Light.

"Here?" Francis asked. He had taken the wheel when they left the inn.

"This will be fine."

He pulled the Raceabout off the road and parked. In the sudden silence they heard the muffled crash of surf from beyond the dunes. The night was clear and starry with a waning moon low in the west. They had seen no one for the last five miles and now Eileen had the eerie feeling that they had left the rest of the world behind and were marooned on a dark island of their own.

Francis walked behind a sand dune to change into his tank top and trunks. When Eileen, in a black-skirted bathing suit, joined him he was standing with his arms folded gazing across the dark waters of the Atlantic.

"There's nothing but water between us and France," she said.

He nodded. His face was pale in the starlight. All at once he ran down the beach, splashed into the surf and dived into an oncoming wave. Startled, she stared after him.

She walked to the ocean's edge, feeling the cold water lap over her feet. Peering into the night, she glimpsed his blond hair beyond the line of the surf.

"Francis!" she called.

She saw his pale arms stroking with a strong steady rhythm. She ran into the water and waded through the surf into the breakers. Diving under the first onrushing wave, she came to the surface beyond the line of the surf. Above her the stars were brilliant, as though the afternoon storm had washed the air clean.

Looking out to sea she tried to catch sight of Francis but she saw only the tossing waves. She swam away from the shore, pausing after a few minutes to look ahead, thinking she saw him. She couldn't be sure so she swam on. A good swimmer, she wasn't afraid of the dark and limitless expanse of the Atlantic.

Surely he'd turned back by now, she assured herself. Yet where was he? An uneasiness gnawed at her. He was so erratic, so mercurial. She never knew what to expect from him. Was that why he intrigued her so?

She treaded water as she looked eastward into the darkness. She saw nothing except the empty ocean rising and falling beneath the stars. She cried out, calling his name. The only answer was the rumble of the surf behind her.

She panicked. He had drowned, there was no doubt about it in her mind. He had challenged the ocean, swimming until he could go no farther and then let the ocean claim him. She moaned, gagging as salt water slapped into her mouth and, with tears burning in her eyes, she turned and began the long swim back to shore.

The surface of the water heaved in front of her and, in the midst of a fountain of spray, Francis burst from the sea. He looked at her, spluttering and laughing as he pushed his blond hair from his forehead.

"I thought you'd drowned," she told him.

"Drowned? Not likely. I was waiting to see if you'd follow me so we could swim back together."

"Go to hell," she said, angry at him for frightening her. Angry at herself for being frightened.

"What's wrong?" he asked.

Without answering, she swam past him and struck out for the distant line of the shore. He caught her after a few strokes, swimming beside her, his face dipping into the water and then resurfacing to gulp in air. The wound on his cheek looked white in the light from the stars and the setting moon.

She let the surf carry her shoreward until her knees touched the sandy bottom. Standing, she ran up the beach. When she found her towel she dried her face. Turning, she saw him walking slowly from the ocean, his body pale against the dark water behind him. He stopped a few feet from her.

"Do you have to go?" she asked, ashamed of herself for asking but unable not to. "Let someone else help save France and poor little Belgium. Didn't you go through enough in Mexico?"

He leaned over and kissed her and she tasted the salt on his lips. The taste lingered.

"We'll walk along the beach," he told her. "Unless you'd rather drive back to Plymouth now."

The choice was hers.

"I love you, Francis," she said huskily.

He kissed her again and walked away from her across the sand toward the darkly looming dunes. She ran to catch him, took his hand in hers, and they walked hand in hand along the deserted beach.

The time wasn't right, she knew. She sensed a wrongness about their being here, tonight, a wrongness she couldn't explain. Yet it was there. She knew it, felt it.

"He's asked me to marry him," she said, trying, perhaps, to break the spell.

She felt Francis hesitate for a fraction of a second. "Your handsome hat-tipping friend?" he asked.

"Yes, Charley Lowell."

"And what did you tell him?"

"I told him I couldn't marry him because I didn't love him but that I hoped we could still be friends. We won't be, you know, it's never the same after you have to turn a man down."

"You sound as though you've had a lot of experience. Turning men down." His voice was flat and emotionless.

"I've had my share."

He let go of her hand as though, she thought, to punish her for having men ask to marry her. She reached for his hand and laced her fingers with his and they walked on. We're behaving like a couple of schoolchildren, she thought. Perhaps lovers, like flyers, were people who had never quite grown up.

They stopped in the shadow of a dune. When he turned to take her in his arms, she put her hands on his wet tank top.

"Wait," she said.

She stepped back and stripped the clinging bathing suit from her body. When she looked up she saw the dark shadow of his naked body outlined against the dim shimmer of the sea.

They came together, standing, and when she felt his arousal she led him to her, into her, and they kissed passionately as they joined. She wrapped her legs about him and he walked a few feet, carrying her, still inside her.

"Francis!" she gasped as he stumbled and fell. They sprawled on the sand, apart now, laughing.

He crawled to her on his hands and knees and, lying on her side in the sand, she opened her arms to him and, kissing her, he rolled on top of her. When he thrust into her she arched to meet him, matching him thrust for thrust, finally crying out in ecstasy.

I'll have his child, she told herself as she lay in the circle of his arms. She knew this with great certainty, there was no doubt at all in her mind. Just as, a short while before, she had been certain he had drowned. She'd been mistaken then, but not now.

You always imagine the worst and the best, she thought. Having his child, his son, would be the best. She wanted to bear his son. Because she loved him. Because she might never see him again. Because, and she pushed the thought away as soon as it appeared, she realized it might be the only way she could keep him.

9

THE storm swept in off the North Atlantic bringing wind and cold rain to France. The dirt in the trenches that stretched like endless gashes from Switzerland to the sea turned to mud and the soldiers, French and British on the one side, German on the other, cursed the rain as they huddled together for warmth while overhead shells whined in a desultory yet death-dealing bombardment.

The rain lashed the desolate Valley of the Somme where the British offensive of June and July had long since ground to a disspirited halt after the high command sacrificed thousands upon thousands of young men in exchange for a few miles of war-ravaged French countryside. In Paris, gray and drab as the war entered its third year, the rain slanted in front of the cafes, the hotels, the shops and the apartments of the capital, leaving the cobbled streets wet and glistening.

During the night the storm passed over German-occupied France, crossed the Rhine into Germany itself, driving east toward Austria-Hungary and the plains and steppes of Russia where the Tsar's Imperial Army still fought to defend the motherland from the hated Hun despite rumblings of discontent in the ranks and in the cities behind the lines, a discontent that threatened to erupt in armed revolution.

Fog followed in the wake of the storm. Near Behonne in northern France, twenty miles from the bastion of Verdun, Captain Georges Thenault, commanding officer of the Lafayette *Escadrille*, woke early, as was his custom, looked out at the gray murkiness covering the countryside, and returned to bed. There'd be no flying this morning. He fell asleep as soon as he closed his eyes.

The other flyers of the *escadrille* stumbled from their cots, glanced at the lowering clouds and, shaking their heads, either buried their faces in their pillows or stumbled wearily to the latrine and then to the messhall on the first floor of their quarters in a villa between Bar-le-Duc and the airfield at Behonne.

By nine the sky still showed no sign of clearing. The pilots gathered in the flyers' lounge, a long, high-ceilinged room with a glowing coal stove in its center. A propeller from a downed Aviatik was nailed to the wall between group photographs of uniformed airmen staring into the camera, arms linked and smiling. Many of the men in the pictures were now dead, even the names of some had been forgotten.

On another wall an American and a French flag

were crossed and to one side of the flags a stern and graying Woodrow Wilson looked down from among smiling photos of Mary Pickford, Douglas Fairbanks, and Charlie Chaplin. Yesterday's flight orders had been erased from the blackboard. On a bulletin board someone had tacked the slogan:

WORK LIKE
HELEN B. MERRIE

The mood of the flyers in the lounge matched the foulness of the weather outside. Lieutenant Charles Nungesser, the French ace, had temporarily joined the *escadrille* in July, startling the Americans when he smiled for between his scarred lips were two rows of gold teeth. The originals were scattered on the battlefields and in the military hospitals of France.

A few days before his arrival at Behonne, Nungesser had been injured and sent to the rear to recuperate but had decided to spend his sick leave with the Americans. He quickly shot down an Aviatik, his tenth kill of the war. The next month, though, he returned to his French unit and with his departure the Americans' luck changed for the worse.

Raoul Lufbery's Nieuport had flipped over on landing and when Lufbery inadvertantly swallowed the gasoline mixed with castor oil spilling from his ruptured tank, he was hospitalized suffering from severe nausea. Jimmy McConnell, trying to land at dusk, overshot the field, sped between two trees that sliced off his plane's wings, and slammed into a ditch, injuring his back. The next day Captain Thenault saw two fellow pilots helping McConnell into his plane and ordered him to Paris on sick leave.

"Our luck's gonna turn," Eddie Fuller said. The men crowding around the stove ignored him.

"You wait and see," Fuller said, as though to himself, "our luck's bound to turn."

He placed a record on the gramophone, turned the crank, flipped the switch beside the turntable and lowered the needle. The sound of a woman's high and scratchy voice filled the room.

"Ah, sweet mystery of life," Fuller sang along with her, "at last I've found you."

No one joined in. The other men didn't like Eddie Fuller. They didn't dislike him, exactly, they just didn't like him. Somehow he was different. The way he talked; the way he thought. And he was a liar. He'd told McConnell he came from El Paso. He'd told Dawes he was from Flagstaff and others remembered him saying he was born in New Orleans. He claimed to have flown with Foulois in Mexico and to have fought in the trenches with the French Foreign Legion. Both, it turned out when his stories were compared, at one and the same time.

Eddie Fuller, knowing he was trapped in his lies, saw no way out. He wanted to be liked, he hungered for acceptance. He had lied to muddy his past to help hide his secret. Eddie Fuller was passing as white when he was, in fact, half black. He preferred dislike to hate.

Raoul Lufbery sat apart from the others with his eyes closed. Lufbery was old for a fighter pilot. Although he had lived more than thirty years, his real life had begun only four years before when he met a French barnstormer, Marc Pourpe, who was flying a Blériot in Calcutta. Lufbery became his mechanic and the two men grew to be close friends.

When war broke out in 1914 they were in France and Lufbery, a Frenchman who had become a naturalized American by serving in the U.S. Army, was forced to join the Foreign Legion. Pourpe helped him transfer to the flying corps. A short time later Pourpe was killed when his plane was shot down behind the German lines.

Lufbery never recovered from the death of his friend.

He claimed his successes in the air were mostly luck, shunned publicity, and rarely left the aerodrome. The evening before he had donned his waterproof coat to walk alone through the sodden woods where, as he usually did in bad weather, he picked wild mushrooms for the flyers' mess.

The other airmen respected Lufbery without understanding him.

Laurence Dawes was the first man in the room to hear the plane. He looked up from the table where he was seated, a pencil poised in his hand.

"A *Bebe*," he said.

"You're out of your fucking mind," Reed Blakely told him. "Nobody's fool enough to be up today."

Dawes narrowed his eyes as he tried to hear above the whine of the gramophone. "You're probably right." He frowned. "I could have sworn I heard a Nieuport," he said as he returned to his calculations. Beneath the table, Whisky, the *Escadrille's* lion cub mascot, chewed on a discarded boot.

"How are you doing?" Reed Blakely asked Dawes.

"I'm $6,240 in the hole," Dawes told him. "My next bet has to be $212."

"This system's a loser too?"

Dawes grunted. "Might be. Can't tell yet. Ten thousand's my stake."

For the past month he'd been working on a mathematical method to beat the roulette wheel. He hoped to go to Monte Carlo on his next leave.

"No system where you keep raising your bet after you lose is ever going to make money," Blakely said. "I know whereof I speak."

"Go to hell," Dawes said indifferently.

Blakely shrugged and dropped into a wicker chair, took a small journal from his jacket pocket, unscrewed a pen and began writing. He was keeping a diary of his service in the *escadrille*.

"After the war," he often said, "I'll be the first American flyer with a book in the stores. I'll make my fortune and retire to California and lie in the sun eating oranges."

"By the end of the war," Lufbery told him, "we'll all be dead and buried."

"Speak for yourself, Raoul," Blakely said. "I don't expect to be dead. They say we all have to die, but I've got a hunch that God made an exception in my case."

Blakely looked up from his journal, head cocked. "Turn that damn thing off," he said.

Eddie Fuller pushed the lever and the gramophone whined to a halt.

"By God," Blakely said, "for once Dawes was right. There is a plane up there in this soup. And she's coming in for a landing."

"The man must be a fool," Dawes said. "The kind of gambler who'd risk his whole bankroll on one spin of the wheel."

"Or he's drunk," Blakely said. "A Tommy who's had too much brandy and milk. God, I don't know how they stomach that swill."

Lufbery raised his head but said nothing. Eddie Fuller slipped the record back in the rack under the gramophone. The other pilots lowered newspapers and magazines or looked up from their letter writing to listen.

They all heard the intermittent pop-pop-pop as a Nieuport taxied down the field. The engine was cut off and the room was quiet.

Ten minutes later footsteps approached the lounge. The door swung open and a flyer swaddled in a scarf and heavy jacket strode in. Stamping booted feet, he pulled off his flying helmit and gloves and held his hands to the stove. The men in the room stared at him.

"I'm Francis Kincaid," the newcomer announced.

"Eddie Fuller." The two men shook hands.

"You actually went up in this muck?" Blakely asked.

"I've flown in worse weather," Francis said. "And in better, for that matter."

"We were just saying," Blakely told him, "that a man would have to be either a fool or a drunk to be up today."

Francis' anger flared. He'd flown to Behonne from Luxeuil against his better judgment after being told the *escadrille* was shorthanded and needed all the pilots they could get as fast as they could get them.

"By my calculation," Dawes said, "Kincaid here makes the thirteenth man in the squadron."

Lufbery glanced at Francis and shook his head dolefully.

Francis knew he should keep quiet but some perverse demon drove him on. He regretted his words as soon as he'd spoken them. "I didn't expect to find all of you huddled around a stove," he said. "I guess you're not the flyers your publicity in the Stateside papers makes you out to be."

There was a stunned silence.

Lufbery stood up. "Why don't you play us another tune, Fuller?" he suggested.

Eddie Fuller pulled a record from the rack and put it on the turntable. Music filled the room, "Oh, you beautiful doll, you great big—beautiful——doll." The gramophone wound down and the song screeched to a stop.

Fuller lifted the needle and started to turn the crank. When Francis looked from one man to the next, they avoided his eyes. He shrugged and walked out of the room, slamming the door behind him.

They can go to hell for all of me, he told himself.

Dodging cabs and carriages, Jerome Kurman crossed Central Park West to the large gray apartment house. When he reached the top of the steps leading from the sidewalk he heard a shout across the street and looked behind him to see a boy slam his heel into the wet ground and place a football tilted backward in the hole. The boy kicked the ball. Another boy, he must have been thirteen or fourteen, ran under the ball, reaching for it, but the football glanced off his fingertips and bounced away on the brown grass.

Jerome went inside the apartment house and crossed the lobby to the elevator.

"Seventeen," he said. The elevator operator, a white-haired black man in a green uniform trimmed with gold, slid the cage door shut.

"You be Miz Stouffer's brother?" the man asked.

"One of them," Jerome said.

"You look like her. Besides, she told me about you. She's real proud of her brothers."

"We stick together," Jerome said. "The three of us."

"Everybody here likes Miz Stouffer. And her boy, too. That Benny's sure one fine boy."

The elevator clanked to a stop at the seventeenth floor. With a nod to the operator, Jerome walked along the hall and pressed the bell of 1701. After his second ring the door opened and Eileen looked at him in surprise before smiling and stepping aside to let him in. Her flowing white dressing gown gave an ashen tinge to her face. Her black hair seemed shorter than he remembered it.

"Eileen," he said, kissing her cheek, "are you all right? After I heard I caught the first train down from Boston."

"You didn't have to," she told him. "I'm perfectly fine. As you can see." She sat on a flowered, chintz-covered divan and folded her hands in her lap. "Benny's at kindergarten." She nodded to the table beside her. "I just made tea," she said. "Would you like a cup?"

Jerome shook his head, tapping a cigarette on the back of his cigarette case and lighting up while

Eileen poured herself a cup of tea. She sipped the tea, her legs crossed beneath the folds of her gown.

"I talked to Martin on the phone last night," Jerome said. "He sailed for France this morning."

The cup and saucer in Eileen's hand rattled. She leaned forward and put them on the table.

"I told him not to go," she said. "I don't understand Marty any more. I used to think I did when we were kids, but not now."

"Ever since father died, he's had the idea he's responsible for the family. For me. Especially for you. He thinks he has to look after you because he's the head of the family. Be your champion, your defender."

"I'm perfectly capable of looking after myself."

"Oh?"

"Don't 'oh?' me! I knew what I was doing. I'm not the innocent little girl you and Marty seem to think I am. That you two want me to be. I don't need a pair of guardians. I don't need my brothers defending my virtue. My God, Jerry, I'm a grown woman with a son."

"I didn't come to argue. I came down because I wanted to be sure you were all right."

"I'm as all right as someone can be who's just gotten out of the hospital. Don't expect me to go bicycling with you in the next few days or ride a horse around Central Park. I'm a little down in the dumps but that's to be expected. Otherwise I'm fine."

"I'm glad, Eileen. And I'm sorry about Marty. I tried to talk him out of sailing but you know what he's like when he gets something in his head. He's just like he was when he was a kid. There's no reasoning with him. One day he was working at Kurkin and the next he'd thrown up his job and was headed for France."

"I feel responsible." Eileen got up and walked to the window and looked down at the street, at the two boys kicking a football, then across the tops of the trees to the buildings on the far side of the park.

"It's not just you," Jerome said. "Something Francis said stuck in Marty's craw. I guess he told Marty he wasn't a real aviator. Told him he didn't know beans about flying. Something like that. Marty's got a notion he's got to prove Francis wrong by becoming a combat flyer."

"I didn't know that. What Francis told him, I mean. I thought it was all because of me. That Marty had the idea he had to defend my honor. My honor! For God's sake, this is 1916."

"Our brother's a trifle old-fashioned. You always accused me of being stuffy, remember? Marty's ten times worse."

Eileen walked from the window and stood looking down at him.

"I wanted to have the baby," she said. There were tears in her eyes.

"You can't mean that."

"Don't tell me what I mean or don't mean." Her voice rose. She swayed, closing her eyes and grasping the back of Jerome's chair.

Jumping up, he took her arm and led her to the divan.

"I'll get you something to drink," he said as soon as she sat down.

"Cold water. In the kitchen."

He returned with a glass of water and handed it to her.

"Better?" he asked after she stopped drinking.

"Much." She smiled wanly up at him. "I wanted Francis' child," she said, "more than I ever wanted anything else in my life. I didn't cry, though, when I lost the baby. Lost *him*. It was a boy, did you know that? I was hoping for a boy and it was."

"I didn't know they could tell this early."

"It was a boy," she said flatly. She looked past him. "My day nurse's name was Patricia Moran. She was a big woman but not too old, maybe forty. Her skin was bad, all broken out like Marty's used to be. She cried when she told me I'd lost the baby. I didn't cry but she did. I haven't cried at all. The nurse did but I didn't. So you see, there's nothing for you or Marty to worry about. I'm perfectly all right."

"If there's anything I can do," he said, "you only have to ask."

She put her hand on his arm. "I know that, Jerry. I don't know what I'd do if it weren't for you. And Marty, too, of course." She paused, frowned. "He's not going to hurt Francis, is he? If he does, I'll never forgive him."

"He said some wild things when he found out you had the miscarriage. Don't worry, he's more talk than action. He'll get over it."

"I can see *you're* worried. I'll write him. You write him, too. That's what you can do for me. You've always been the family peacemaker, Jerry. Write a letter to Martin. Tell him to come home. That's what I want. I want him to come home."

"I'll write him tonight. I'll send a cable."

"We'll be in this war soon, won't we?"

"I think so. Everyone I talk to in Boston thinks it's just a matter of time."

"Mrs. Moran said I could come to the hospital two days a week to work as a volunteer."

"A volunteer?"

"To learn to be a nurse, Jerry. If war comes I don't intend to sit here in New York. Knitting socks. Folding bandages. Whatever women are supposed to do in a war. You didn't expect me to do that, did you?"

"Eileen," he said, "I've given up trying to guess what women, including you, are going to do. I gave it up a long time ago."

10

THE day after Francis Kincaid joined the *escadrille*, Captain Thenault assigned him to a patrol making a sortie over the Verdun battlefield. The five planes circled the aerodrome, forming a Vee with Thenault at the point and the others stairstepped up behind him.

As they neared the Meuse Valley, Raoul Lufbery peeled away from the formation to hunt Germans on his own. Francis nodded. At Luxeuil he'd been told that Captain Thenault, the commander of the *escadrille*, had been given no authority to discipline the American flyers if they chose to ignore his orders.

A piss-poor way to run an air service, he thought, but one he meant to take advantage of. Just as the German ace, Hans Reinhardt, the Black Falcon, usually flew alone, just as Lufberry flew alone, Francis intended to throw off the constraints of formation flying. He hunted best who hunted alone.

Not today, though. Today he would docilely follow Thenault while familiarizing himself with the terrain and his Nieuport. He smiled. He liked the feel of the *Bebe*; the plane, nicknamed Baby because of its small size—it was only nineteen feet long—climbed well and was hummingbird quick. If only Kurkin could come up with a model half as good. Damn Martin Kurman.

The four remaining planes flew north with the ghost of the setting moon to their left and a few stars still shining overhead in the pale light of the predawn. As the flight approached the lines at—Francis consulted the map in his map case—Avocourt, Francis drew in his breath in awe at the destruction he saw below him.

The ravaged land that extended for miles on both sides of the trenches reminded him of the Texas high plains country he had once flown over after a disastrous prairie fire. The ground, pockmarked by shell holes so close together that they often merged, looked like an artist's conception of the craters of the moon. The shattered trunks of occasional trees pointed at the heavens. Villages in the path of battle or within range of the artillery had only fragments of walls or chimneys remaining.

The sun had not yet risen and the artillery batteries behind the lines flashed in the dimness. Like obscene winks. Francis couldn't hear their irregular thump-thump-thump above the roar of his engine.

Smoke drifted over the desolate land, across the trenches and the No-Man's-Land between them and over the concealed artillery emplacements to the rear. From two to five miles behind both lines, observation balloons—"sausages"—floated lazily on the ends of the long cables tethering them to trucks on the ground.

As the flight of Nieuports crossed into German territory, puffs of smoke appeared a few hundred feet below them. Francis stared from his open cockpit at the black and white bursts of the Archies, the anti-aircraft shells, as they sought out the French planes. By God, he thought, uneasy yet somehow proud, they're shooting at *me*. Thenault ignored the ground fire and flew on to the north and east.

Though they patrolled along the front for almost two hours, returning to Behonne only when their fuel ran low, they saw only distant planes that fled at their approach or that they were unable to overtake. Francis noted that Thenault, for whatever reason, had avoided flying near the German stronghold at Fort Douaumont where Fokker air activity was reported heaviest.

After landing, Francis slammed his fist against the side of his padded cockpit in frustration. He was in France to fight the Boche, not to see the sights. Tomorrow, he vowed, would be different.

The next morning Francis shaved hurriedly, donned his flying suit, pulled on fur-lined boots, grabbed helmet and goggles and went downstairs to the messhall.

Thenault, he found, had already eaten. Francis joined Lufbery, Fuller, and Ostrander, the flyers assigned to the dawn patrol. The three men said little as they ate eggs and French rolls. As they sipped second cups of black coffee, Fuller whistled snatches of "Ah! Sweet Mystery of Life," Ostrander, who had returned from leave in Paris the day before, kneaded his forehead as though still recovering from a hangover, while Lufbery stared vacantly at a tapestry left hanging on the wall by the owners of the villa.

Francis snapped open his cigarette case and the others, after a slight, almost imperceptible hesitation, accepted cigarettes and lit up. They smoked silently as they were driven in a staff car from the villa to the field.

Francis walked around his gray Nieuport 11, nodding to one of his three mechanics. Satisfied with the plane, he ground out his cigarette under his boot, placed his foot on the step on the side of the fuselage and pulled himself up, swinging his leg into the cockpit. With his hands on the cockpit rim, he brought his other leg inside and lowered himself into the seat.

He breathed in the familiar odors of gasoline, castor oil, and the dope used to patch the surfaces of the Nieuport.

Francis pulled a webbed belt tight across his abdomen and locked it into place. Putting his feet on the rudder bar, he kicked left and right while looking behind him to make sure the Nieuport's rudder swung freely from side to side. As he pushed the stick forward and pulled it back, he heard the squeak of the cables and the thump of the elevator on the tail lowering and raising. When he shoved the stick from side to side the ailerons on the outer part of the upper wings of the biplane changed position, one up, the other down, then one down and the other up.

Good. The controls checked out. The other four

planes of his patrol were already idling nearby. Francis waved and the waiting mechanic walked to the propeller and put his hands close together on the thick upper part of the wooden blade.

"*Coupe!*" he called to Francis. Two French enlisted men walked to the plane, one on each side, and grasped the ends of the lower wings.

Francis checked the ignition switch to make sure it was off. The fuel cock was in the full on position. The mechanic swung the propeller to suck fuel through the crankshaft into the cylinders.

"*Contact!*" the mechanic shouted.

Francis switched the ignition on.

"*Contact!*" he yelled back.

The mechanic snapped the propeller down. The Le Rhone nine-cylinder engine roared to life, spewing blue-white smoke from the cowling. As the air-cooled rotary engine settled into a steady whine, Francis saw the last of the patrol's Nieuports lift from the field. His mechanic ran around the wings to the side of the vibrating aircraft, grabbed an oily pair of ropes and yanked the wooden chocks from in front of the wheels. The two men holding the wings let go.

The mechanic and the two enlisted men turned their backs as the prop wash hurled gravel and dirt behind the plane. The Nieuport, gathering speed, bounced across the field into the wind.

Francis held the stick forward until he felt the plane's tail lift from the ground. As he gained more speed, he eased back and the plane climbed, the horizon dropping away beneath him. Overhead, large patches of blue showed between drifting cumulus clouds. With the stick held back, he flew into the limitless reaches of the sky.

As the last of the five Nieuports to leave the field, Francis took his place at the right rear tip of the Vee, behind and above the other planes in the formation. They approached the lines farther to the east than they had the day before, near Chattancourt, with the scarred remnants of a forest falling away behind them.

They flew to the rear of the French trenches at ten thousand feet with the Meuse a pale ribbon a mile ahead. Lufbery, as he had the day before, veered off and flew north alone. After flying with the formation for a few more miles, the morning air cold on his face, Francis banked to the right and headed toward the battlefront north of Verdun.

He saw Thenault wag his wings and imagined the captain's exasperation, but he shrugged and flew on with the Meuse far below him, the French lines to his right and the German to his left. He had seen no aircraft other than two Blériot trainers since leaving the aerodrome.

Suddenly Francis tensed. Ahead of him, flying serenely in his direction from German territory, was a two-seater biplane. Francis maneuvered to put the sun at his back, remembering the cardinal rule of fighter tactics—always attack out of the sun if you possibly can.

He climbed with the rising sun behind him, the other plane above and to his left. Now he could see the machine gun tilted skyward in front of the observer's rear cockpit. The other aircraft took no evasive action. He was in luck, they hadn't spotted him.

He brought his Nieuport up from behind and beneath the other plane, trying to keep in its blindspot where the observer's fire couldn't reach him. His finger caressed the trigger of the .303 Lewis machine gun mounted on top of his upper wing where it could fire over the Nieuport's propeller. He closed to a hundred yards. The other plane flew on. Neither the pilot nor his observer had seen him.

He'd been right to leave Thenault's flight. He pictured his bullets tearing into the enemy plane, imagined the two-seater catching fire and hurtling to the ground trailing flame and smoke. He saw himself returning to the aerodrome.

"Any luck?" they'd ask.

"Middling," he'd tell them. "Shot down an Aviatik in flames."

He smiled as he anticipated the slaps on the back signaling his acceptance into the fraternity of the Lafayette *Escadrille.*

Sixty yards now. Fifty. His finger tightened on the trigger. He meant to rake the other plane's fuselage with all of the forty-seven rounds in his drum. Francis caught his breath. With a feeling of shock and near panic he saw the *cocarde* insignia on the bottoms of the wings of the other aircraft, concentric circles of red, white and blue. The plane was French!

Francis swept past and saw the startled looks on the faces of the pilot and observer. He wondered if they had seen the shocked expression on his own face. He'd been so damn close to firing. God! He'd been so sure the plane was a German scout.

An explosion rocked his Nieuport. Francis looked to his left and saw the menacing puff from a bursting Archie. Too close for comfort. He swerved to the right, speeded by the torque of his rotary engine, and climbed. Glancing down, he saw two more shells explode several hundred feet below and behind him. The Archies startled you at first, he thought. He wasn't ready yet to treat them with the disdain shown by the rest of the *escadrille*.

Flying just beneath mountainous clouds, he saw that he was behind the German lines headed for Beaumont. He hunched in his seat, angry at himself for mistaking the French plane for a Boche. It had been a close call. That's one mistake, he told himself, he wouldn't make a second time.

Below him he spotted a single aircraft flying from German territory toward the battlefront. With its lower wing shorter than its upper and with a heart-shaped elevator, he was willing to swear it was a German Aviatik. Coming out of the sun, he bore down on the plane. He'd be damn sure what his quarry was before he fired.

The plane below him flew steadily to the south. Francis drew closer. At three hundred yards he recognized the tell-tale German Maltese crosses on the wings, tail and fuselage. He swooped lower to attack from behind and beneath the other plane. He wanted to fire but held off, knowing he should get closer.

At a hundred yards his finger closed on the trigger of the Lewis gun and he fired, exulting in the steady tac-tac-tac-tac of his weapon. He swept past the German. Where was the other plane? Had he hit him? Brought his down? Climbing, he looked back. No, the Aviatik—and there was no doubt now that it was an Aviatik—had swerved at the last moment and had now resumed its course to the south.

Francis brought his Nieuport about. He wouldn't miss a second time. He heard the chatter of a machine gun and the thud of bullets striking his plane. He jerked his head around. Two Fokker monoplanes were on his tail, the lead plane's guns winking yellow flame.

They'd tricked him. The Aviatik had been a decoy to lure him into range of the two Fokkers waiting above. He'd been a fool and swallowed the bait.

Francis shoved the stick forward and the Nieuport dived. His plane hurtled earthward. He heard a tearing. His lower right wing? His heart lurched as he remembered the fabric tearing from the wing of the Kurkin. He swore. He cursed the two Fokkers and he cursed himself for falling into their trap.

He pulled back and zoomed out of the dive. The wing held. A Fokker was on his tail. Climbing toward him. Francis knew with a grim certainty that the Hun had him dead to rights. Machine gun fire spit at him. The Nieuport shuddered. The cloth on the shoulder of his flying suit tore. Had he been hit? He felt no pain, saw no blood.

He flew south. The one German followed, neither gaining nor losing. He didn't see the other Fokker. He hoped the Hun would only follow him as far as the French trenches. The Germans seldom risked flying over unfriendly territory. At least that's what he'd been told.

The hell with turning tail and running. If his number was up, so be it. He climbed in a *retournment*, mounting steeply, stick well back, turned, looping, right foot well forward, plunged down again, stick centered, twisting the Nieuport sharply to the right, bringing the controls back to center and still slightly forward, his feet straight as he resumed his original course. He was behind the German.

He pulled the trigger of the Lewis machine gun. The gun barked and tracers streamed at the Fokker. They swept off to the German's right. Not even close. At a hundred and fifty yards he was too far away. In his excitement, he pulled the trigger again, knowing he had less than a chance in a hundred of even hitting the enemy plane, much less one of the vital spots. What the hell.

Tac-tac-tac.

He looked behind him. The second Fokker was plunging at him like the avenging angel of death, his Spandau firing through the propeller. Francis accelerated until his exhaust blackened and his plane stalled, going down tail first. The Hun roared past him. Francis brought the Nieuport out of its dive and he sped in a wide arc until he was above the second German. Where was the first one? A quick glance failed to spot him.

Francis bore in from the left rear and fired the rest of his drum. Half-standing in the whip of wind from the prop, he pulled the gun down and wrestled another drum into place as he gripped the stick with his knees. There, the drum was locked in position. The Fokker was circling to get behind and below him. And nearer, into killing range.

The Nieuport's engine sputtered, sounding like a frying pan spitting bacon grease. The Hun fired. Short bursts, one after the other. Holding his position behind Francis and firing. Again Francis climbed steeply, the Nieuport sluggish but responding. He hoped the Hun expected him to repeat the *retournment*.

He kept climbing. The Fokker circled below him, ready to come in on his tail when he completed the maneuver. He kept climbing. No loop. No dive. Climb, climb, climb. The Fokker, realizing his mistake, started up after him.

A Nieuport 11 in good condition could outclimb a Fokker EIII. Could a Nieuport with a shot-up engine? With a tattered lower wing? Francis climbed higher. The Fokker was overtaking him. The answer to his questions was no. The German, though, had still not reached effective range.

Francis saw the welcoming billows of a cloud in front of him. He climbed with the Fokker in close pursuit. He was almost there, could almost feel the cooling wisps of vapor on his face. Tac-tac-tac. The Fokker was firing. The bastard wasn't close enough, only a lucky shot had a chance of hitting home at that distance.

Then Francis was in the cloud. Despite the cold, he was sweating. After wiping his face with his sleeve, he throttled down and rode with the wind on his tail. Heading east. The wrong way, farther into German territory and away from the French lines, away from the aerodrome. Even the prevailing winds seemed to favor the Germans.

He'd leave the cover of the clouds and fight if he was sure there was only one Fokker waiting for him. Or if his Nieuport was up to snuff. To leave the clouds now to face two Fokkers would be suicidal. No matter what Eileen may have thought when he swam out past the surf, he had no death wish. He remembered his last night with Eileen, the drive to the Cape, their lovemaking on the sand as the waves pounded on the beach near them.

He jerked his attention back to the here and now. The clouds were wispy around him, thinning.

He saw the halo of the sun. His compass told him he was heading northeast. The Nieuport climbed from the top of the clouds and he searched the blue sky. There was no sign of the Germans.

He ducked back into the protective cloud cover. He should wait at least ten minutes, he told himself, until he could be reasonably sure they'd given up the hunt. Then swoop from the clouds and scoot south as fast as his sluggish plane would carry him. So he'd live to fight another day.

He glanced at his fuel gauge. Less than a quarter of a tank left. The tank must have been hit, must be leaking. He blinked back a sudden vision of fire, the image of Leon Kurman standing amidst flames on the wing of the Kurkin as though crucified.

No, there was nothing wrong with the tank, he'd been up over an hour and three quarters. Probably he had enough gas to reach the aerodrome but little more. Eight minutes had gone by since he entered the clouds. He'd wait two more. The time dragged. He willed the hands of his watch to hurry. There, ten minutes.

Francis pushed forward on the stick and the Nieuport responded, a trifle sluggishly, nosing down as he circled to fly southeast. Cloud vapor swirled past him, the moisture cool on his face.

He dropped from the underside of the clouds and saw the French countryside below him, dappled by sun and shadow. A village lay off to his right with fields and woods beyond. He didn't recognize any landmarks. He glanced left. No planes. He looked right, twisting his head to see on his blind side.

A Fokker circled in wait a thousand feet above him. As he cursed his luck, the Hun plane swooped down. Francis shut off his motor and threw all of his controls to the left. The Nieuport fell, spinning at the same time, its tail up, circling around and around.

He'd dropped five hundred feet when he again heard a tearing on his right. Shreds of fabric streamed behind the lower wing. Shit. Had he lost the Fokker? Not likely. He centered his controls and his plane stopped spinning and dived straight for the ground. He pulled back, held his breath, fearful the lower wing would tear away and send the Nieuport into a final, fatal spin.

The machine straightened and he switched on the motor. The wing had held. A long strip of fabric tore free and whipped past his face. He turned but didn't see the German. The chatter of the Fokker's Spandau startled him. Still he didn't see him. Where was the bastard?

The German plane hurtled past, climbing from below, firing. How in hell had he gotten down there? The Fokker monoplane climbed to come around again. Francis knew he had one chance and one only. He had to anticipate the other pilot. He wouldn't get a second opportunity if he guessed wrong.

He climbed to his right with the Nieuport even more sluggish than before. The Hun circled and came around. Francis grunted in satisfaction. He'd guessed right. The two planes were on a collision course. He held the Nieuport steady. The Fokker came at him, not wavering, looming closer. He glimpsed the German pilot through the two whirling propellers. At a hundred yards the Hun's Spandau winked fire. Tracers streamed over the top of Francis' plane.

He waited a split second before he fired, got

off three rounds before the Lewis jammed. Damn! Instinctively he started to swerve to avoid the on-rushing plane. He stopped, holding steady. That would only give the German his vulnerable belly as a target, he told himself.

He'd ram the bastard first. He yanked at the cocking lug on the Lewis to try to clear it. The Fokker was on him. He saw the pilot's goggled face, the flashes of the Spandau firing through the propeller. He braced himself for the crash. At the last minute the Fokker veered up and away. Francis felt the wash of the other plane's prop. The large Maltese crosses on the German's wings imprinted themselves on his mind. As did the markings arrayed on the side of the Fokker's fuselage. They looked like tombstones. A record of victories? Of missions?

The Fokker circled to come in behind him. All he could do with his disabled Nieuport was wait and, at the last moment, take evasive action. And pray. Finally he cleared the gun and fired a few rounds. Damn, he thought, next time he'd make sure of the gun, of the ammunition. He smiled ruefully, wondering if there'd be a next time.

The Fokker climbed toward him from behind and below. Gaining on him slowly, steadily. The German wasn't taking any chances this time. He realized the Nieuport had been hit, was wounded and limping. The pilot meant to finish him off and circle like a vulture to watch him fall behind the German lines. They must still be over German territory, Francis knew. The German pilot would have a confirmed kill to add to his record. Another tombstone for his fuse-lage.

The Fokker was a hundred yards from him. Ninety. The Hun didn't fire. Eighty. Seventy. Still he held his fire. Give him twenty more yards. Francis planned to swerve to his right and dive. The other plane should have no trouble following him. Francis braced himself, expecting to feel the impact of bullets.

Sixty yards. He gripped the stick, looked back and down. The German plane dived. Francis lost sight of him. The Fokker hadn't fired. His gun must have jammed. A plane zoomed up past the Nieuport and Francis saw the red, white and blue *cocarde* on the wings. Two other French planes, both Nieuports, were above him, pursuing the fleeing German.

Francis let out his breath. *Vive la France,* he muttered under his breath. The motor of his Nieuport spluttered, then caught again. He looked at the gas gauge. Empty. Flipping open his map case he tried to match the landscape spread below him with the symbols on the map.

Ahead he saw low hills and shattered trees. Off to his right piles of rubble marked the site of what had once been a village. In the devastation of war, everything looked drearily alike. In the far distance he saw a winding river. The Meuse, it had to be the Meuse. But he knew the river snaked from German territory into French so he could be on either side of the lines.

His motor coughed a last time and died. He had no choice but to glide south as far as he could, land, and hope to hell he'd reached friendly territory. He was flying at three thousand feet. He'd be able to glide at least a mile for every thousand feet of altitude. Three miles, then, before he'd be forced to land.

I've probably nothing to worry about, he told

himself. I'll find that I'm well into France. When I land I'll be ten or twenty miles south of Verdun. Three explosions sounded to his right. The sounds startled him in the silence of his glide. Three more below to his left. Puffs of black and white smoke. Bursting shells fired from the ground. The German antiaircraft was trying to bring him down. So much for being over France.

Again he heard the bursts of Archies. Should he take evasive action and lose altitude? No, he'd risk the Archies, knowing his slow speed and unswerving course made him as vulnerable as a duck in a shooting gallery.

If a shell hit the plane, he hoped the end would be quick.

Another trio of shells. Closer, the explosions shaking the plane. Another burst, closer still. They were zeroing in on him. He wondered if they were deliberately taking their time, toying with him, making him sweat. Not likely. He hunched down in the cockpit, irrationally trying to make himself as small a target as possible as he waited for the next salvo, the one that must surely bracket the Nieuport and rip it asunder.

None came. He waited. Still nothing. He let out his breath. He must have glided out of range of the Archie battery. Odd, though, that other guns hadn't picked him up. He was at two thousand feet now. What other reason could they have for silencing their guns? Only one. He jerked his head up and looked over his shoulder.

A Fokker EI was a hundred yards behind him, a second above and behind the first. Francis saw a black insignia on the side of the nearer German plane.

He looked again. Not a Maltese cross. A bird, a diving falcon. So this was the Black Falcon, in at the kill.

When Francis swerved to the right his plane responded with agonizing slowness. The Fokker had closed half the distance between them. He heard short staccato bursts from the German's gun, heard the rounds tear into the fabric of the Nieuport's fuselage.

The Black Falcon swept past. The Nieuport had been riddled, Francis knew, but he hadn't been hit. The second Fokker was almost on him, firing as he climbed. Tracers streamed far above Francis' head. Thank God this one was a bad shot, he thought.

The second plane soared over him and Francis saw the French *cocardes* on the wings and the screaming Indian symbol of the Lafayette *Escadrille* on the fuselage. Lufbery? No, Lufbery had no more fuel than he'd had. Lufbery must have returned to the aerodrome long ago.

The shell-churned ground was less than a thousand feet below him. The other two planes fought their way to the north, circling, diving, firing. Francis saw trenches ahead of him. The rear German line. In some sectors each army had two, three or more trenches, one behind the other.

Soldiers in the trench fired up at him. He prayed that no machine guns would join in. He heard the thump-thump of artillery, the hum of the wind in the wires and struts of his Nieuport. The earth below was barren and pockmarked with shell holes. He passed over a second trench. More rifle fire. Faces turned up toward the plane. A bullet slammed into the wing below him.

He looked for a cleared level space to land. One spot seemed as bad as the next. The ground was uneven with water laying in the bottoms of the shell holes and in smaller puddles on the scarred earth. Blackened tree shards reached skyward. Smoke drifted across the battlefield from his right.

Francis saw a relatively flat strip directly ahead. He brought the Nieuport down as gently as he could, his wheels probing for the ground. The plane struck the earth, bounced up, came down again, the wheels smashing into the far edge of a crater he hadn't seen.

He felt the undercarriage buckle. The plane slammed down on its belly and, with a grinding screech, skidded forward. The lower right wing struck a stump and the plane swung around the stump as the wing crumpled. The Nieuport tilted up on its nose. Francis pitched forward, held in the cockpit by his harness. He smelled castor oil and damp earth. In the distance the artillery boomed. A machine gun rattled a short way off, fell silent, rattled again.

He unbuckled and looked around. The ground where he had crashed was relatively level. There were several small craters nearby and a much larger one ten yards in front of him. The plane had gouged a furrow in the wet earth as it landed, showing him that he now faced the way he had come. Smoke drifted from left to right over barbed wire entanglements just beyond the large shell hole. He hoped it was only smoke and not poison gas.

Looking over his head he saw that the sun had risen a third of the way to its zenith. The sun was to his right so he was facing north in the direction of the German lines. But was he between two German trenches or in No-Man's-Land? He had no way of telling. He had seen no sign of life since he crashed.

For the first time he wished he'd worn a pistol. Many *escadrille* pilots flew armed but Francis had scorned wearing a gun just as he'd refused to wear spurs as a few of the American airmen did. This wasn't the shootout at the O.K. Corral, he'd told himself. Now he wished he was armed. If a German patrol appeared, at least he would be able to defend himself.

Don't be an ass. Armed or not, he'd have to surrender if he was actually behind the German lines. Better to be sent to a prisoner-of-war camp where he'd have a chance to escape than to be killed.

He clambered from the Nieuport's cockpit and dropped to the ground, hunkering down beside the fuselage. Feeling his shoulder, he explored the slash in his flying suit where the Fokker's bullet had grazed him. His fingers came away dry. He'd been lucky, he hadn't been hit. Glancing up at the wrecked plane, he muttered, "Some luck." He'd been shot down on his second day in combat.

Taking his cigarette case from his pocket, he lit up. Out of gas and with little to lose if the Nieuport burned, he didn't worry about fire. This might be a hell of a long wait. He wasn't about to chance leaving the plane in daylight in the hope he'd stumble on a French outfit. If he did set out to the south, he'd make an easy target for German snipers and machine gunners. Better to wait till dark and then make his way south.

A shell exploded fifty yards ahead of him, sending a fountain of dirt and rocks showering down on Francis and the plane. A stray shot, he told himself.

He heard a whine and the earth erupted. This one was ten yards closer. He sat up. Again he heard the deadly whine of a shell. Another explosion, closer still.

He tossed his cigarette away. By God, the Huns were zeroing in on his downed plane, intending to blow both the Nieuport and Francis Kincaid to kingdom come. At least they'd told him one thing. He was in No-Man's-Land and not behind the German lines.

Crouching, he sprinted to his left, angling away from the Nieuport and the exploding shells. Another whine, another blast behind him, only a few yards from the plane. Dirt sprayed down on him. He smelled the acrid stench of gunpowder. He heard the bark of a machine gun and threw himself face first into a shell hole, rolling down its side into the water and muck at the bottom.

Francis crouched in the mud as three shells whined overhead in rapid succession. The explosions followed one after the other—whoomp-whoomp-whoomp. Flying dirt and rocks splashed water onto his face and clothes. He waited a moment and then crawled on his hands and knees to one side of the crater where he lay still, listening.

He heard no more shells. The Germans seemed to have lost interest in the downed plane. Clawing his way to the lip of the shell hole, he looked back the way he had come. The Nieuport was a black, shattered ruin. Nearby, smoke curled from a burning fragment of the fuselage.

Francis shook his head as he stared at the remains of the plane. He was saddened by its loss and angry at himself. She'd been a good ship, fast and maneuverable. Gallant. He'd served her poorly . . .

The day was warm, the noon sun high overhead. Only the distant rumble of the guns broke the stillness. Impatient, tired of waiting, Francis crawled over the lip of the shell hole and lay on the ground. He didn't know what to expect. Looking ahead, to the south, he wondered how far away the French lines were. There was one sure way to find out.

He started crawling on his hands and knees. He expected to hear shots, the whine of bullets. He didn't. The silence was absolute. No birds called. It was as though nothing lived here. He crawled on, saw a dark gash in the earth ten yards in front of him. A trench. It looked deserted. He hunched his way ahead, climbed over the sandbags piled in front of the trench and dropped down.

He stared into the black muzzles of rifles. Turning, he faced more rifles. *Poilus,* French infantrymen.

"*Americain?*" he shouted.

They smiled and nodded.

"*Americain,*" they repeated. "*Americain.*"

A soldier put his rifle down and embraced Francis.

They led him through a series of zig-zagging trenches past soldiers who followed him with curious eyes. The soldier with him, short with a thin moustache, jabbered at him in French as they clumped over the duckboards laid above the water and mud at the bottom of the trenches.

The soldier nodded as he told Francis that he had seen his plane come down. Seen him crash in No-Man's-Land. A French officer took charge of Francis next. They entered a dugout with a single lamp glowing in the gloom. The officer telephoned.

"Escadrille Lafayette," he said over and over. Finally he nodded and handed the phone to Francis who identified himself and reported the loss of his plane. He gave the phone back to the officer.

"They want to know where I am," he said in his ungrammatical French. He had been born in France, and as a boy had spoken the language fluently, but had forgotten most of it after a few years in Boston.

The officer spoke into the phone. Francis heard the word "Tavannes." The conversation over, the officer led him from the dugout. They stopped at an officers' mess where they ate and drank wine, talking of the war.

They trudged farther to the rear. The officer left Francis near a field hospital where he waited, watching the wounded being brought in on litters and in ambulances. The injured soldiers groaned in pain, calling out in French. One repeated a woman's name, Bernadette, over and over. A corporal, a bloodied bandage over the stump of his right arm, whimpered and then was still. Francis walked over to him. The soldier, tall and thin, was dead.

At last the staff car came and Francis climbed in beside the driver. They were halted near the hospital by a sentry to let a column of lorries pass. Later the driver became lost and had to ask directions. It took them two hours to reach Behonne.

The sun was low in the west when they drove onto the aerodrome road. Francis was hungry and tired. His body ached and he realized he had been more bruised in the crash than he had thought.

When they drove past the field he saw a pilot standing near one of the hangars, smoking a cigarette. Francis asked the driver to wait and he got out and walked over to him. It was Lufbery.

"I heard you'd crashed," Lufbery said.

"I lost the plane," Francis told him. "The Boche blew it to smithereens."

"The French say any landing's a good one if you can walk away. You walked away."

"I was lucky. Somebody in a Nieuport, from the *escadrille*, saved my ass. I came here to find out who it was."

"It was me," Lufbery said. "I came back to the field. Found you were still up. I refueled and went looking for you." He spoke English in short bursts. Like the firing of a machine gun.

"I thought you didn't give a shit about me."

"You're one of us. One of the *escadrille*," Lufbery said. "We're in this rotten mess together. All of us."

"I made an ass out of myself today," Francis admitted. "Not once but twice. I almost shot down a French plane and then I let myself fall for the oldest Boche trick in the book. I chased a decoy."

"Don't worry," Lufbery said. "You'll do. You know how to fly."

"I thought so once. Now I'm not so sure."

"You'll do," Lufbery said again. "You can tell about a man when you see him up there. Give me ten minutes with a man in combat. Ten minutes, no more. I'll know more about him than I could in a year of living with him. A man shows what he's made of up there."

Lufbery ground out his cigarette and they walked

"Did you get him?" Francis asked as they drove to the waiting car.

"Did you get him?" Francis asked as they drove to the villa. "The Black Falcon?"

"Not a chance. I was lucky. He didn't get me."

Francis nodded. They went inside and entered the lounge. When the flyers looked up at them, Lufbery put his hand on Francis' shoulder.

"Why don't we have music?" Lufbery asked. Eddie Fuller started to look for a record.

Francis sat at the battered piano and picked out a few chords.

"Do you play?" Fuller asked.

"A little. By ear."

The pilots gathered around the piano. Francis struck up a lively tune and one by one they joined in until they were all singing:

You made life cheery when you called me dearie,
'Twas down where the blue grass grows.
Your lips were sweeter than juleps,
When you wore a tulip and I wore a big red
*   rose.*

11

COLONEL Jean Dubonnet was a martinet. He was also a dedicated French flying officer passionately concerned with the welfare of his men. To some, the two traits were contradictory, but not to Colonel Dubonnet.

Because he was a disciplinarian with little patience for what he called "citizen soldiers," he was thankful when Martin Kurman completed his training in *chasse*—pursuit—aircraft at Pau. Because he was also a conscientious man, the colonel summoned Martin to his office.

Martin saluted perfunctorily.

"Stand at ease," Colonel Dubonnet told him.

Martin, stocky, with dark brown hair and brown eyes, clasped his hands behind his back and waited.

"I congratulate you on successfully completing your course of instruction at Pau," the colonel said in English. "Your assignment to a combat *escadrille* should be forthcoming in a few days."

The colonel placed his elbows on his desk and rested his chin on his folded hands. His eyes were gray, the same color as the fringe of hair that circled his balding head. While his face and manner seemed cold, his eyes were sad, almost wistful.

A plane roared past the window and the colonel turned to watch a Caudron two-engine bomber climb into the overcast sky. He stood abruptly and faced Martin.

"I suggest," he said, "that you request your release from the Foreign Legion and return home to America."

Martin stared at him in surprise. "I'm afraid I don't understand the colonel," he said as he tried to recover his aplomb.

"I believe I have made my meaning quite clear."

"But why? France needs flyers. Every day there's a new call for volunteers for the air service."

"To send you against the Hun will help neither France nor yourself. You will be a dead man within a week."

"I've flown for years," Martin protested. "Not only flown, I've designed aircraft. I've completed the course here at Pau. I'm a qualified *chasse* pilot."

"Each word you speak is the truth. Technically, you are ready to be sent to the front. That means nothing. I have seen many other aviators such as yourself. Today they are all dead. In a sense I killed them by signing my name to certify that they were qualified to fly in combat when they were not. You are an American. You can do more for France if you serve a brief tour of duty as a non-combatant and then return to the United States to encourage others to give their money and their support to our cause."

"You still haven't told me why, sir."

"When some men leave Pau"—the colonel touched his fingertips to his lips—"ah, they are aviators of excellence. Many of them, if they are fortunate enough to remain alive, become aces. Others, aviators such as yourself, though they know how to guide an aircraft from the ground and how to maneuver in the air and to descend, lack the touch of the combat aviator. They are—how can I express it? —inflexible in flight. They fly their aircraft as though they were heavily loaded drays, not the delicate machines they are."

"Many aces," Martin said, "almost failed in flying school. You know that's true, colonel."

"What you say *is* true. Some of them have stood before me in this very room where you stand now. Yet their failings were those of excess. They possessed an exuberance of spirit, an *elan*. An attitude of what the English call the devil-may-care. A wild beast can often be tamed, or half-tamed. As for yourself, it's too late to make a predator of you."

"I wish to thank the colonel for his advice," Martin said stiffly.

"I am clumsy with words," Colonel Dubonnet said. "If I have wounded your pride, I am contrite. Consider my words not as the orders of your commanding officer but as the guidance of a man old enough to be your father. Ignore them if you must, but do not take them lightly."

"I thank the colonel for his advice," Martin said again. "If that's all, sir . . ?"

"Dismissed," Colonel Dubonnet snapped.

As soon as the door closed behind Martin, the colonel walked to the window where he stood with his hands behind his back. Another Caudron G.4 rumbled across the field, roared past the window and climbed into the wind. The colonel glanced at a framed photograph on the wall behind his desk, a picture of a young man in the uniform of the French Air Service who looked much as the colonel must have looked twenty years before.

His eyes went from the photograph to the plane receding in the gray distance. Why won't they listen? he asked himself. The waste. The agony. The heartbreak.

The first klaxon sounded at twenty minutes after midnight. Soon the air was shattered by one raucous blast after another.

Martin threw off his blankets and, in the dark, struggled into his pants and shirt. He searched for his boots, found them beneath his cot, and yanked them on. All around him men cursed as they stumbled to and fro.

Martin hurried out into the dark, cold night. To the north of the field a machine gun rattled, then another. He looked up and saw only a scattering of stars. Slowing his pace, he passed the aircraft graveyard where broken wings, tail sections and fuselages were black outlines against the lesser darkness of the night sky.

"Raumm-raumm-raumm."

The familiar unsynchronized thunder of German bombers. Martin increased his pace. He tripped. A dog yelped and growled. Martin cursed, kicking at the animal.

He looked around him and realized he'd taken a wrong turn. The bombers were closer. Again he heard the French machine guns firing futilely. Saw their tracers arch into the night. The German bombers would be unopposed in the air. French planes weren't equipped for night fighting.

Bombs began falling on the far side of the aerodrome. Hundred pounders, two hundred and fifty-pounders. He saw the flash of the explosions and heard the dull thumps of the detonations. He ran past the rear of a hangar. There was a shelter a hundred yards ahead between this hangar and the maintenance shop. He saw no one, heard no one. The aerodrome seemed deserted.

A bomb struck two hundred yards from him, the flash lighting the field, the hangars, the barracks. Darkness again. Another blast, fifty yards closer. And another, fifty yards closer still. Martin pictured the bombs as they arced down from the German planes, one behind the other, pictured the explosions marching toward him.

He dashed to one side and hurled himself to the ground. An explosion rocked the earth nearby, pelting him with a shower of dirt and rock. He knew with a dread certainty that the next bomb would kill him. He heard the whine, screamed, threw both arms over his head and, his heart thudding, waited for death to come.

The bomb exploded beyond him. A good fifty

yards away. Thank God, he thought. Martin pushed himself to his feet and trotted toward the shelter. The crotch of his pants was wet. He cursed.

Another wave of planes approached. Martin stumbled down the steps into the shelter, opening the door, pushing the dark curtain to one side. A lamp hung from the ceiling and in its light he saw Sergeant Auger look up at him and smile sourly. He'd had trouble with the sergeant only the week before over mess privileges for guests. Martin considered the man an overbearing ass. The kind who fawned in the presence of officers while bullying subordinates such as Martin.

"You were frightened, eh?" The sergeant nodded at the dark stain on the front of Martin's pants.

Martin ignored him and sat between two French mechanics on a bench along one wall of the dugout.

"Our Jewboy is afraid of the Hun," Sergeant Auger said in a loud voice. The murmur of talk in the shelter quieted.

"What did you say?" Martin asked, blinking as he looked at the sergeant.

"You are evidently afraid of the Hun." Auger paused. "Jewboy." He spat the word.

Martin leaped from the bench and grasped Auger by the throat. His hands tightened, his thumbs pressing in. He felt the sergeant flail his fists at his arms and head. He ignored the blows as he tightened his grip. The sergeant's face was turning blue. His tongue came out and he gasped for breath. His eyes bulged.

Martin smiled as he increased the pressure. He shook Auger, who was a small wiry man, making his head bob back and forth. Martin felt hands grip his shoulders. An arm locked around his neck and pulled back. Hands gripped his hands, prying his fingers from Auger's neck.

Martin gasped, choking. Fought for breath. The dugout spun before his eyes. Still he held to Auger's neck. Even as blackness swirled around him.

When Martin recovered consciousness he was lying on the dirt floor of the shelter looking up into staring faces. Sergeant Auger sat with his back against the wall, his head in his hands, gulping in air. So he hadn't killed the bastard. Just as well, Martin thought. If Auger had died there would have been no end of inconvenience.

Auger meant nothing to him. The man he was going to kill was Francis Kincaid.

Two days later Martin drove to the front in a sidecar of a courier's motorcycle. He was still waiting for orders assigning him to the Lafayette *Escadrille*. Colonel Dubonnet, he suspected, was dragging his feet.

To hell with Dubonnet. The orders would come. It helped to have friends in Washington like Oliver Latham, the Kurkin representative who knew Dr. Edmund Gros, the director of the American Ambulance Corps in France and the man who had helped create the squadron of American flyers early in 1916.

The motorcycle roared past occasional old shell holes and villages with here and there a wrecked house. Luckily, Martin told himself, the sound of the cycle's engine made conversation difficult. The courier, a talkative young man from Sedan, would have liked to call Martin's attention to every point of interest along the way. Like a peacetime tour guide. Martin wasn't interested. He had other matters to attend to, more important matters.

As they neared the front, the sound of artillery fire increased and the shell holes beside the road became more frequent. The cycle jounced along rough dirt lanes and sped through hamlets where French troops were quartered.

So far, the fear Martin had felt during the German air raid had not returned. But he had to find out, had to plumb his courage. Not because he was a Jew, he told himself, though he was acutely aware of being one of the few Jews in the French air service. He had to discover for himself what kind of a man he was.

The interview with Colonel Dubonnet had shaken him more than he had wanted to admit. Could Dubonnet be right? Martin slammed his fist against the rim of the sidecar as he recalled Francis' similar words.

They were both wrong. He'd prove they were both wrong. He might not be the daredevil Francis was, yet he knew how to fly. Was, in fact, a damn good flyer. You didn't shoot down Fokkers by looping-the-loop or spinning earthward in *vrilles* or by any of the other aerobatic maneuvers they were taught at Pau. You killed Germans by being methodical, by waiting until all the odds were in your favor and then swooping in for the *coup de grace*.

Martin glanced around him. They were passing through what had been a town. Not a building remained standing. Rubbish and broken stones lay in the streets. Every tree had been shattered as though struck by lightning and the ground was a succession of shell holes, the bottoms of their craters filled with muddy water.

On the far outskirts of the town the ditches on both sides of the road were choked with the debris of war, smashed wagons, a treadless tank with a gutted turret, a twisted wheel from a cannon, the carcass of a horse. The courier gestured to a cemetery where thousands of small wooden crosses marched away from the road and up and over a slope in seemingly endless rows. As they slowed, Martin read one of the inscriptions: "Pierre Duellin, Killed in Action, June 26, 1916."

An ambulance sped past them heading for the rear. The courier pointed ahead, telling Martin in a mixture of English and French that they were almost to their destination. When they arrived they found that the village, in the British sector of the front, had been heavily shelled during the morning. Smoke still hung in the air. Tommies trudged by them, weary, some limping, others supporting wounded comrades.

The command post had been relocated so the courier had to stop to ask directions. After an English noncom gestured off to the right, they wove their way along a dirt road between shell holes to a building camouflaged with draped nets. The big guns rumbled ahead of them and an occasional shell exploded with a whoomp. Overhead, balloons floated above the lines, manned by spotters using telephones to direct the British artillery fire.

The courier parked next to two staff cars concealed beneath an open-sided shelter roofed with canvas.

"Remain here," he said. Martin nodded.

As soon as the courier disappeared inside the

building, Martin climbed from the sidecar and walked in the direction of the front lines.

The smell of gunpowder was all around him. A Tommy ran from a stone shed off to his right, one of the few buildings that hadn't been leveled. When an officer approached him, the soldier pointed back at the shed.

"There's a bloody unexploded shell in there," he said.

"Leave the blighter be," the officer said. "I'll send for the bomb squad."

As the officer walked off, another Tommy, a corporal, hurried up, nodded to the first soldier and started toward the shed.

"There's a bloody Hun shell in there," the first soldier warned.

"I've a week's provisions stored inside. Help me get them out."

"Not on your life. Nobody's getting me to go in there. I damn well don't want to get blown to kingdom come."

The corporal shrugged and went into the building.

Martin went on and dropped down into a trench. Two Tommies lay sleeping nearby, their heads resting on their knapsacks. He walked quickly forward on the duckboards and after ten minutes came to a group of exhausted men huddled together, some sitting, some leaning against the timbers supporting the trench's dirt wall.

He climbed up to look over the top of the earthwork in front of the trench. A hand grabbed his arm but he shook the soldier off and stood looking out across the devastated land between the British and German trenches.

Nothing happened. The thump-thump-thump of the guns, so familiar to him now that he almost didn't hear it, went on and on. He heard a droning in the sky and looked up to see a lone Nieuport flying two thousand feet over the lines.

A rifle cracked and then another. A bullet zinged past him, another embedded itself in a sandbag at his feet. He smiled. He wasn't afraid. By God, he wasn't afraid. Another crack of a gun, another whizzing bullet.

Martin dropped to his knees and leaped backwards into the trench. The Tommies stared at him as though they suspected he was ready for the loony-bin. Or whatever they called it. He ignored them and made his way back along the trench. He passed the two Tommies sleeping with their heads on their knapsacks.

Stopping, he looked more closely at the two soldiers. He saw flies buzzing around them. A fly landed on one of the men's faces. Only then did he realize they were dead. While he stood watching, two litter bearers plodded up, knelt by one of the dead men and lifted him onto their stretcher and carried him away.

Martin walked on toward the rear. The stone shed still stood, evidently the German shell hadn't exploded. Probably a dud. The Tommy he had seen first, the man who had warned of the unexploded shell, was watching the shed from a slit trench.

"The bloody fool's gone back in there," he said to Martin as he passed.

Martin nodded, then frowned. An idea had been forming in his mind and now the man's words had made it elude him. Give it time, he told himself, and it would come back. He walked on.

An explosion shook the earth, hurling Martin to the ground. Debris crashed down around him. A stone struck his back. He hadn't heard the whine of the shell. You never hear the one that hits you, they said. He was, though, unhurt.

Picking himself up, Martin looked behind him. The roof of the shed was gone and three of the walls had been blown asunder. Only the rear wall still stood. The Tommy who had been watching from the trench was brushing himself off. There was no sign of the corporal.

"I warned the bloody fool," the Tommy said. "He wouldn't listen to me." He turned to Martin. "You heard me warn him, didn't you?"

"I heard you," Martin said.

He wondered if the corporal would have lived if the other soldier had helped him remove the provisions from the shed. If he, Martin, had helped him. Martin sighed and returned to the vehicle shelter. One of the staff cars was gone but the motorcycle was still there.

He climbed into the sidecar and after fifteen minutes the courier returned. He glanced at Martin.

"Everything quiet?" he asked.

"A delayed action Hun shell went off in a shed a few hundred yards up the line," he said.

The courier straddled the cycle and started the motor. "That happens all the time," he said.

"One man was killed I think," Martin told him.

"He was warned to stay away but he didn't pay any heed."

"*C'est la guerre.*" The courier eased the cycle onto the road. "You tell some people a fact a hundred times over and they will not listen. Not if they do not wish to hear."

They drove away from the command post and back through the destroyed villages, past the sheltered trees, past the cemetery.

As he looked at the rows of crosses, the idea returned to Martin, full-blown.

I'll be a delayed action bomb, he told himself. *Francis will never suspect because he thinks I'm long on talk and short on action. I'll declare a truce between us and I'll wait. Wait as long as I have to and then, when the time is right, I'll kill him.* He smiled.

When Martin returned to Pau he found his orders waiting for him. He'd been assigned to the *Escadrille* Lafayette now operating from Luxeuil in northeastern France.

12

"SOMETHING big's brewing at Luxeuil," Walt Mc-Cready, the driver of the staff car taking Martin to the aerodrome said. "I'm usually in the know but this time I haven't the foggiest notion what it is."

"Why do you think it's going to be big?" Martin asked.

"Would they bring in fifty pilots and more than a thousand men for a routine hit and run raid on a Hun airfield? And build new hangars? And pack them with Sopwith 1½ Strutters and Farmans and Breguets? Not on your sweet life. Not in an out-of-the way place like Luxeuil."

They were driving through mist-shrouded meadows where streams meandered peacefully beneath a somber October sky. Ahead, hidden by the overcast, were the Vosges Mountains, while thirty-five miles to the east was the Swiss frontier.

"A raid into Germany? An attack on Strasbourg or Ettenheim?" Martin guessed, naming two Rhine Valley cities.

"Who knows?" McCready said. "But just between you and me, it's going to be one hell of an operation, whatever it is. The Red Corsair wouldn't be here if it wasn't."

"The Red Corsair?"

"Captain Felix Louis Maurice Happe of the French Air Service," McCready said in a tone that let Martin know he was probably the only person in France who hadn't heard of the Red Corsair. "The Germans have a price of 25,000 marks on his head. Four times he's flown to Friedrichshafen, just him and his mechanic, to bomb the Zeppelin sheds. You wouldn't believe the chances Happe takes."

"I'd believe anything," Martin said. "The way some aviators fly you wonder if they're tired of living."

McCready glanced in the rearview mirror at Martin, his only passenger.

"I'm pretty good at telling what a man does just by looking at him." McCready, for his part, had told Martin he'd been a timber appraiser in British Columbia before joining the Royal Naval Air Service. "Now you, I pegged you right off as a businessman. Am I right?"

"I suppose you could call me that," Martin said. "In Massachusetts."

"I'm not often wrong, even when it comes to you Yanks. Not that I have anything against Yanks, they're a great bunch. Why, I thought I was a good poker player until I ran up against these Yanks in the *escadrille* at Luxeuil."

"I've never cared for cards much myself," Martin said.

"You'll learn fast enough at the aerodrome. What else is a bloke to do while he's waiting for this foul weather to end? They've three poker leagues, the Yanks, penny-ante, minor and major. One dollar limit, four dollars, and no limit at all. Most of your Americans play in the majors with us Canadians shuttling back and forth between the penny-ante league and the minors. Once in a while one of us wins a big enough pot to go up to the majors for a time. You Yanks have too much money for your own good. No offense meant."

"None taken." Martin was used to hearing the complaint.

McCready turned off the road and drove onto the aerodrome. French Farman pusher biplane bombers and an aircraft Martin had never seen before sat on the field in front of the hangars.

"Breguets," McCready told him. The Breguets, like the Farmans, had the propeller mounted on the rear of a central nacelle.

They drove past two Nieuport 11's with the Lafayette Indian insignia on their fuselages.

"All I can say," McCready told him, "is that I pity Captain Thenault. It must be hell to have to lead men into battle and not be able to discipline them."

They stopped in front of the *escadrille* headquarters. "The name's Walt McCready," the driver said as Martin got out. "If you ever need anything from Paris, anything at all, keep me in mind."

When Martin entered the commander's office, Thenault rose from behind his desk. The captain, of below average height, was a dapper man with a trim moustache and black hair balding at the forehead. A graduate of the academy at St. Cyr, he was twenty-nine years old.

"I welcome you to the *Escadrille* Lafayette," he told Martin in precise English.

"Thank you, sir," Martin said.

"Your papers make mention of the fact that you are already acquainted with one of our aviators, *Monsieur* Kincaid."

"I know him, sir," Martin said stiffly.

"A good airman, Kincaid." Thenault sat behind his desk. "You can learn a great deal from him. I will suggest he help you to—What do you say in America? Help you to experience the ropes. Is that correct?"

"Yes. Learn the ropes. Exactly, sir."

"I try to make myself familiar with the American idiom." The captain nodded at several books on his desk, all the titles of which, Martin saw, were in English. "I do all I can to better understand the aviators under my command. They are a most intriguing and diverse group as you will discover for yourself. All France salutes them. Honors them. They and you are the vanguard of what we hope will soon be an army that will be the salvation of civilization. You will help us remain free just as the Marquis de Lafayette helped your countrymen win their freedom."

"I expect America will be in the war within a year."

"I pray to God it will be sooner." Thenault stood and walked past Martin to the door. "Come," he said, "I will escort you to meet your new comrades."

As they walked beside a camouflaged hangar, Thenault said, "I must present you with a word of warning. New aviators such as yourself are apt to be brash. They have a great fear that they will not show up well against the Boche. They take chances that are unnecessary."

"*I* don't intend to," Martin said.

"Ah, very good. Remember, you do not have to prove yourself all in one day. Take time to learn your trade. Study the appearances and the capabilities of the Hun planes. Study the terrain. Take care. I never thought I would live to hear myself, Georges Thenault, advocate caution. But you Americans, you are so rash, so impetuous. As though there were no tomorrow. In France we have learned there is always a tomorrow so it is best to be prepared for it."

They entered the hangar and Thenault stopped beside a trim Nieuport fighter. The machine, Martin saw, was a newer model of the *Bebe.*

"This is a Nieuport 17," the captain told him, "the creation of Gustave Delage. The 17's have new Le Rhone engines of 110 horsepower and reach 10,000 feet in nine minutes. The *Bebe* took at least fifteen. And they are faster in level flight as well."

Martin looked up at the machine gun mounted in front of the cockpit below the top wing.

"At last we have a single-seater with a synchronized gun," Thenault said. "More than a year after the Boche had theirs. And no more drums, the gun is a Vickers fed by a belt. Later you must see the British Sopwiths. Bombers and fighters. Marvelous craft."

"The driver who brought me here," Martin said, "thought a great raid was being planned."

"The greatest of the war! Where will we attack? I

do not know. When will it occur? Again, I do not know. I only hope and pray that we of the *Escadrille* Lafayette will have an opportunity for glory when the time comes. We were blooded in the skies over Verdun. Now we are ready to accomplish whatever Captain Happe asks of us."

They left the hangar. When they came to the pilots' lounge, Thenault opened the door and ushered Martin inside. The first man he saw was Francis Kincaid, sitting in an overstuffed chair, reading. Francis looked up and then stared in surprise.

Martin walked across the room with his hand extended. Francis laid his book on a table—it was Zane Grey's *Riders of the Purple Sage*—stood and, after a brief hesitation, shook hands.

"I will leave you," Thenault said to Martin. "I am pleased you have a friend in the *escadrille*."

"How do you like it?" Martin asked.

"Bloody boring," Francis said. "We haven't had a good flying day in two weeks."

"I meant the book you were reading." *He's different*, Martin thought. *Around the eyes especially. Tired. Older. When he looks at me it's almost as though he doesn't really see me. As though he's looking at something else, far away.*

"I like it." *The same old Martin*, Francis thought. *The uniform hasn't changed him. What's he doing here at Luxeuil? Especially now. Eileen wrote that he'd sailed for France but I never really expected to see him. He won't last a week in combat, the supercilious bastard.*

"It takes place in Utah," Francis went on. "The hero's name is Lassiter. One good man pitted against the world."

Martin nodded. *That's how you see yourself, isn't it, Francis?* he thought. *You against the world. Francis Kincaid first and the rest of us be damned. You were always that way and combat hasn't changed you.*

"How was everyone when you left the States?" Francis asked. *Eileen?* he wanted to ask. *How is Eileen? Why doesn't she write?*

"Jerry's working full-time with Henry at Kurkin. Business is booming, what with the war. Henry's still spending money as though it grew on trees. Bought a new touring car for himself and a pony for the kids." *You want to know about Eileen, don't you? You'll have to ask.*

"And Eileen?"

"Better. Still in New York. In her last letter she said she was working part time in a hospital there. Presbyterian, I think."

"Better? Was she sick?"

"Didn't you know?"

"She never said a word about it to me. What was wrong? She's all right, isn't she?"

You bastard, Martin thought. *You were what was wrong.* He clenched his fists and glanced across the room. Why didn't that fool stop playing the same record over and over? "Ah! Sweet Mystery of Life." He'd never liked the song anyway. Francis did seem surprised about Eileen. He might be telling the truth. Maybe he didn't know.

"She had influenza, I think. Eileen was never quite clear what it was exactly. She's all right now."

He's holding something back, Francis thought. *I can see it in his eyes. In the smug curl of his lips.*

"I've been doing a lot of thinking," Martin said. "About you and me. I'm offering you an olive branch,

Francis. For the duration of the war. Why should we be fighting each other when it's more important to fight the Boche?"

"I was never the one who wanted to fight. It was always you."

"Yes, and you damn well know why." Martin checked himself. *Don't spoil it.* In his mind he saw the stone storage shed, heard the blast as the delayed action shell exploded. "I'm sorry," he said. "I mean it when I say I want a truce." *Be humble,* he told himself. *Ask him to help you. He'll like that. Francis enjoys showing everyone how much he knows. Particularly about flying.*

"I've got a lot to learn," Martin said. "About combat. About flying. I realize that now." He looked down at his hands so Francis couldn't see his eyes. "You were right," he said. "I've found out I'm not the flyer I thought I was. Just like you said."

"You mean at Plymouth? I was angry. You're not as bad as all that." *You're worse,* Francis thought. *You never did have the feel for flying. I can't teach you that. You either have it or you don't.*

"Aerial combat's a whole new game to me," Martin said. "Do you know what they told us back at Pau? They had statistics about how long a new aviator lasted at the front before he was killed. How long do you think?"

"I'd say two or three weeks is average."

"Ten days, they said. My God, Francis, ten days and you're dead."

"Unless you're good. Or lucky." *The son-of-a-bitch is scared. That's the reason for his so-called truce. Can I trust him? What difference does it make, he can't do me any harm. And there's always the outside chance he means what he says. And he is Eileen's brother.*

"Will you help me, Francis? I'd appreciate it awfully." *God, he must see through me. He can't imagine I'm as humble as I sound.*

"I'll do the best I can."

"Great." Again they shook hands.

"Does he always play that same song?" Martin asked, loud enough for everyone in the lounge to hear.

Eddie Fuller lifted the needle from the record and stared at Martin.

"You don't like it?" he asked, a challenge in his voice.

"He likes it fine, Eddie," Francis said. "This is Martin Kurman. I knew him Stateside."

"Just say you don't like the song if you don't," Fuller said to Martin. He lifted the record from the turntable and flung it against the wall, shattering it.

Althouse, who was sitting at a table writing, looked up, shrugged, and went back to his letter. The door opened and Dawes stuck his head inside.

"The news is out," he said. "The target's Oberndorf. The raid's tomorrow afternoon."

"Oberndorf? That's 220 miles!" Fuller crossed the room to stand in front of Dawes. "Are you sure?"

"I'll lay you ten to one," Dawes said.

"Can't you bastards take anything seriously?" Fuller demanded. Dawes glanced past Fuller at Francis, raised his eyebrows slightly, then left the room and eased the door shut behind him.

"I'm not going on the Goddamned raid," Fuller said. "It's lunacy."

"No one's ordered you to go," Francis told him. "You know the *escadrille's* short on Nieuports."

Fuller grabbed a handful of records from the rack

below the gramophone. "I"—he hurled a record at the wall—"won't"—another record smashed into small black bits—"go"—the final record hit the wall.

Martin stared in amazement. Was Fuller crazy? Francis seemed unconcerned. Was this behavior normal? Had he been assigned to an *escadrille* of madmen?

"My best guess is that we can't put more than five Nieuports in the air tomorrow," Francis said. "I think they'll send de Laage, Prince, Lufbery, Althouse and maybe me. Don't you agree, Eddie?"

"Stop trying to make me out a coward." Fuller's mouth worked and he licked his lips.

"I'm not doing anything of the sort," Francis said. "I know you're as brave as the next man."

"I'm not afraid for me," Fuller said, his voice rising. "It's the Frogs and the Limeys. They're sending them over Germany to be killed. It's the Limey's turn tomorrow and it'll be ours the next day. You know that, Kincaid. We're just numbers to them."

"Oberndorf's a munitions town. Mauser rifles. If we can destroy the factory, we might shorten the war."

Martin had never seen Francis so patient. The war had changed him, there was no doubt of that. Maybe for the better as well as for the worse.

"The Farmans," Fuller said. "How fast can they go? Sixty miles an hour when they're loaded with bombs? The Breguets aren't much better. Death traps, both of them. Clay pigeons. And their bombs. Have you heard them? The damn things gurgle. They leak azote fumes, you know that, Kincaid, as well as I do. They're as likely to disable the French in the planes as the Huns on the ground."

"They're the best we've got," Francis said.

Fuller slammed his fist against the wall, making the framed photographs jump. He drew in his breath with a sobbing gasp and slumped into a chair, lowering his head into his hands.

Francis walked to him and put his hand on his shoulder. The other man's body heaved as he sobbed silently. Francis stood over him, waiting until the tremors stopped before taking his hand away. He walked to the door, gesturing with his head for Martin to follow.

Fuller leaped to his feet, knocking his chair to the floor. He ran after Francis. "Kincaid," he shouted.

Francis turned. Fuller threw his arms around him and hugged him, his head resting on Francis' chest. Francis put his hand on the other man's back. After a moment, Fuller drew away.

"Sorry," he told Francis in a low voice.

Francis nodded and, with Martin a few steps behind, walked from the lounge . . .

The assignments for the Oberndorf raid were posted the following morning: De Laage, Lufbery, Kincaid, Fuller.

Francis requested to see de Laage, who was the *escadrille's* acting commandant. Captain Thenault had been ordered to go on leave.

"Fuller shouldn't fly on the raid," Francis told him. "He's been acting strangely. He's not himself. We think he needs a rest."

De Laage shrugged. "*M.* Fuller is one of our best aviators. I have no choice. Captain Thenault himself made the assignments before he left."

Francis started to object but, realizing the uselessness, nodded, sighed, and walked away.

The pilots began crossing the field to their planes

at 1245 hours on 12 October 1916. They wore sheep-skin-lined coveralls above layers of heavy clothing, knee-length fur boots and, on their hands, heavy leather mittens over white silk gloves.

The first Farman lifted awkwardly from the ground at 1300 hours. The Breguets took off next, their engines straining to lift the 4,235 pound bombers from the field. The lighter, more bouyant Sopwiths followed. The four Nieuports rose into the air last and circled above the bombers while the air armada formed and headed to the east.

Visibility was good as the raiders flew over the autumn-tinted foothills and then above the dark green pines of the Vosges Mountains. As they crossed into German territory, Archies opened up from below. The bomb-laden Farmans, unable to rise above 2,000 feet, were raked with antiaircraft and machine gun fire. One staggered, hit by a 77 mm shell. The plane dipped below the formation, began to rise, fell again, righted itself, then plunged to the earth.

They crossed the pale ribbon of the Rhine. Five miles ahead was Ettenheim, the limit of the Nieuports' range. The four fighters banked, left the bombers and headed for home to refuel before returning to escort the raiding party back to Luxeuil. The Sopwith fighters, with a greater range, would accompany the bombers to the target and back.

The shelling stopped. A flight of Fokker EIII monoplanes dropped out of the sun and made passes at the bombers, but the Sopwiths drove them off. Twenty minutes later the bombers reached the Neckar and turned to follow the river north to Oberndorf. The bombardiers adjusted their sights for the single pass at the target.

The Sopwiths made their run first, twenty-four single-seater bombers guarded by two-seater fighters. Wing Commander Davies led the way down the valley, expecting machine gun fire from the hills on both sides. None came. He lined up his sights on the buildings of the Mauser *Waffenfabrik.*

Davies released his bombs and watched them tumble earthward. The other British bombers followed. Explosions thundered from below and behind the planes. Smoke billowed up in dense black clouds.

Happe's Farmans and Breguets lumbered down the valley. Unable to see the target area because of the smoke, their bombardiers released their bombs into the mdist of the fires and, lighter now, the planes climbed to 6,000 feet and headed for France.

The Allied planes were fifty miles from their rendezvous with the Americans and seventy from the French lines when the Fokker EIII's returned to attack in swarms. Evading the umbrella of Sopwiths, they struck at the slower French planes. A Sopwith fighter dived after an EIII, firing. The Fokker spun away and fell to crash in flames in the Black Forest below.

Another Sopwith 1½ Strutter attacked a Hun. A Farman bomber drifted into the Canadian pilot's line of fire, burst into flames and exploded in a violent orange ball. The Americans—de Laage, Kincaid, Lufbery, and Fuller—arrived to find the dogfight spread across the sky. Francis saw a Sopwith, trailing smoke and fire, hurtle into the clouds. Another spun earthward, the pilot dead at the controls.

De Laage plunged into the melee, opening fire on a Fokker who, in turn, was on the tail of a Breguet bomber. The Fokker shuddered and fell. Francis saw three Fokkers circling a Farman, dashing in to fire at the slow bomber and then zooming away. He flung his plane to the attack. Coming up under one of the Fokkers, he fired and saw the tracers from his belt-fed .303 Vickers bite into the enemy machine. The Fokker banked away, refusing to fall.

A second Hun swooped down on Francis from behind, overshot him, and Francis saw his tracers lace their way across the Fokker's belly. The Fokker spiraled away and nosed into a spin, trailing smoke.

He'd drawn blood at last.

He had no time to exult. Two Fokkers closed in behind him; bullets thrummed into his fuselage. Francis banked to his right and one of the Huns shot past on his right, his blind side. The other held his position, still firing. A Nieuport appeared from nowhere and bore down on the Fokker. Fuller's plane? Yes, he glimpsed Fuller's white scarf billowing in the wind.

The Fokker started to climb. Too late. The Nieuport closed to fifty yards, firing as he came. Closer. Still firing. Why didn't he veer off? The Nieuport slammed into the Fokker and the German plane's wing buckled. Locked together in a deadly embrace, the Fokker and Nieuport plunged from the sky shedding struts and shreds of fabric as they fell.

The returning bombers and their escort flew over the trenches. The Fokkers, low on fuel, broke off and headed for home as the Allied force droned toward Luxeuil. In the gathering dusk the pilot of one of the Sopwith 1½ Strutters lost his bearings and finally landed in Switzerland. He was interned for the duration of the war.

* * *

Martin Kurman, standing in the shadows beside a hangar at Luxeuil, watched the returning aircraft circle the field. The bombers landed first, then the Sopwith fighters. A Nieuport came down too fast and bounced across the field. When the plane taxied to a stop in front of the hangar, Francis climbed from the cockpit and dropped to the ground. His shoulders slumped with weariness.

Martin turned away. He was confused. He wanted Francis dead. There was no doubt in his mind that he wanted him dead. Yet when he saw him climb from the Nieuport he had felt a thrill of pride in his fellow American, his fellow pilot. He shook his head, puzzled.

The French dropped 9,548 pounds of bombs on Oberndorf.

The Germans claimed that production at the Mauser works was unhindered by the raid.

Six French and three English bombers failed to return to their base.

Six German planes were destroyed.

Captain Felix Happe, also known as the Red Corsair, was removed from his bomber command because of the raid's "excessive losses." He was re-assigned to the French infantry.

Corporal Edward Fuller of New York City received the *Croix de Guerre*. The award was posthumous.

13

SHORTLY after the raid on Oberndorf, Francis and Martin left for Paris on a three-day leave.

They rode toward the French capital in a rattling, swaying railroad coach, gazing from the windows at a countryside untouched by war, undamaged houses clustered in small villages, fields covered with the brown stubble of autumn, woods bare and stark.

A Tommy sat across from them, a slight, sandy-haired young man whose eyes peered through the thick lenses of steel-rimmed glasses. Every five or ten minutes he looked up from the slim book of poems he held open in front of him and quoted a line or stanza that struck his fancy. After nodding approval, he returned to his reading.

The train slowed and stopped, passengers boarded

and the train started again with a lurch and the wail of its shrill whistle. Another passenger train rushed past and from their window Martin saw a bearded man, an old woman with a kerchief over her head, a laughing girl. Again their train slowed, bumping across switches. On both sides of the tracks he saw drab streets alive with the bustle of early morning and, in the distance, the Eiffel Tower.

Paris.

The Tommy looked up. "Listen to this," he said. "It's by Rupert Brooke." He put his forefinger on the page to follow the words as he read:

Ye are men no longer but less and more,
Beast and God.

Francis smiled and nodded. Martin frowned. Beasts? Gods?

As train rumbled and groaned into the station, Martin felt a growing excitement, a thrill of anticipation. He didn't ksow what to expect from Paris, but he was certain it would be different from anything he had ever experienced. He remembered feeling the same way years before when he first visited New York with his father.

The two aviators walked along the platform carrying their duffel bags. The station, the Gare du Nord, was big and dingy and smelled of soot. People were everywhere, hurrying, talking, smoking, calling out, embracing, crying. A unit of French soldiers sat along one wall, waiting, their packs of dangling boots, canteens and shovels on the floor beside them.

A taxi took Martin and Francis to a small hotel near the Champs Elysees.

"We won't be in our room all that much," Francis said. The excitement of Paris had effected him as well, Martin noted. He talked faster, seemed more alive. Martin watched as Francis combed his blond hair. He's a good looking son-of-a-bitch, Martin thought, scar and all. I'll give him that.

Later, in the Crillon bar, Martin stared enviously at the French officers with their elegant ladies. A British major sat at a corner table, smiling easily at the woman across from him. She took a long cigarette holder from her mouth and gestured with it as she exhaled a thin stream of smoke. Her eyelids, Martin noticed, were blackened, and her face was an unnatural white.

"They say this is the best bar in Paris," Francis said.

"We don't have anything like it in Boston."

"We sure as hell don't."

"Not in New York, either," Martin said. "*Garcon*," he called. When the waiter came, he ordered two more whiskey and sodas. "It doesn't seem right," he told Francis, "to be drinking before lunch."

"There aren't any rules like that here," Frances said. "This is France."

"I'll have to be careful. I might grow to like it."

They heard a stir in the corridor. As they turned, a short dapper French aviator entered and walked through the bar. Men and women stood and clapped as he passed. "*Vive la France!*" one called and the cry was echoed around the room.

"What was all that about?" Martin asked when the room was quiet again.

"He's Rene Fonck, the French ace. I've met him. A cocky little bastard, but good, awfully good."

"It's his kind that keeps the average as high as it is." Martin lit a cigarette and sat watching the smoke curl upward.

"I don't think—"

"The ten days they say a new pilot has before he cashes in his chips. If it weren't for the likes of Fonck and Lufbery, the rest of us wouldn't last a week at the most." He tapped his cigarette on the ashtray. "Don't mind me, Francis. I'm the original wet blanket."

Francis leaned across the table. "The aerodrome is there and this is here," he said. "They're different worlds and the twain doesn't meet. The front's a killing ground. Paris is for living, for enjoying life. Don't get the one mixed up with the other."

Martin ran his fingernail down the white cloth on the table. He stared at the line and then made another that intersected it to form a cross.

Francis reached over and added two more intersecting lines. He put an X in the center box. "Your play," he said.

Martin made an O with his fork. In three plays Francis had a straight line of X's.

"You always were better at games," Martin said.

"A drink for the road?"

Martin nodded and ordered.

"Pretty soon you'll be speaking French like a native," Francis told him.

"Little good it'll ever do me." After glancing at the woman with the black eyelids, he leaned across the table and said in a voice made over-precise by whiskey, "I wouldn't know what to say to a woman like that."

"There's nothing to it. Just tell her how you shot down six Fokkers. In one day. The last two with a pistol after your machine gun jammed."

"I'd make a fool of myself."

"Listen," Francis said, "there's something I want to tell you. Some things you have to keep separate. Like I said, the front's one thing and Paris is another. Flying's a different world, too. I don't think a man who hasn't flown his own plane has lived. Not to the fullest. After you've been up above the clouds where you can see to the far horizons of the earth, you're never the same again."

He stared into the distance. As though he saw something that no one else could see.

"I've never felt that," Martin said. "To me flying is just a faster way to get from one place to another. Or will be one day."

"Flying's the most exciting thing a man can do in this world. Better than being with a woman. There's nothing like it."

Martin shifted uneasily in his chair.

"I got sidetracked," Francis said. "What I wanted to say is this. France isn't America, it's different. The same rules don't apply here and not only your rules about when to drink and when not to. What we do in France doesn't count after we go back home. France and the States are separate and distinct. What some people might think wrong at home isn't wrong here. *Comprehends?*"

"I understand what you're telling me but I can't say I agree with you."

"Good God, Martin, we only have two and a half more days in Paris. You understand that, don't you?"

Martin nodded.

"Then let's see if we can't make the most of them . . ."

They were walking down a tree-shaded street in the purple dusk. Martin's throat felt raw from singing and he was a bit unsteady on his feet. Francis, he noted with envy and a touch of irrational anger, seemed unaffected by the liquor.

Francis led him through an archway opening off the sidewalk. Behind the brick wall was a garden with several small, bare trees. Someone approached from the shadows, a short, heavy-set, mustachioed man.

"*Monsieur!*" he cried out when he saw Francis. He raised his cap.

Francis nodded as they walked past him. The *concierge?* Martin asked himself. Francis climbed a flight of stairs with Martin a step behind and rang the bell on the first floor. A thin woman in a black dress and slippers opened the door, standing aside and bowing when she recognized him.

Seeing Francis lay his hat on a table in the hall, Martin did the same. He glanced at himself in a mirror. His face was pale. Was he going to be sick?

"*C'est toi, mon ami?*" A woman's voice came from inside the apartment.

Francis paused in the open double doorway to the salon. Martin looked past him. The room reminded him of an illustration of a princess' chamber in a book of fairy tales. The light from two lamps glowed through their multi-colored glass shades. The carpet was light gray, the drapes a deep blue and gold. The bowls on the table were decorated with delicate Chinese figures.

A woman rose from a divan. Martin had an impression of black eyes, red lips, and a long, billowing green gown. Her hair was blonde, almost white, though her face was young and vivid. Her green eyelids matched the color of her dress. As she came toward them with her arms extended to Francis, the folds of the gown fell away to reveal slender pale arms and slim hands with long silver fingernails.

"Francis," she said.

Her voice was expectant and exciting, Martin thought. Francis opened his arms to her and they embraced as Martin stood to one side watching, wondering if they had forgotten he was there.

Francis held the woman away from him as though to admire her loveliness. Martin coughed and Francis turned to him. "This is Denise," he said . . .

They were in a restaurant, a large room of white and gold with a tree rising through an opening in the center of the ceiling. There was white damask on the tables and gilt mirrors on the walls. So many mirrors, Martin thought. The French must never tire of admiring themselves.

Another girl had joined them, a friend of Denise's named Andrea. Martin hadn't caught her last name. He hadn't expected to like her and so was surprised when he did. Even though, at least at first, her eyes kept drifting away from him to Francis.

Andrea was petite, a head shorter than Martin. Her auburn hair had just been marcelled, she told him, explaining it was something hairdressers did with curling irons. Her nose turned up; she smiled constantly. Everything amused her—Francis, Denise, Martin, the waiter, the restaurant. Everything. She liked to laugh. And to flirt. With Francis. With him.

When she looked at him from beneath her long lashes, her brown eyes sparkled in the candlelight.

Their waiter arrived with a great platter covered with small dishes of mushrooms, anchovies, sardines, hearts of artichokes, eggs, grated cucumbers and radishes. They ate, laughing, Francis describing Thenault, making fun of him. He was angry at Thenault, Martin knew, because he blamed the captain for Fuller's death.

The waiter returned with a bottle that was lacy with cobwebs.

"Chateau Lafitte," he told them, "from Paullac."

He poured the wine, Francis sipped it and nodded. They raised their glasses in toasts to France, the United States, the *Escadrille* Lafayette, the women of Paris.

Martin, who had sobered up in the cab on the way to the restaurant, shook his head to clear it. There were cobwebs on the bottle, he thought, and cobwebs in his mind. Francis seemed unaffected as he sang a snatch of a song, *"For 'tis love and love alone the world is seeking."* Fuller's favorite.

"In the United States," Martin told Andrea, "I design aircraft. My name is Kurman and Francis' name is Kincaid and we put the two together and called the company Kurkin. Our factory's near the city of Boston."

"Ah, Boston," she said, "I have heard of Boston. Is it near New Orleans?" Her cousin, she said, had visited New Orleans and found the city charming.

"No, Boston's a great distance from New Orleans," he told her. "New Orleans," he said, feeling daring, "is no more charming than you are."

Laughing, she covered his hand with hers. Andrea

was so easy to talk to, he thought. And she listened to what he said. She was charming, just as he'd told her. So gay and lively. She didn't glance at Francis now, she looked only at him. She was the kind of girl, he told himself, that a man could easily fall in love with.

The main course came. *Puree St.-Germain, Artichaux Lyonais, Cepes a la Bordelaise, poulet roti,* and *salade.* Francis poured champagne from a large dark bottle. They drank more toasts. To the Nieuports. To gallant aviators. To Denise. To Andrea. To love.

"Tell me more of your magnificent factory in the United States," Andrea said.

"Actually it's quite small. Someday, though, Kurkin will be the largest aircraft manufacturer in the country." He described the foundry, the testing shops, and the rooms where they asembled the airplanes. She was fascinated. How lucky he'd been to find a girl who understood business.

Andrea leaned toward him to straighten his tie and he glimpsed her pale flesh under the Vee of her neckline. He couldn't help staring at the tops of her small breasts. She looked down and then smiled at him. "Ah, *cheri,*" she murmured.

The night was cold and mist haloed the streetlights as they walked hand in hand through the deserted midnight streets. It had showered while they were in the restaurant and the cobblestones shone wetly, reflecting the blue light at the entrance to a Metro station. Andrea walked close beside him with her hand on his arm and he breathed in the fragrance of her, a strange intoxicating scent that made him think of veiled Oriental women in diaphanous gowns lying on cushions beside shimmering pools.

They entered a square with a fountain at its center, the water bubbling up from a Cupid's mouth to fall in cascades, first into a basin and then to a pool below. Andrea dipped her hand in the pool and flicked water at him. Martin leaned down, intending to splash her, and she ran. He chased her, caught and held her in his arms. Before he realized what he was doing, he was kissing her. She opened her mouth to him, clung to him.

He heard footsteps and turned from Andrea to see Francis and Denise watching them. Francis' face was expressionless. Denise, her hand holding Francis' arm, smiled in a superior, almost supercilious way.

The hell with them, Martin thought.

Andrea pushed him away and went to stand near the low stone wall that circled the pool. She stared down into the dark water. Martin came to stand behind her, looked over her shoulder and saw their reflection. She leaned over and put her hand in the pool and roiled the water. The reflection vanished.

"You do not like me," Andrea said softly.

"I do," Martin said. "I love you."

There, he had said it. He did love her. After the war he'd come back and take her with him to the States. She was the most beautiful girl in all of Paris, the most desirable woman in all of France.

"You are not serious," she said. "All soldiers say the same."

"I am serious. I swear I am."

She looked up at him, her eyes misted, her mouth partly open. Leaning forward, he kissed her and she put her arms around his neck and held him to her . . .

He was with Andrea in a bedroom in Denise's

apartment. Francis and Denise had disappeared into a room on the far side of the parlor. Before they'd closed the door, Martin had seen, in the glow of a candle flame, a vanity with a mirror above it.

"Now I know you don't like me," Andrea said from the bed. "I'm so cold, so lonely."

Martin removed his clothes and laid them carefully on the back of a chair and then walked to the bed. Suddenly he was completely sober. He heard the soft rustle of sheets in the darkness.

He slid into the bed and lay still. He began to tremble. Stop, he told himself, but he couldn't stop. Lips touched his upper arm. Andrea's tongue teased his flesh.

"Kiss me," she told him.

He reached for her and took her into his arms. The touch of her warm bare body sent excitement pulsing through him. His mouth covered hers and they kissed, their tongues meeting and entwining. Her small breasts pressed against his chest, her hands caressed the nape of his neck, her legs opened and closed around his, imprisoning him.

He thrust into her, their arms locking their bodies together, her legs wrapped about his, her sex drawing him deeper and deeper inside her. He thrust again and again, out of control, driving into her and exploding inside her as he heard her cries, her moans, and felt the bite of her fingernails on his back.

He rolled away and lay staring into the darkness. Andrea whimpered. Had he hurt her? he wondered. Had she been a virgin? He didn't know.

"Are you all right?" he asked.

Saying nothing, she turned away from him and

lay huddled on the bed with her hands around her knees. He nestled his face in her hair and smelled her exotic fragrance.

"I love you," he murmured as he drifted into sleep.

When he awoke, Andrea was gone. He sat up in the bed. He could make out the footboard and the chest of drawers across the room.

"Andrea," he whispered.

There was no answer. Where was she?

He rolled from the bed and pulled on his pants and shirt. Going to the window he pushed the shade to one side and looked down. On the other side of the street a tall black man was sweeping in front of a grocery and, as he watched, a horse-drawn cart piled high with turnips rolled past the apartment house.

Martin walked on bare feet to the bedroom door. It was open.

"Andrea," he called softly. He wanted to take her in his arms again, hold her, kiss her. Love her.

Furniture loomed blackly in the empty parlor. Martin walked slowly across the room with his hands outstretched for fear of knocking into a table and breaking a vase or bowl. He heard a woman's soft voice. Someone laughed.

He saw that the door to the other bedroom was open and remembered it had been closed earlier. Martin approached the doorway, curious yet afraid of being discovered. He stopped and looked into the room where he saw a single candle flickering on a high table. He heard voices, then silence followed by sounds he couldn't interpret.

From where he stood he could only see the foot of a large bed. Edging nearer the door, he peered into the room and saw a reflection in a mirror. Of Francis. He was on the bed, naked. Denise sat in a chair beside the bed murmuring words he couldn't hear.

Andrea was on the bed with Francis, facing the other way. Martin drew in his breath as, naked, she crawled over Francis on her hands and knees, straddling him, crawling forward until her legs were on either side of his head and her face was above his distended sex. Slowly she lowered her body and they joined. Denise spoke to them as though offering amused advice.

Martin closed his eyes. Gagging, he turned and hurried across the parlor to the other bedroom. He finished dressing and crossed the parlor on tiptoe, unlatched the door and trotted down the outside stairs.

As he walked along the almost deserted streets on his way back to their room, he remembered the English soldier on the train. *God and beast*, he had quoted.

They were beasts, all three of them.

14

THE night was dark and rain fell intermittently as their train rattled from Paris to the *escadrille*'s new base at Cachy. Martin sat with his arms folded and his eyes closed, pretending he was asleep. Francis, seated across from him, held a large bottle of champagne in one hand and a longstemmed glass in the other. Each time he drained the glass, he immediately refilled it.

"Here's to Captain Georges Thenault." Francis raised his glass. "May the bastard rot in hell."

Martin watched him through slitted eyelids. He had caught only brief glimpses of Francis during the last two days. Neither had mentioned Denise or Andrea and Martin didn't know whether Francis was aware he had seen him with the two girls. He didn't give a damn, he told himself, whether Francis knew or not.

"Here, have some champagne." Francis held out an almost full glass.

Martin opened his eyes and shook his head.

"You only live once," Francis said.

Martin had to admire the man's capacity for liquor. And his endurance. He wondered if Francis had slept more than a few hours during the leave. Once back at Cachy he'd have to sleep for twenty-four hours straight.

"I don't want any champagne," Martin said. "I think I drank more these last three days in Paris than I did all last year."

"One more glass won't hurt you. We'll drink a toast to Captain Thonault."

"It wasn't his fault Fuller was killed. Thenault didn't realize the state he was in."

"It's the commanding officer's duty to know."

"Give me that glass." Martin took the champagne from Francis and raised his hand in a toast.

"Here's to Eileen," he said.

Francis' head jerked up. For a moment Martin thought he was about to lash at him with his fist but then Francis relaxed and smiled his slow, lazy smile. He grinned. Taking the glass from Martin, he raised it to his lips.

"To Eileen," he said before he drank. "She's one of a kind." He stared at Martin as though challenging him to mention Denise and what he'd seen in Paris.

You hypocritical bastard, Martin wanted to shout. *How can you pretend to care for Eileen after what happened in Paris?* All that bullshit about France and the States being two separate worlds. Claiming that what a man did here didn't count back home. Meaningless words. Excuses to let Francis do whatever he damned well pleased.

Martin leaned forward with his hands on his thighs.

"You act like you have something on your mind," Francis said.

Martin swung his open palm and struck the empty glass from Francis' hand. It struck the side of the coach next to the window, shattered, and fell to the floor in pieces. Most of the other passengers slept on; an old man glanced at them and shrugged; a woman frowned.

"You've had enough to drink," Martin said.

Francis stared at him as though unperturbed. If anything, he looked mildly amused, Martin thought. Francis' unconcern infuriated him. He clenched his hands into fists.

"I may have had a bit to drink," Francis said calmly, "yet you're the one making the row."

Martin fought to control himself. At last he drew in a deep breath and sank back in his seat.

"You'll be in no shape to fly," he said as though he had to justify himself.

"The *Escadrille* Lafayette has an unwritten rule," Francis said. "A very practical rule. No pilot's ordered to fly until at least eight hours after he returns from leave." He raised the bottle to his lips, drank the last of the champagne and placed the bottle on the floor under his seat. "I'll admit I'll need every minute of those eight hours." He leaned his head against the corner of the seat and stared from the window into the dark night. It began to rain and water slanted across the pane.

Ten minutes later the train ground to a halt and they climbed down to the platform where they walked through billows of smoke hissing from the locomotive. They passed a porter in a blue smock hauling a hand-cart loaded with baggage up onto the platform. The train whistle squealed and a French soldier ran from a *urinoir* at the side of the shed, grasped the handhold beside the coach steps and jumped aboard. The train jerked ahead, gathered speed, and was gone.

They waited for a ride to the aerodrome in the high dark train shed as water fell from the edge of the roof to the platform with a steady drip-drip-drip. An hour later a lorry pulled up outside and they hurried into the drizzling rain to hail the driver. They rode crowded in the cab as the truck crawled through the rain with its lights out. Francis stared straight in front of him while Martin dozed, jerked awake, and dozed again.

The lorry skidded to a stop. "Here you are, mates," the driver told them.

They jumped into the mud and retrieved their bags from the rear of the truck. The rain was falling harder. The airfield was dark and quiet. It must be well after midnight, Martin thought. They trudged to their hut-like quarters and, once inside, walked down the aisle past the partitions separating the sleeping men. As soon as Francis dropped his duffel bag beside his cot he started back toward the door.

Martin followed. "Where in God's name are you going?" he whispered.

"Got to find Thenault and report back from leave," Francis mumbled.

"Tell him in the morning. He sure as hell doesn't want to see you now."

"Why should that bastard get to sleep when I'm awake?" Francis stumbled as he reached for the door handle.

He was, Martin saw, staggering drunk. As though all the liquor Francis had consumed in Paris was at last having its effect. Martin took him by the arm and began leading him to his cot.

"Take your Goddamned hands off me." Francis shook loose and reached for the door again.

"Knock it off," one of the pilots said.

"Get some sleep first," Martin told him.

"What's between me and her is none of your business."

"Her?"

"Eileen. Your fucking sister," Francis said.

Martin froze. Rage engulfed him. He'd kill Francis for that. He lunged at him but the door slammed in his face. Francis was gone.

"For Christ's sake," someone said.

Martin plunged from the barracks into the rain. He saw Francis' dark form striding away from him in the direction of the officers' quarters. He ran after him. His shin struck a railing and he cursed, hopping on one foot as he massaged his leg.

A door opened ahead of him and for a moment he saw Francis silhouetted in the light. The door closed. Martin ran to the building and flung the door open. There was no sign of Francis. Halfway down a long corridor a single lamp glowed on the wall. Martin had never been in the officers' quarters and had no idea where Thenault's room was. If that was really where Francis was going.

As he ran along the corridor he looked right and left at the closed doors. Some had names lettered on cards thumbtacked to them, some did not. The corridor ended in a T with one hallway leading right, one left. Martin stopped, undecided. He recalled his vow to kill Francis. At the same time he was trying to stop him from disturbing Thenault. He didn't know what he wanted. He realized his head was beginning to pound.

A sound came from the right-hand corridor and Martin ran that way. A fall of light came from an open door near the far end. He slowed as he neared the door, then stopped and looked inside.

The room was long and narrow with a single window at its opposite end facing the door. Rivulets of water streamed down the panes. Thenault's cot had been overturned and his blankets lay in a heap. Captain Thenault, dressed in a long white nightgown, sat on the floor staring up at Francis.

"Get up, you bastard," Francis shouted at him. "Get up, get up."

Martin stood staring at the two men.

As Thenault pushed himself to his feet, the captain glanced at a clock on a stand near the overturned cot.

"It is two in the morning." Thenault's voice was muzzy with sleep.

"I'm up, why aren't you?" Francis demanded.

"You are drunk," Thenault said. "You don't know what you're doing."

Martin crossed the room and took Francis by the arm and started to pull him away while at the same time talking over his shoulder to the captain.

"I'll take care of Kincaid," he said. "I'll see he gets to bed."

"You Americans are children," Thenault said. In his nightgown he reminded Martin of a picture illustrating a poem he'd read as a child, *The Visit of St. Nicholas*.

"It's time you knew what it feels like," Francis told Thenault. Martin wondered what he was talking about.

"Children," Thenault repeated. As he came wider awake his face reddened with anger.

"And you're a bastard," Francis said to Martin as he tried to shake off his hand.

"If you Americans persist in acting like children," Thenault said, "I will be required to treat you like children. You have too much money, you drink too much, you gamble too much, all of you. You have no idea what it means to be a soldier."

"I'm not a fucking soldier," Francis shouted. "Is that what you think I am, a soldier? I'm an aviator."

"You are a soldier in the service of France," Thenault said, "and I am your commanding officer. You seem to have forgotten that fact, *Corporal* Kincaid. And this is not the first time."

"I'm tired of listening to him," Francis said to Martin. "It's time I hit the sack."

Thenault walked up to Francis and, with his face inches from the American's, said in a deathly calm voice, "You will listen to what I have to say first. I order you to fly in the dawn patrol tomorrow morning. This morning. You will be prepared at zero four hundred hours."

"Sir," Martin said, "he's in no condition to fly. You can see that."

"Do you understand what I say, *Corporal* Kincaid?" Thenault demanded.

"I understand," Francis said. "If you think I won't be ready, you're wrong." He turned on his heel and walked from the room with Martin a step behind him.

"Nobody will be able to fly today," Martin said as he followed Francis down the corridor. "Not in this rain."

When they left the officers' quarters they found that, though the night was dark and damp, the rain had stopped.

"You'd better get some shuteye," Martin said.

"He thinks I won't be able to fly today," Francis said, "because I had a few drinks." He seemed completely sober. "I'll show the bastard."

"You've time for a few hours' sleep before dawn," Martin said.

"I'm not going to bed. Once I lie down I'll never get up again. What I need is some black coffee."

The two Americans sat in the deserted messhall with a pot of coffee on the table between them. Francis grimaced as he drank. His blue eyes were bloodshot and from time to time his head nodded forward and he had to jerk himself awake.

A sense of impending disaster seemed to have gathered about them, Martin thought, a feeling of doom as somber and real as the murky night. Francis was determined to fly with the dawn patrol. If he did, Martin was sure, he would never come back. If the Huns didn't shoot him from the sky he would fall asleep at the controls, go into a spin, and crash.

Martin gripped Francis' wrist. "I'll take your place," he said.

Francis stared at him in surprise. "Don't be a fool."

"Thenault will never know. Not with my helmet and goggles on."

Francis smiled thinly. "He'd know as soon as you got the Nieuport off the ground. You don't fly like me. Never did. Never could even if you wanted to."

The old anger rose in Martin. He bit his lip to hold it in check.

"You'll only kill yourself if you go up," he said. "What good will that do? It doesn't make sense."

"War doesn't make sense." Francis stared at the dregs of the coffee in his cup. "The hell with all of it," he said. "The hell with Thenault. I'm flying and that's the end of it." As he left the messhall to return to the barracks to put on his flying clothes, he said, "When you see her, tell Eileen I was thinking about her."

"I will. And I won't say a word about the other," Martin promised.

"The other?" Francis frowned. "Oh, you mean Paris. I didn't expect you would. Like I told you, that has nothing to do with Eileen."

Isn't this what you wanted? Martin asked himself as he stood looking after Francis. *You hate him, don't you?*

Yes, he told himself, he did. And yet there was a bond between them that he couldn't explain. If he didn't know he hated Francis, he could almost believe he loved him.

A half hour later Martin watched the first flight of the day leave Cachay. Lufbery, Althouse, and Kincaid. As the three planes rose into a gray and cloudy sky, Francis' Nieuport climbed straight and true.

Martin began to relax. Francis might pull it off. Suddenly Francis' plane drifted off to the west, recovered and followed the others for a few minutes only to veer away again, this time to the east. And then the three planes were in the clouds and he could no longer see them.

Martin strode to the barracks and pulled on his flying clothes. Thenault intercepted him as he was hurrying to his Nieuport.

"I thought I'd go up and orient myself to the *escadrille's* sector," Martin told him.

"It's a poor day for flying." Thenault stared at the cloud cover to the east, the direction taken by the three Nieuports. "I expect the aircraft will soon return with nothing to report."

Martin guessed the captain was regretting his decision to send Francis on the patrol.

When Thenault turned away, Martin climbed into the cockpit of his plane and signaled the mechanic. He let the motor warm briefly before lifting off into the wind. The cloud cover hugged the ground, the ceiling under five hundred feet, and he climbed into the overcast intending to fly in the direction the other planes had taken once he was above the clouds. Somehow, he told himself, he'd be able to help Francis.

Would he ever reach the top of the clouds? Martin peered upward, searching for the first glimmer of the rising sun, but saw only the enveloping mist. He seemed to be flying through an endless tunnel that opened in front of him only to close in behind.

He realized how tired he was. His headache had returned. He shut his eyes for a moment. No, he couldn't afford to doze. Without a horizon, he was in danger of losing all sense of direction, he risked falling into a spin. The Le Rhone engine droned, the wires sang, the mist of the clouds beaded his face.

He seemed to be traveling between two worlds. Below him was the world of trenches and guns, of muck and mud and barbed wire, where death lurked behind every barricade. And above? He looked past his Vickers machine gun, past the whirling prop, into the cloud. He saw nothing but darkness.

Five minutes later a glow appeared off to his right. As he climbed, the cloud thinned and he broke through into the light. To the southeast the rising sun shone pale and yellow a short distance above the clouds on the horizon. His altimeter read 3,000 feet. The cloud cover below him stretched away on all sides like a calm and endless sea.

Though he looked above him and to all points of the compass, he saw no other planes. Where in the hell was the patrol?

As he flew into the rising sun toward the Somme Valley, Martin felt a great aloneness and, at the same time, a sense of rising excitement. As though he was venturing where no man had ever been before. This must be what Francis meant when he talked of the joy of flight, he thought.

Early navigators must have felt this same excitement as they sailed for the Indies over uncharted seas, defying the threat of lurking monsters and waterfalls ready to sweep their ships over the edge of the Earth. Columbus, Drake, Magellan, all of them must have known this sense of aloneness, this frightening yet awesome thrill of venturing into the unknown.

Below him the ocean of clouds extended as far as he could see. The sun shone in front of him at eleven o'clock and the sky overhead was an unvarying pale blue. If he had fuel enough he could fly on and on until he eventually circled the globe. Here in the sky, the artificial boundaries and borders of man meant nothing. There were no frontiers in the air. Only the sky itself was a frontier. The last frontier.

He looked to the south and saw a wisp of cloud rise above the others. As he watched, the wisp grew, swelling and filling in, becoming larger and larger until it towered above its fellows. He was witnessing a small miracle, he realized, the birth of a cloud.

When the sun caught the mist around the new cloud, a rainbow formed. Not an arc reaching from horizon to horizon but a perfect circle of color in the sky. Like a multi-hued halo, an omen of good fortune.

Martin breathed deeply as the events of the past days and weeks, the bitter memory of Paris, of Luxeuil, of Pau and the colonel who had suggested that he return to the States, the memory of Francis, all fell from him. His world consisted only of the comforting vibration of his Nieuport, the glory of the rising sun, the carpet of clouds below him and the limitless blue sky above.

He looked at the sun and blinked as the light dazzled his eyes. Someday, he told himself, not in his time but his children's, men would escape from this envelope of air around the earth. They'd soar to the moon, to the planets, and beyond. Perhaps to the stars.

He was the lord of all he surveyed. Flyers were akin to gods. He was like a god. He was a god.

He remembered the line from Rupert Brooke: Beast or God.

After taking a last look and seeing no other aircraft, he angled his Nieuport down. Ten minutes later he broke under the cover of the clouds. A quick glance told him he was still alone in the sky.

The ceiling had risen since he'd left the aerodrome and, off to the west, he thought he saw patches of blue between the clouds. Below him the ground was still shadowed. To the north he saw the flash of artillery fire.

Martin studied the countryside trying to make out landmarks in the gloom of early morning. He didn't see the Fokker drop from the clouds and swoop beneath him. The enemy plane held its fire until it closed to less than a hundred yards and then the pilot fired a series of short bursts into the Nieuport.

Martin heard the tac-tac-tac of the machine gun. Startled, he looked around just as a bullet slammed into his back. The impact hurled him against his harness. Another bullet tore through his helmet into the side of his head. He slumped forward, his Nieuport nosing down into a spin as the Fokker, a plane with a black bird of prey, a falcon, painted on its fuselage, hovered in the sky above him.

Francis Kincaid walked slowly through the temporary morgue near Amiens. The attendant, a short man with vacant, staring eyes, led him to a wooden coffin, lifted the cover, and Francis glanced inside. He looked quickly away.

Francis nodded and the attendant replaced the wooden cover. As Francis turned, he heard a steady drip-drip-drip and he remembered the train shed where he and Martin had waited on their way back from Paris as the rain dripped from the edge of the roof to the platform. In his mind he pictured blood leaking from Martin's coffin and falling to the concrete floor. When he turned there was no blood. Water dripped from a pipe along the far wall into a dark puddle on the floor.

He walked to the door and went out into the cold November sun.

15

"LIEUTENANT Jerome Kurman reporting for duty, sir."

Colonel Billy Mitchell pushed back his chair and stood up. He saluted casually and then extended his hand.

"Good to have you with us, lieutenant," he said.

"Thank you, sir."

"I'm driving up toward St. Mihiel," Mitchell said. "Like to come along? We can talk on the way."

"I'd like that very much, sir," Jerome said.

A staff car was waiting outside the headquarters building. The chauffeur, a corporal, saluted and opened the door for the two officers.

"I'll drive, Davis," Mitchell told the corporal. "I won't need you again until thirteen hundred hours."

The chauffeur saluted, stepped back and watched them drive off.

"Being my chauffeur is considered one of the cushiest jobs in this man's army," Mitchell said.

"Yes, sir. It would appear so, sir."

"Relax, lieutenant. Once you know me better you'll find I don't stand on ceremony. That's only one of my many faults, at least according to the army brass. Not that I give a hoot in hell what they say. I like to think I'm a fighting man, not an armchair soldier."

"I've heard you're that, sir. A fighter, I mean."

"What do they say about me in the States? Go ahead, be candid. I doubt you'll tell me anything I don't already know."

"They say you're an aggressive son-of-a-bitch who doesn't give a damn what he says or who he says it to. They say you want a separate air service of 20,000 planes or more with Billy Mitchel las its commanding general."

Mitchell took his eyes from the road long enough to glance at Jerome. All at once he smiled. "Well," he said, "maybe there's hope for you after all, lieutenant."

"I'm afraid I don't understand, sir."

"Did you know I once met your father?" Mitchell's thoughts seemed to have veered off at a tangent. "Leon Kurman tried to interest us in one of the new Kurkin planes but I'm afraid I wasn't buying. Those planes from before the war! They were animated kites compared to what the French and British are building today. And what the Germans have."

"They were good planes for their time."

"That time has passed but we Americans don't seem to realize it. We insist on building the same clumsy aircraft. We've come so far since then. When the war broke out there was a total of 400 planes on both sides. From 1914 to the end of this year more than 175,000 planes will have been built. That's eighteen times the number of all the planes built in the whole world between 1903 and 1914. Aviation's come of age. Except in America. We should be building or buying French planes, Spads, Breguets, Nieuports. I suggested as much to the War Department. Do you know what they said?"

"No, sir, I don't."

"Nothing. They didn't answer. That's Washington's way of handling difficult field commanders. With liberal doses of benign silence. My father was a United States Senator so I've had some experience with the Washington breed. The generals back home have as much knowledge about air fighting as a hog has about ice skating. Which isn't a whole hell of a lot."

Mitchell was speeding north through the remains of French villages at a steady fifty miles an hour.

"The trouble with our regular army officers is that they're always fighting the wrong war. The last war. Because the last war was their war. Today they'd like nothing better than to order a cavalry charge up some new San Juan Hill. Jesus Christ! George Patton has the right idea with his tanks. And, I have to admit, at the risk of appearing immodest, that I have the right idea. Aircraft. We need enough planes to fill the sky from horizon to horizon."

For a time they drove in silence along a road bordered by the littered debris of war. Beyond the rubble, the French countryside was green with spring.

"Enough of William Mitchell of the U.S. Army

Air Service," the colonel said. "Tell me about yourself, lieutenant."

"I'm twenty-eight," Jerome said, "and I've been flying almost as long as I can remember. You know about Kurkin Flight Research. When the U.S. got into the war last year I enlisted and was commissioned a lieutenant. I believe in the airplane and its future, colonel. From now on, wars will be fought in large part in the air and anyone who doesn't think so is an ass." Jerome paused. "That's about it."

Mitchell slowed the staff car and stopped at the side of the road, nodding to their right between two blackened treess. "What do you see?" he asked.

"Shell holes. Blasted trees. What looks like a French gun emplacement a hundred yards to our right. Sausages over the lines. A plane, it looks like a Spad, south of us at two thousand feet."

Mitchell grunted. "I like to bring visiting brass here. Now hold on."

The car shot forward, twisting and turning along a narrow winding road that led up a small hill. Mitchell skidded to a halt at the crest of the hill and jumped out, motioning Jerome to follow him. They walked to a vantage point overlooking the Moselle Valley.

Below them the battlefield was laid out like a map with the trenches of the Americans on the left and those of the Germans on the right snaking away from them to the north. Artillery rumbled in the distance. A shell whined over their heads. Jerome glanced uneasily from side to side as he looked for cover but Mitchell ignored the shell. It exploded several hundred yards behind them.

"Our generals," Mitchell said, nodding to the spot

where he had first stopped the car, "insist on fighting the war from down there. Because that's what they've always done and they don't want to change. Hardly a one of them has ever set foot in an airplane. They see the trenches and barbed wire entanglements and bunkers and they think they've seen the front. If only they'd fly they'd know they haven't. They squander thousands of lives fighting for a few square miles of mud when they could be sending armadas of bombers with fighter escorts to strike at the heart of Germany. Before this war is over we'll see a thousand Allied planes in the sky at one time. Two thousand. And someday, by God, we'll see more."

"I agree with you, sir," Jerome said. Why is he showing me this? he wondered. I don't have to be convinced of the future of aviation.

The Spad droned overhead and Mitchell stared up at it. The colonel was a handsome man, spare and athletic, with a dimpled boyish face. The only decoration he wore was a pair of Air Service silver wings. What struck Jerome most forcefully was the man's energy. Even when, as now, he was standing still, he seemed coiled and ready to leap into action.

"Have you ever commanded men?" Mitchell asked suddenly.

"Not exactly, sir. I've supervised workers at the Kurkin plant."

"Command is a lonely business." Mitchell walked away from Jerome and stood gazing across the French countryside. "You have to stand apart. You have to be able to guess what's beyond the next hill and the one after that and the one after that. You're damned when you're wrong and you're called lucky when you're right and then the next day you have to do the same thing all over again. You send aviators into the sky to fight without parachutes because your superiors say they haven't been perfected and when the aviators don't come back you wonder if it's your fault. Could you have prepared them better? You can never be sure. And the next day you have to do the same thing all over again."

He turned to Jerome. "Why do men do it? Why do they claw and fight for promotion? I'll tell you why. I've been in the army for twenty years. At one time I was the youngest officer in the service. I'm thirty-seven now and I intend to be a general before I'm forty. I've learned this. Leading men is the most exciting challenge in the world. The higher you climb, the farther you can see and the more you can do. And that's the heart of the matter, Kurman. We're here to do. To fight, to win, to leave our command in better shape than it was before we came. That's the challenge."

"I intend to do my best, sir," Jerome said.

"Have you ever flown in combat?" Mitchell asked.

Jerome hesitated. "No, sir," he admitted, "I never have. In fact I was surprised when I learned you'd selected me as a flight commander in the 7th Squadron."

"I once heard a sermon in a Methodist Church when I was stationed in Washington," Mitchell said as he led the way back to the car. "I don't recall a damn thing the preacher said but I remember his subject. It was 'We must use what we don't choose.'" The colonel let out the clutch and the car jounced onto the road. "I didn't choose you, Lieutenant Kurman, you were given to me, but by all that's holy I intend to use you."

"I realize Air Service officers are in short supply."

"Building planes is child's play compared to training competent pilots to fly them. And finding men to lead those pilots. Well, I have to play my hunches there more often than not. What do you know of the 7th Squadron, lieutenant?"

"I've heard it's called the Unlucky Seventh," Jerome said cautiously. It was common knowledge that the 7th was the worst squadron in the U.S. Air Service.

"It has the poorest record of all our combat squadrons," Mitchell said. "It's loss-to-kill ratio is three to one. That's the reason I put Captain Cornwall in charge. He's the best man I've got. He'll be able to whip the 7th into shape if anyone can."

"I've heard nothing but praise for Captain Cornwall," Jerome said. "It will be an honor to serve under him."

"Charley's a leader as well as a commander. That's what the 7th needs, a leader. He'll be up over the lines as often as any of his pilots. I told him, by the way, that I'd be talking to you before you reported to him at the aerodrome. I believe in having a word with all the new officers in my command."

"I appreciate it, sir."

The car skidded around a curve and onto the road leading back to headquarters.

"I'd feel better if I could be of more help to you," Mitchell said. "Though every officer has to meet and solve his own problems. If you ever need advice, I'm sure Cornwall will be a great help. He has combat experience with the French. So few of our commanders do."

"I intend to feel my way along," Jerome said. "Perhaps I'll even pray a bit."

"Prayer never hurts. You'll find out what's what at the squadron when you get there, of course, but I'll tell you what the situation looks like from where I sit. The 7th has a few experienced byers from the Lafayette *Escadrille* and the other French air units. Those men are the backbone of the squadron but there aren't enough of them and some of the ones we have are an undisciplined lot. They're not used to taking orders. One of them, Kincaid, has nine Huns to his credit but his last commander threw up his hands after Kincaid tried to set his Nieuport down on top of him at two thousand feet. Just as a prank."

"I know Francis Kincaid from before the war. I knew him in the States."

"That's right, you were both with Kurkin, weren't you? I didn't make the connection before."

"My brother Martin flew with him in the Lafayette *Escadrille* for a couple of weeks. Before Martin was shot down by the Huns and killed."

"Kincaid's a great flyer," Mitchell said, "but he's undisciplined. He thinks these are still the early days of the war when aviators were like knights who challenged the Huns to individual combat. Today we fight as a team in formations of nine or ten or more. The day of the lone wolf is almost over. Probably is over. What we have to do is convince the lone wolves of the fact."

"Francis was never one to listen to what he didn't want to hear. He's charming and I like him but—" Jerome left the sentence unfinished.

"The new men in the 7th are as much a problem as

the old-timers," Mitchell said. "They're like lambs letting themselves be led to the slaughter. They don't have enough flight time or enough machine gun practice time. They haven't a chance in hell of lasting more than a couple of weeks in combat if they last that long. Unless they're lucky. So there you have the problem of the 7th in a nutshell. Experienced men who won't listen and inexperienced men who will but are dead before you have the chance to teach them anything."

"You paint a bleak picture."

"I don't believe in blinking at the truth. The squadrons' record bears me out. Give Captain Cornwall six weeks and we'll see what happens."

Colonel Mitchell stopped in front of the headquarters building but made no move to leave the car.

"I always hate to go back to my desk," he said. "I'd rather be up there." He glanced above his head where they saw a flight of Handley-Page heavy bombers droning to the north.

"Yes, sir," Jerome said. Once he had felt the same way. Before Curt was killed, before he became afraid. His fear was his secret and his curse. If only, he thought, he could find some way to exorcise it.

"When I was younger," Mitchell said, "I was forever searching for a magic formula. To win at cards. At polo. At war. A way to lead men. A surefire method for getting ahead in the army. If I discovered nothing else I discovered that there isn't any formula. You can learn from others, true enough, but what works for one might bring disaster to the next. In this busines, you're always flying by the seat of your pants."

"One thing you might be able to tell me," Jerome said. "When I was in Paris the officers at Air Service headquarters all praised your communications. No one ever had trouble understanding your messages. If I've heard one complaint in the army and at Kurkin, too, it's that nobody knows how to communicate. How do you do it, sir?"

Mitchell smiled. "My secret's a simple one. When I took over here I inherited most of my predecessor's staff. I had to make do with what I had. One of my new officers had great difficulty understanding what I considered the simplest of messages. If there was a way to misinterpret what I was trying to say or write, this officer managed to do it. I decided to make use of his unique talent. He became my message coordinator. Every message that leaves my headquarters is routed through him. If he can't understand it, it's sent back to be rewritten. If he completely understands a message, anyone in this army can understand it."

Jerome, who'd often been accused of having no sense of humor, nodded uncertainly. He wasn't sure if Colonel Mitchell was pulling his leg or not.

The colonel was smiling as though to himself. "When I took over my first command," he said, "I found out the hard way that the men like to test you, particularly the noncoms. They come running to you with all manner of unimportant questions to be answered. Do we do it this way now or that way? The answer isn't as important as letting them know you have a mind of your own. They're testing you to find out if you can make a decision on the spot or if you're the type who hems and haws forever."

Jerome smiled. "How did you handle them?" he asked.

"Very simply," Mitchell said. "I used what I call the two yea and two nay approach. What is it—"

A lieutenant walked rapidly from the headquarters building and approached the car. Saluting, he said, "Colonel, General Pershing has been trying to reach you on the phone for the last hour. And General Foulois is waiting in your office."

Mitchell sighed. "Thanks, Garwood. I'll be right there."

As soon as they got out of the car Jerome saluted.

"Good luck, lieutenant," Mitchell said as he returned the salute.

"Thank you, sir." He knows I'll need all the luck I can get, Jerome thought.

A chauffeur from the headquarters pool was waiting to drive him north to the aerodrome at Toul. After they had been on the road for a few minutes, Jerome leaned forward.

"Stop at the hospital, please," he said.

The driver nodded and pulled up in front of a large, barracks-like building with red crosses painted on its sides and roof. Jerome climbed the steps two at a time, went through a crowded entry hall and hurried along a corridor that smelled of ether, excrement and disinfectant.

He waited at the nurses' station. When he first saw her walking toward him, her head was bent over a chart held in her hand so she didn't see him. She looked up, stared, then cried out and ran to throw her arms around him.

"Eileen," he said, "I've only a minute. I'm on my way to Toul. I've been assigned to the 7th as a flight commander."

"Oh, Jerry," his sister said, "not the 7th. You know what they say about that squadron."

He nodded. "I'll make the best of it. There's a new

commander, that'll help. The car's waiting for me. I just ran in to see you and tell you the news before I went to the aerodrome. I wanted to see you one last time."

"Don't talk rot. We're both going to live through this war. After all, we're the last of the Kurmans, the adult Kurmans. We have to live through the war."

"Francis will be one of the pilots under me. At least I think so."

She was silent for a moment. "Say hello to him for me," she said. "I wrote yesterday to tell him I was here. I don't know if he'll drive down to see me or not."

"It's all over then? Between the two of you?"

"What there was is over. I guess it was over almost before it began. But I would like to see him again. For old times' sake."

"I never thought he was right for you, Eileen."

"You always told me to marry a nice Jewish boy, not a *goy*. You and father both. If I ever marry again, I'll probably take your advice."

"You'd have let yourself in for more heartache if you had married Francis. You remember how it was with Stouffer."

She looked away and when he saw the pain in her eyes he was sorry he'd mentioned her dead husband.

"I never pretended to be a good judge of men," she said.

A horn honked outside and Jerome kissed her quickly on the cheek. At the door, he turned and waved.

"Gosh," Eileen said, "it was good to see you. If only for a minute."

"You look just great," Jerome said. "More beautiful than ever."

I wonder if she means what she says about Francis, he asked himself as they drove on toward Toul. Women like to deceive themselves when it comes to men. At least Eileen always had.

They stopped to let a company of French soldiers march past. The *poilus* wore blue coats and carried packs with dangling boots, shovels, and brown mesh sacks holding bottles of red wine. The bayonets on the rifles on their shoulders pointed at the sky. The company trudged wearily toward the front as though they had been marching for the entire three years and more the war had lasted.

Ten minutes later the staff car drove onto the aerodrome along a gravel road. The chauffeur swung into a parking area beside squadron headquarters and Jerome climbed out. The breeze that fluttered the Stars and Stripes above his head was warm with the promise of spring.

To Jerome's surprise, the sergeant in the orderly room came to attention and saluted as he entered. The man's face was unnaturally solemn.

"Will you tell Captain Cornwall that Lieutenant Kurman is reporting for duty," Jerome said.

"I can't, sir, though I wish to God I could." The sergeant drew in a deep breath. "The captain was shot down north of St. Mihiel early this morning. He landed his plane behind our lines but by the time anyone could reach him he was dead."

Jerome stared. "I'm sorry to hear that," he said slowly. "I'll do whatever I can to help until the new commander arrives."

"We had a wire from Colonel Mitchell a half hour ago. A new commander's already been named, sir."

"Who is he?"

"You, sir."

16

THE four pilots—Francis Kincaid, Davenport Kearney, Hugh Ross, and patrol leader William Mackey—sat hunched over their breakfasts of eggs, coffee and rolls. It wasn't like the old days with the Lafayette *Escadrille,* Francis thought, when the pilots about to go up on patrol had joked among themselves while the ones left behind watched enviously.

Francis tried to experience again the joy he had felt then, the mounting anticipation as he prepared for takeoff and the soaring excitement as his Nieuport lifted from the ground and climbed into the limitless sky. Though he recalled the feeling, it was only a memory he now had no way of reliving.

Somewhere he had lost the joy of flying he had

once known. Not all at once and for no one reason he could put his finger on. Perhaps the feeling had been smothered by the routine of patrol, the hovering threat of death, the shock of injury, and the memory of comrades he would never see again.

Laurence Dawes, the gambler, had still been trying to perfect his roulette system when he was shot down and killed near Belloy-en-Santerre. Reed Blakely, who planned to write a book about the *escadrille*, was luckier. He'd lost his nerve, crashed his Nieuport twice on the same day and been invalided home. Walter Althouse had been wounded over Ham and, the last Francis heard, was still in a hospital near Paris learning to walk again. Raoul Lufbery, now in another American squadron at Toul, seemed indestructible.

As the four aviators finished their second cups of coffee and trudged silently from the messhall, planes from the 95th flew overhead while others warmed up on the field. Four American squadrons were stationed at Toul with a total complement of eighty to ninety planes and as many pilots.

The aerodrome was square, a half mile on a side, with each of the hangars around the periphery holding ten or twelve Nieuports or Spads. The mess and quarters for the pilot-officers faced the field while the barracks for the enlisted men, the mechanics, truck drivers and maintenance personnel, were behind the hangars.

Francis made a perfunctory check of his Nieuport 28, the newly-designed French plane that was routinely issued to arriving American aero squadrons. The Nieuport 28 had a speed of 123 mph at 6,500 feet, a ceiling of 20,000 feet, and could stay in the air for two hours or longer without refueling. It was armed with two fixed Vickers machine guns synchronized to fire through the propeller.

The plane's only fault was its distressing and often deadly habit of shedding the fabric from its wings while in a dive.

"Contact!"

The 160 hp Gnome engine roared to life. Francis waited until the other three Nieuports in the patrol were airborne before he taxied into the wind. He sped across the field, put his tail in the air, rose from the ground and climbed into the bright blue sky.

Not even the crystal purity of the day could dispel his lethargy. He remembered how, after surviving his first month with the Lafayette *Escadrille*, he had felt himself to be immortal. By God, he'd live forever! Hadn't he passed through the trial by fire of his first weeks of combat? Confident, he'd flown with *elan*, with *sang-froid*, with daring.

Lately, he'd started to suspect he'd outlasted his luck. As though the days remaining in his life were a finite number, a number known only to God. And the days left to him were constantly dwindling as an unseen hand marked its daily X on the calendar of his life. He lived on borrowed time.

He frowned as he remembered yesterday's letter from Eileen. He'd stared at the envelope for long minutes before tearing it open and as soon as he finished reading the letter he tore it across and across again and across still again before letting the shreds scatter in the wind. Though she'd traveled three thousand miles to France, she seemed farther away from him than she'd ever been.

He remembered the night they swam in the Atlantic—was it almost two years ago?—and had made love in the shadow of the dunes. This was different, he'd told himself then. Eileen wasn't just another woman, a woman for a night or for a summer. *She* was different.

What went wrong? Blame the war, the distance between them, the passage of time. Time killed everything eventually. What had her letter said? She'd like to see him "for old times' sake." He smiled. Once the words would have been a challenge to meet and conquer. His smile faded and he shrugged. What difference did it make? Eileen didn't seem important anymore. Nothing did.

Francis shook his head angrily. He'd let his Nieuport, at the rear upper point of a diamond formation, drift off to the right. As he swung the plane back into position, he saw, far below, the desolation of the battleground east of St. Mihiel. The only sound was the steady roar of his engine. He scanned the horizon. Clouds clustered in the west but otherwise the day was clear, sunny and cold.

He looked up, suddenly alert. Above him to the north, over German territory, he'd glimpsed movement. A lone Hun? Not likely. The Germans clustered like sheep these days. Not that the Americans were any better. Or the French or the British. He shook his head. The days of real flying, of man against man, were almost gone.

He banked, turning, and began to climb. Behind him he saw Mackey dip his wings to call him back into formation. The hell with that. The hell with Mackey. He'd had all the routine patroling he could stomach. The names of the towns along their sector of the front had long since been imprinted on his mind: Apremont, Xivray, Flirey, Pont-a-Mousson, Toul.

Still climbing, he headed east so the sun would be behind him when he approached the other plane. It was, he saw, one of the new Fokker D VII's. The Hun flew serenely on. Good. He studied his opponent's biplane carefully, thinking he recognized his markings but, at the distance, he couldn't quite make them out.

Francis dived and swooped up on the other plane from behind and below. At ninety yards he began firing. And then the Fokker was gone. Damn! Francis glanced over his left shoulder in time to see the Hun flash away. A black bird of prey was painted on the fuselage. A falcon. This was the German who'd attacked him before he'd crashed in No-Man's-Land just after joining the *escadrille*. He had a score to settle with that bastard.

Crack-crack-crack.

The Fokker's Spandaus opened up with a short burst followed by a long. Short-long, short-long. Francis had never had a Hun slip behind him so quickly before. He climbed, turning, and fell away to his left. The Fokker was in his sights again. He fired with both machine guns. And once more the Fokker disappeared.

Banking, Francis looked down and saw the German zoom out of a dive and climb toward him. Francis put his Nieuport's nose up, keeping the controls well back as he climbed steeply. At the apex of the climb he turned and, diving, brought the Nieuport back to head in its original direction. Now the Fokker should be in front of him.

The enemy plane was nowhere to be seen. Again bullets cracked from behind on his blind side, thudding into his fuselage. Francis swore. He threw the control stick abruptly to the right as far as it would go while at the same time pulling back hard while pressuring the rudder slightly with his left foot. The plane climbed and turned, jarring him back against the seat.

He'd changed direction without losing altitude. He held his breath, half expecting to hear the tac-tac-tac of the Fokker's guns from behind him. He didn't. Looking over his shoulder, he saw the German above him, out of effective range. As he watched, the Fokker nosed down in a dive and Francis veered to the left.

All at once he realized the Black Falcon had been forcing him deeper and deeper into German territory. Common sense told him to break off the duel, dive, and race for the American lines. He shook his head. He wasn't going to let this bastard get the better of him again.

The Fokker D VII held to his tail but the German's guns were silent. Could his Spandaus be jammed? Was the Hun out of ammunition? Francis felt a rush of hope. At the same time he experienced a sinking sensation, a realization—a suspicion at least —that the Black Falcon was more skilled than he.

The hell he is, Francis told himself.

Still the Fokker pilot didn't fire even though he was less than a hundred yards from him. Francis threw the controls to the right, hoping to surprise the German by repeating his change of direction maneuver. As he regained level flight he looked behind him to see the Fokker closing from above. The German pilot leaned from his cockpit to point to the ground. He wanted Francis to land.

As though to emphasize his demand, the Black Falcon squeezed off a short burst. So his guns were okay. The arrogant bastard can go to hell, Francis thought.

He pulled back on the controls and the Nieuport zoomed skyward, slowed as it gained height, turned onto its back with Francis suspended upside down from his harness in the open cockpit, the plane coming around in an inside loop, dropping behind the German, his Vickers' guns chattering, the tracers arcing into the Hun. Francis grinned. For a moment the old feeling of joy returned as he saw the bullets strike the tail of the Black Falcon's plane.

The other plane slid away with Francis in close pursuit. The Falcon dived earthward in a *vrille*, spinning down and down with Francis aping each of the German's maneuvers. He heard a tearing and glanced up to see fabric shred from his upper wing. He swore but refused to pull out of his dive. More fabric tore and he felt the Nieuport wobble. He pulled back and the plane leveled.

Banking, he looked down and to his right. The Black Falcon was five hundred feet below him making a beeline for the rear of the German lines.

"I'll be damned," Francis muttered as he stared after the retreating Hun. His elation was tempered by the realization that the Fokker had abandoned the fight not because he'd been bested but because he was running low on fuel. We'll meet another day, Francis told himself.

He followed the German for a few minutes. As he reluctantly swung his Nieuport south he thought he saw the Fokker pilot lift his hand and wave. Francis shook his head. He'd be damned if he'd wave back.

He would have once. At first, with the Lafayette *Escadrille*, he'd considered air combat a sport. As hunting was a sport, only now the Germans were the game. He'd heard pilots call dogfights "jolly parties" and describe patrols as "good hunting."

"It doesn't matter to me what a Hun might do if he were in my place," he remembered Althouse telling him once, "I'll never shoot at a German that I have at a disadvantage. Out of ammunition, say, or with his guns jammed. It simply isn't sporting."

Today Althouse lay in a Red Cross hospital with his right leg amputated above the knee and suffering from a supperating wound where a Hun explosive bullet had torn away part of his buttocks. He wondered what Althouse would say about chivalry today. War was no longer a sport to Francis, it was a grim battle to the death. Kill or be killed. No quarter asked, none given.

Francis caught sight of a flash of white from the American side of the lines. He recognized the smoke puff as a signal from an antiaircraft battery that had spotted a German air incursion.

He flew at 10,000 feet in the direction of the signal. As he crossed the lines he saw a Halberstadt two-seater below him. He was cautious—he'd been lured too many times into rash attacks on decoys—as he approached slowly, scanning the sky above and behind the German reconnaissance plane.

There. A Fokker D VII lay in wait to the rear and above the slower plane. Francis searched the sky for more Huns but saw none. Perhaps, after watching Mackey's patrol pass on to the east, these two planes had decided to venture into Allied territory to scout the preparations for an expected American ground attack.

Ignoring the Halberstadt, Francis climbed behind

the Fokker. The enemy plane began taking evasive action at once, zigzagging this way and that but refuisng to leave the Halberstadt unprotected. After positioning himself above the Fokker, Francis dived and swung up behind the other plane.

At a hundred and fifty yards he fired a short burst. The Fokker began to climb and seemed about to turn or dive when a thin stream of black smoke began trailing behind him. The smoke thickened into the size of a comet's tail and Francis saw a spurt of flame on the fuselage behind the engine at the Fokker fell away in a dive, out of control. He glimpsed the pilot fighting to bring the plane from its dive and imagined his growing terror as the burning plane plunged toward the ground.

The Hun pilot stood in his cockpit and leaped free. As he fell, arms extended, his figure grew smaller and smaller. Off to the right the Fokker spun through space trailing smoke. When Francis glanced back he could no longer see the pliot but saw instead a mushroom of white. A parachute. The German pilot drifted slowly to earth behind the American lines.

Francis banked to his left and saw the Halberstadt was making its way back to the German lines. He gave pursuit and after five minutes was within four hundred yards. Flame flickered from the rear of the German plane as the gunner fired. He must be inexperienced, Francis thought, to fire at this distance.

Francis approached with care, flying toward the underside of the other plane inside the thirty degree blind spot beneath the German's tail. The Halberstadt veered right, then left, the gunner pressing off round after round at the rate of 550 per minute whenever he thought he had the slightest chance for a hit. Frances narrowed the range to a hundred yards. He held his fire as he drew closer. To fifty yards. To forty.

The Halberstadt climbed and again her gunner fired. Francis, directly behind the other plane, returned the fire and saw his tracers miss low. He leveled and again came up beneath the Halberstadt as the Boche turned and went nto a dive. For an instant the Halberstadt was in his sights, seemed to hold steady in his sights. Francis squeezed off a blistering fusillade, grunting with satisfaction as he saw the tracers stream along the length of the upper side of the German's fuselage from between the wings to the tail.

The other plane flew steadily on. Francis heard the crack-crack of the German gunner's fire. Without warning the Halberstadt stalled in midair and pitched on its nose, falling like a leaf as it spiraled down and down.

Francis dove after the reconnaissance plane, fearing a trick. Down and down the Halberstadt fell, now obviously out of control. This was no trick, the German pilot must be dead or dying. Francis pulled his Nieuport out of its dive. When he glanced down for the last time the machine gunner in the rear had abandoned his gun and was standing in his cockpit with his arms folded in front of him as his doomed craft fell. Either he hadn't been issued a parachute yet, Francis thought, or else the German disdained using one.

Francis flew on to the east above the trenches but he saw no more enemy planes. With a feeling of elation, he turned his Nieuport back toward Toul. Today's kills had come quickly. And relatively easily.

Sometimes you could pour round after round into an enemy aircraft with no apparent result. Other times, like today, you hit a vital spot almost at once.

Two Huns downed in a single patrol. That made thirteen kills in all. Not bad, he thought, not half bad. Not when you considered the unconfirmeds he was sure of.

Francis circled the aerodrome at Toul and landed into the wind. As he taxied to the hangar he noticed a strip of fabric flapping beneath his lower wing. He cursed the Nieuport under his breath.

Nothing, though, could dampen his spirits today. He intended to make sure his two kills were confirmed—two sightings including one from an observer noit with the 7th Squadron were needed for confirmation—and then he'd stand drinks all around. The numbing despair that had gripped him earlier was gone and, as he climbed down from the cockpit, he grinned when he saw Mackey hurrying toward him.

Francis leaped to the ground and turned to face Mackey. The flight leader had probably already had word about at least one of his victories and wanted to congratulate him before anyone else had the chance. Francis waited beside the torn section of his Nieuport's wing.

"You fucking bastard!" Mackey shouted. His face was white with rage.

Francis stared at him, frowning and shaking his head. Puzzled, he wondered if he'd heard Mackey right.

The flight leader gripped the front of Francis' jacket in his fist and pulled Francis to him. Mackey's mouth worked but no words came. Francis stood, not moving, making no attempt to defend himself.

At last Mackey's spasm of anger subsided and he released Francis.

"Ross," Mackey said. "Ross was shot down. Killed. An hour ago."

Ross. Hugh Ross. A good pilot. Steady. Something of a loner. Mackey had been his only friend. Ross' request to live separately from the other pilots had been denied. He'd recently planted a small garden beside the boneyard of discarded planes and parts, and only the week before he'd boasted about the first radish sprouts of the spring.

"What's Ross got to do with me?" Francis demanded. He war becoming angry. Why didn't Mackey mind his own business?

"His motor must have been missing," Mackey said. "He was lagging behind me and Kearney when a flight of five of the new Fokkers jumped him. If you had been where you were supposed to be, you could have helped."

Francis shrugged. "If, if, if," he said.

"You think because you were with the Lafayette *Escadrille* you can do as you please. You can't. If the captain can't make you shape up, we can."

"We?" Francis repeated.

"All right. *I* can. *I* can, Kincaid."

Francis glared at Mackey for a moment before he shrugged again and turned away. He walked slowly to the hangar. He couldn't see Mackey staring after him but he could feel the man's eyes boring into his back.

Henry Gaspard, standing near the hangar doorway, looked up at Francis. "The new C.O. wants to see you," he told him.

"O.K.," Francis said.

He walked across the field to the headquarters building. All the pleasure from his two victories had drained from him. He felt empty. The hell with the confirmations, he told himself, they either came or they didn't. It made no difference to him.

When he walked into the office, Sergeant Ingram jerked his thumb in the direction of the captain's open door. Francis went in and stopped, staring in surprise at the officer standing beside the desk.

"Well, I'll be a son-of-a-bitch," he said. "Jerry Kurman. Eileen wrote that you were in France but I never expected to see you here."

"I'm acting squadron commander," Jerome told him. "Cornwall's dead. I've been reading Lieutenant Mackey's report." He shifted a sheet of paper on his desk with his forefinger. "Do you have anything to say, lieutenant?"

Francis glanced down at the report and shook his head. "I expect it's accurate enough," he said. "As far as it goes."

"You're not to leave a formation again without authority or without cause," Jerome said. "Is that understood?"

Francis stared at him. "I hear you," he said.

"Good. You're dismissed, lieutenant."

"One question. How much combat experience have you had, Kurman? How many Hun planes have you shot down?"

"I said you were dismissed."

"I've been fighting the Boche for two years," Francis said. "I think I know a bit more about how to do it than you do. I brought down two Huns today, a new Fokker and a Halberstadt. That should be worth something."

When Jerome didn't answer Francis spun about and walked to the door. As he pu this hand on the knob, Jerome said, "Lieutenant!"

Francis turned.

"I expect you to address me as 'sir,' " Jerome said.

Francis stared at him. Smiling, he sketched a lazy salute. "Yes, *sir*," he said with exaggerated courtesy.

Jerome clenched his fists as he watched Francis leave the office. You were warned, he said under his breath. Don't say you weren't warned.

17

"I HAVE some matters that require your attention, sir,"
Master Sergeant Ben Ingram said.

"This is as good a time as any," Jerome told him.

"I've written them down, sir," Ingram said stiffly.
"Let me get my list."

As Jerome watched the sergeant leave the office,
he remembered Colonel Mitchell's warning that a new
commander faced a time of testing. He had a feeling
that his was about to begin.

Ben Ingram returned and sat across the desk from
him. The Regular Army sergeant was short, wore
glasses, and had hair as black and curly as Jerome's.
Jerome suspected he was Jewish.

"There's the matter of Captain Cornwall's funeral," Sergeant Ingram told him. "It's scheduled at 1000

hours tomorrow at the military cemetery ten miles south of Toul. Will the lieutenant want to attend himself or will he send a representative?"

Jerome frowned. He hadn't known Cornwall. On the other hand, as the captain's replacement, however temporary, he should attend his funeral. If only as a matter of respect. The time, though, could be better spent here at the base. He was sure Captain Cornwall himself would have understood that. Yet what would the pilots think if he didn't go?

Ingram, expressionless, sat with his pencil poised above a pad of yellow paper on his lap. Perhaps I should ask the sergeant what he thinks I should do. No, Jerome told himself, this is my decision. Yet the pros and cons seemed so evenly balanced.

He remembered Mitchell starting to explain how he had solved these minor yet troublesome problems. Something about a system of two ayes and two nays. Of course. What he'd been suggesting was an automatic way to settle routine questions. It wasn't what you decided that mattered, Mitchell had said, as much as the ability to make up your mind.

"I plan to attend the funeral," Jerome said.

Ingram made a notation on his pad.

"Captain Cornwall held meetings for all officers," Ingram went on, "at 2000 hours every Thursday. In the officers' lounge. Do you want to continue the meetings? If you do, will you keep the same day and time?"

"Yes to both questions," Jerome said.

Ingram glanced at him as though surprised at his quick response. "Very good, sir," he said. Again he wrote on his pad. "Then there's the matter of the squadron's supply requisitions. The headquarters' courier should be here for them now. He's late. Does the lieutenant want to review them before they're sent?"

"No," Jerome said. "Leave copies on my desk, I'll have a look at them later. I'd like to review any future requisitions, though. At least until I'm oriented."

"Very good, sir." Ingram glanced at his list. "Two days ago," he said, "we received copies of the Army medical reports on our pilots who entered the Air Service from the Lafayette *Escadrille* and other French units. The men were approved *in toto* by the examiners. Shall I file the reports?"

Jerome could think of no reason the reports shouldn't be filed. Yet if he followed Mitchell's two ayes and two nays approach, a no answer was required.

"No," he said. "I'd like to take a look at them before they go in the files."

Ingram glanced over his glasses at Jerome as though he was having trouble following the logic of his new commanding officer's answers. "Yes, sir," he said, "I'll bring you the medical folders." He stood and placed several copies of a form on the desk in front of Jerome. "This is our requisition for replacement personnel. We've lost several flyers in the last few days. Lieutenant Ross yesterday. Captain Cornwall. The form needs your signature."

Jerome scanned the list. He raised his eyebrows at one notation.

"What's this?" He looked up at the sergeant. "What does it mean, 'Piano player preferred'?"

"Lieutenant Kincaid played the piano when he first joined the squadron but he hasn't for the last few months. A squadron has to have a piano player, sir. Good for morale. Lifts the men's spirits."

"I agree," Jerome said, "so I'll go you one better." He took a pen and drew a dark line under the words "Piano player preferred."

"That's very good, sir. As for myself, I prefer the classics. Bach, Beethoven, Wagner. The music most of the officers play sounds like noise to me."

"Wagner?"

"Yes, sir. Damn his black German soul."

Jerome smiled. "I'm afraid my musical tastes run more along the lines of tunes like 'Good Morning, Mr. Zip-Zip-Zip.'"

"'With your hair cut as short as mine,'" Ingram sang in a remarkably good tenor. The sergeant frowned and drew himself up. "I'm sorry, sir, I quite forgot myself." He picked up the signed personnel requisition from Jerome's desk. "That's all I have this morning. Does the lieutenant have any questions?"

"We'll go over the squadron routine later," Jerome said. "I do have one question. Who's the best combat pilot here on the base?"

Without hesitating, Ingram said, "Major Raoul Lufbery of the 94th Aero Squadron. There's none better."

"Thank you, sergeant." Jerome nodded to himself as Sergeant Ingram left the room, knowing he'd made a beginning he'd be able to build on . . .

Major Lufbery waved Jerome to a seat in his office at the 94th Squadron. "How can I help you, lieutenant?" he asked. His French-accented speech was rapid-fire and precise. "I've heard, of course, of Captain Cornwall's accident. Most unfortunate."

"Quite frankly," Jerome said, "I did come to you for help. You're the best combat pilot at Toul, perhaps in all of France. You've been flying against the Germans for almost four years."

"And you want me to tell you my secret?" Lufbery smiled. "I have no secret. There is no secret."

"I realize that, sir. And I know the part that luck plays. And opportunity. Being in the right place at the right time. But there's more to it than that. There must be reasons why one man succeeds and another fails."

"Work is one reason," Lufbery said. "There is no shortcut. You must work and work hard at your job. I fly as often as I can. At times my Spad seems almost a part of me. Like an arm or a leg. I can't count the hours I've spent at the target butts where I practice firing the swivel-mounted machine guns. Hundreds of hours. Hundreds upon hundreds."

"I intend to work hard."

Lufbery stood up behind his desk and walked back and forth, gesturing with his hands. "The ammunition is so important," he said. "I can't count the chances I lost because of faulty ammunition! My gun jams, I work the lever, I look up. *Voila!* The Fokker is gone, escaped. The new man curses his luck and does nothing more. That does no good. You must prepare. I never fly unless I have checked the ammunition for my Vickers. Listen to what I say, *M.* Kurman. I check each and every round of ammunition I take aloft. My guns still jam. But not as often. Has this saved my life? Perhaps. I do not know. How can you ever know?"

"And in combat?"

"One word tells all. The word is patience. When I

was younger I thought I possessed a certain *elan*, a certain dash. As Americans might say, I leaped before I looked. Early in the war I was almost killed because of my *elan*. I said to myself, 'Raoul, do you wish to be a daring aviator who dies young? Or do you wish to be a cautious one and live to an old age?'

"The choice was not difficult. When I'm in combat, I protect myself and I protect my comrades. I take care. I stalk the Hun as I would stalk a dangerous beast. Because that is precisely what he is. I prepare; I wait; I am patient. When the conditions are right, I strike. For the heart. From pointblank range. And if the odds turn against me, I retreat. This war is almost four years old. I know another day will come."

"You make it sound so difficult," Jerome said. "The hours of preparation, the target practice, the checking. Having patience when you're in the air."

"Nothing worth doing is easy," Lufbery said. 'Defeating the Hun is worth doing. As is staying alive. Both are difficult these days."

A sergeant appeared in the major's doorway.

"Thanks for taking the time to talk to me," Jerome said.

"If there is any other way I can help you, I will do it." Lufbery put his hand on Jerome's shoulder. "After all, you have taken the first step. You have admitted to yourself you are not all-knowing. You cannot learn if you don't admit there are things you don't know. I admire you for that. I wish you luck."

"Thank you, sir," Jerome said.

Jerome admitted something else to himself as he drove back to the 7th Squadron. He'd need all the luck he could get . . .

Jerome assigned himself to fly with the next morning's patrol. Before the aviators went to their planes, he drew William Mackey aside.

"You're an old hand at this," he said. "I'm not. I'd like you to lead the patrol."

"Sure," Mackey said. "Be glad to. Fact is, I think it's a good idea. You have to get your feet wet before you can swim."

As Jerome started to turn away, Mackey stopped him.

"I don't want Kincaid in my patrol," he said. "He was okay when he first came to the squadron, taught us a lot, as a matter of fact, but lately he's been nothing but a pain in the ass."

"Is he scheduled to fly this morning?" Jerome knew he was.

"Kincaid's on the flight roster but Parsons won't mind taking his place."

Jerome shook his head. "If Francis is scheduled to go up, he'll go up. I had talk with him the day before yesterday. I don't think he'll give you any trouble."

Mackey shrugged. "It's your funeral," he said. "By the way, our signals once we're in the air are quite rudimentary. If I sight Huns I waggle my wings for an attack. If a pilot has to head back to the base for one reason or another, he does the same. When I want the flight to re-form I'll dip my wings again. All right?"

"Sounds good," Jerome said.

The pilots walked to their planes in the gray light of the pre-dawn, Mackey, Kincaid and Banning to their Nieuports, Jerome and Gaspard to their Spad XIII's, planes named for the initials of their manufacturer, the *Societe Anonyme Pour l'Aviation.* Jerome ran up his engine quickly and waited while Mackey,

Banning and Gaspard took their planes into the air. He rolled his Spad down the field, lifted his tail, and climbed. Behind and below him, he knew, Francis was taxiing into position for takeoff.

Mackey circled to the east of the aerodrome as he waited for his flight to form behind him. When they were all airborne they flew toward the lines in a V with its tail high. The spring day promised sun and showers. Off to the west Jerome saw clouds with the dark slant of rain beneath them. The horizon to the north was clear but the sun was rising beneath their right wings in the midst of a warning red glow.

He noticed Mackey gently dipping first one wing and then the other. Damn it, he thought, have I forgotten all I've ever learned? He followed suit so he could search for enemy planes below him as well as on both sides and above. He saw none.

So far, so good, Jerome told himself. A routine patrol. He was tense, he realized, and his flying must appear wooden to Francis, but today that didn't bother him. He pulled his map case from its rack to follow the course of their flight. Mackey climbed to 15,000 feet and, when he reached the northeast corner of their sector, led the formation to the east.

The Spad's ceiling, Jerome knew, was over 20,000 feet, 21,820 feet to be exact. Four miles above the earth. He shook his head, marvelling at the war-spurred progress in aircraft design. Only a few years ago no one would have dreamed of routinely flying at this altitude. Before 1914, the world altitude record was only slightly more than 20,000 feet.

Mackey wagged his wings. Jerome jerked erect, scanning the sky around him. He saw nothing. Mackey pointed the nose of his Nieuport up and the rest of the flight followed. At 18,000 feet they leveled and, looking down and ahead, Jerome saw a flight of six Germans. No, there were seven. He felt his heart pounding.

The Huns were Pfalz's for the most part, but he also recognized the distinctive silhouettes of two Fokker DR I triplanes. The three-winged Fokkers had arrived at the front in 1917 and Jerome knew that Manfred von Richthofen and the other pilots in the Red Baron's Flying Circus now flew the highly maneuverable but hard to handle planes.

The Germans were some three thousand feet below them, flying north. In a few minutes, if the Americans kept to their present course, the enemy planes would pass beneath and in front of them. With the sun at their backs, the Americans, though outnumbered, had the advantages of altitude and surprise for the Germans gave no indication they had spotted them.

Attack! Jerome murmured to himself.

As though he had heard him, Mackey wagged his wings. The flight leader put his nose down and dived with the two Spads and two Nieuports behind him. Jerome gulped in air as his plane plunged downward.

The Germans saw them. The Pfalzs and Fokkers scattered, their pilots flinging their planes right and left. The routine patrol turned into the chaos of a dogfight. Planes streaked past Jerome, firing as they dived, twisting and turning to gain an advantage.

Jerome climbed beneath a Fokker only to have the other plane climb, dive, and come up on his tail. He heard the deadly crack of the Fokker's two Spandaus, saw tracers stream over his head. The Fokker veered swiftly away to the right with the help of the torque from its rotary engine.

Another German, a Pfalz, was ahead of him, firing at one of the Nieuports. Jerome fired in turn and thought he saw his tracers bite into the side of the Pfalz's fuselage. Nothing happened. The Pfalz, still on the Nieuport's tail, flew serenely on as though untouched.

Jerome pressed off a last burst before swinging away. A Nieuport lurched past him, out of control. Smoke trailed from the American plane as it angled earthward and disappeared into a cloud.

Crack-crack-crack. Twisting to look behind him, Jerome saw nothing. Crack-crack-crack. Bullets pounded into his Spad. He smelled singed fur. His flying suit, he found, had been creased but, untouched, he felt nothing.

He slipped the Spad to one side, climbed and dived. The other plane was off to his right and slightly ahead of him. He stalked the Pfalz. Another Pfalz angled down past him trailing smoke. From the corner of his eye he saw Mackey waggle his wings and dive. He was breaking off the action.

Jerome fired three bursts at the Pfalz at two hundred yards, knowing the distance was too great. He put his nose down and followed Mackey, again gulping air as his plane went into its dive. He pulled out and saw a formation of five more Fokker triplanes approaching from the north. No wonder Mackey wanted to head for home.

Leveling off behind Mackey, he followed the flight leader as the formation sped southward. Francis was to his right and slightly ahead of him, but there was no sign of Gaspard or Banning. The Fokkers were flying north.

Mackey swung to the east to avoid masses of rain-laden clouds. Jerome, following him, was surprised to see Francis fly directly into the clouds. Jerome watched for him to come out. He didn't. A few minutes later, glancing behind and below him, he spotted Francis' Nieuport pursuing a lone German toward the north.

Mist drifted around Jerome's Spad and he tensed. He flew out of the cloud and took up a position above and behind Mackey. As they neared the lines from the German side, Mackey dropped slowly down to 3,000 feet toward a Hun observation balloon floating at the end of its tether. God, what a tempting target.

Mackey circled and came up under the balloon with both guns firing. Archies puffed around his Nieuport as he attacked, the shells pre-set to explode at the altitude of the balloon. Mackey swooped away, both he and the balloon seemingly unscathed.

Jerome climbed toward the balloon. When he was within fifty yards he opened fire and watched round after round pour into the bulging fabric as the observers crouched in their basket below. An explosion jarred his plane, hurled him to one side of the cockpit. The Nieuport's engine stuttered and the balloon loomed up ahead of him. He pulled back on the stick, the plane responded and his wheels grazed the balloon as he climbed. Two Archies burst in front of him and, flying through their puffs of smoke, he smelled the tang of gunpowder.

He was clear. Looking back he saw the balloon floating placidly above the German rear. Mackey was above him and to the south near the American lines.

Evidently he didn't intend to have another go at the balloon. Jerome debated whether to return to the attack. Shaking his head, he followed Mackey south toward Toul.

He circled the aerodrome as he waited for Mackey to land first. Jerome lined up the field, headed into the wind, then cut back his throttle and eased the stick forward. When he tried to pull the stick back to level out for the landing it refused to move.

He grabbed the stick with both hands and yanked. It didn't budge. He looked up and saw the field rushing at him. In a panic, he sat paralyzed, staring through his propeller at the ground rising to meet him.

Desperate, he reached down the length of the stick. His gloved hand found the map case jammed between the stick and the seat. The case must have worked loose during the flight. Jerome pulled the case up, thrust it to one side and pulled back on the stick. Just in time. The Spad's nose lifted and the plane slammed down onto the field, bounced high, and settled once more onto the grass.

When Jerome climbed from his cockpit he expected every eye on the aerodrome to be watching him. Wondering what had caused one of the roughest landings he'd ever made. No one, though, seemed to pay any attention.

Mackey walked toward him.

"Any word on the others?" Jerome asked.

"Gaspard's back," Mackey said. "His engine started to miss and he broke off. I thought I saw Banning on fire but I couldn't be sure. I don't know what became of Kincaid. He was with us through most of the fight and then I lost sight of him. He'll turn up. Like a bad penny."

Jerome started to tell him that Francis had left the formation in pursuit of a Fokker but held his tongue. He nodded and, as Mackey walked off the field, returned to his Spad. He found three bullet holes below and behind the cockpit. Fascinated, he stuck his forefinger in each in turn.

The drone of an approaching plane made him look up. A Nieuport. Francis? The plane landed gently and rolled across the field toward the hangar. When Jerome saw the miniature Indian insignia on the tail he nodded. It *was* Francis.

"Lieutenant."

Jerome turned and saw Sergeant Ingram standing beside his Spad's wing.

"Banning landed at an emergency field near Apremont," the sergeant said. "He's okay, considering his Spad's a total loss. They expect to have him patched up in a few days."

"Good."

All the pilots from the patrol were safe, then. Jerome turned from the sergeant to see Francis climb from his plane to the ground.

When he saw Jerome watching him, Francis walked to him with one hand raised, palm out. "Don't say it, Jerry. Hear me out first. No one saw me sneak off after that Hun. Just you. So there's no sense making a mountain out of a molehill." Francis shook his head. "The bastard got away," he said.

"I warned you not to leave the formation," Jerome said.

"Don't be hardnosed. What do you want me to do, tell you I'm sorry?"

"No, I want you to obey orders."

"Like I said, no one's the wiser. Live and let live." He smiled.

Jerome was tempted to do as Francis suggested. No one knew Francis had disobeyed orders. Why not just forget it? Except that he, Jerome, knew. And Francis knew.

"After all," Francis said, "you need me more than I need you."

Jerome flushed with anger. "You're grounded, Kincaid," he said. "Grounded indefinitely."

He spun on his heel and walked from the field, leaving Francis staring after him.

18

THE next new pilot to arrive at the 7th Aero Squadron was Alfred Enright of Houston, Texas. He was twenty years old, the tall and slender son of a cattle rancher who was attempting to grow a moustache with a marked lack of success.

The pilots in the officers' lounge greeted him perfunctorily with nods and brief "hellos." Enright crossed the room and sat on the stool in front of the piano. After resting his fingers on the keys, he got up and spun the stool three turns lower.

"You fellows mind if I play?" he asked once he was seated again.

"Go ahead," Alex Banning told him.

"I'm not very good," Enright said. "I just like to

fool around at the piano." He ran his fingers up and down the keyboard. Then he began to play.

" 'Come on and hear,' " he sang to himself, " 'come on and hear, Alexander's Ragtime Band.' "

One by one the pilots gathered around the piano. " 'It's the best band in the land,' " they sang.

Jerome, passing the lounge, paused to listen. After moment he smiled. The 7th Aero Squadron had found a moment he smiled. The 7th Aero Squadron had found its piano player.

Eileen heard a scream in the night.

She sat up, all her senses alert. The scream came again, a wail of helpless terror that rose and fell and finally died away, leaving echoes in her mind.

She walked through the familiar hospital ward between the beds huddled darkly on both sides of the aisle, smelling the pungent hospital odors of ether and disinfectant. A soldier, talking in his sleep, mumbled words she couldn't understand.

She passed through a doorway into a smaller room where a lamp on a table burned low. Men lay in three of the four beds, the fourth had been empty since the death, the day before, of Corporal Rabinowitz.

Johanson screamed again. Even though Eileen expected it, the nearness of the sound startled her, sent a frisson of fear running down her back. She leaned over Johanson's bed, placed her fingers on his wrist and felt his pulse. It was slow and weak.

Johanson stirred and opened his eyes. There was sweat on his forehead and, around his mouth, his black beard was wet. Eileen used a cloth to wipe the moisture away.

"It's all right." She put the palm of her hand on his hot forehead.

"They attacking through the fog," Johanson said. "I can't see them. Can you see them? Can you hear them? They'll kill us all."

"No one's going to kill you. You're all right, you're in the hospital."

Johanson laughed, more a grunt than a laugh. "All right, in hospital," he repeated. Mouth open, he stared at the pale rectangle of the window.

"Listen!" he whispered urgently. "Listen and you'll hear them, too."

Eileen raised her head. Artillery rumbled like the roll of distant thunder.

"Hold my hand," Johanson said. There was fear in his voice. When she took his hand in hers she found it cold and damp. He trembled. "Listen to the guns," he said again, "listen to the Boche guns . . ."

For more than four hours the German bombardment saturated every trench, every battery, every headquarters and every supply dump with high explosives, tear gas and mustard gas. Dawn found the front blanketed by a dense fog.

Johanson, deafened and dazed by the artillery fire, couldn't see more than six feet in front of him. At 0930, mortars opened fire on his section of the line and five minutes later the Germans, led by their Storm Troops, swarmed across No-Man's-Land to attack the trenches.

The defenders fought back with rifles and Lewis machine guns. After two hours twenty-six men of

Johanson's platoon of thirty were either dead or badly wounded.

Captain Hoover crawled up beside him. "Can you see them?"

"Not in the last ten minutes."

"I can't go on much longer." The captain was bleeding from wounds in his legs and lower back.

They were lying behind hurriedly-piled sandbags. The captain fired a Lewis gun while Johanson worked to clear another machine gun.

A bullet struck the captain's gun and ricocheted to hit him in the mouth. He slumped forward. Johanson turned him over, gagging when he saw his face.

"The gun," the captain said, "fire the gun. Kill the bastards." Blood spattered from his mouth onto Johanson's face and tunic. Johanson lifted the captain in his arms and carried him to the trench where he laid him on the duckboards. He returned to his gun and began firing . . .

"Did you hear them?" Johanson asked. "Did you hear the guns?"

"I heard them," Eileen said.

Johanson nodded, sighed, and closed his eyes. In a few minutes he was asleep. Eileen wiped the sweat from his face and walked quietly back through the ward. Though it was almost morning, the rooms were still dark. Through the windows she saw a heavy, gray fog.

When, an hour later, she passed Johanson's bed, he still seemed to be asleep. She hadn't heard him scream again. She stopped, frowning. Going to him, she lifted his wrist.

He was dead.

Mademoiselle from Armentieres, parlee-voo,
Mademoiselle from Armentieres, parlee-voo,
Mademoiselle from Armentieres,
She hasn't been fucked in forty years,
Hinky dinky, parlee-voo.

On April 8, 1918, the mobile air fighter group *Jagdgeschwader* 1, commanded by Captain Manfred von Richthofen, was ordered to the Somme.

The German ace was depressed. "I'm in wretched spirits after every battle," he said. "When I set foot on the ground again I go to my quarters and don't want to see anyone or hear anything."

On April 20, Richthofen shot down two Sopwith Camels. The pilot of the second British plane, who was only slightly wounded, reported that Richthofen "flew down to within 100 feet of the ground and waved."

At his base at Cappy, the Red Baron seemed to have regained his high spirits. "Eighty!" he said as he climbed down from his red Fokker. "That is really a decent number."

That night his fellow pilots toasted their captain as "the one-man army, our leader, our teacher, and our comrade, the ace of aces."

The next morning, a Sunday, Richthofen led a six-plane patrol from Cappy. Above the battlelines, the Germans met five Sopwith Camels flying under the command of Canadian Captain A. Roy Brown and the planes scattered in a dogfight that raged over the roaf between Sailly-le-Sec and Le Hamel.

Richthofen swung into position behind a withdrawing Camel. Brown attacked the German triplane.

"A full burst ripped the side of the airplane," Brown said. "The pilot turned around and looked back. I saw the glint of his eyes behind the big goggles, then he collapsed in the seat."

Richthofen managed to fly another mile before crash-landing his Fokker near Australian trenches. By the time the Aussies reached the plane, the Red Baron was dead.

Later that day Captain Brown went to the tent where Manfred von Richthofen's body had been laid on a sheet of corrugated iron.

"He looked so small to me, so delicate," Brown said. "His cap had been removed. Blond, silk-soft hair, like that of a child, fell from the broad high forehead. His face, particularly peaceful, had an expression of gentleness and goodness, of refinement. I did not feel like a victor."

Late on a sunny April afternoon, Captain Richthofen's funeral procession made its somber way through the budding French countryside. The British officer leading the cortege was followed by an honor guard of thirteen Australians who carried their rifles upside down beneath their arms. Behind the Australians, a motorized tender held a wooden casket garlanded with wreaths sent from nearby Allied air squadrons.

Under the poplars in a small cemetery near the village of Bertangles an Anglican chaplain conducted the burial service. Three rifle volleys shattered the stillness and a bugler played *The Last Post*. A large wreath from British headquarters was laid on the grave, the tribute inscribed to Captain von Richthofen, "our gallant and worthy foe."

Over there, over there,
Send the word, send the word over there

*That the Yanks are coming, the Yanks are coming
The drums rum-tumming everywhere.*

Jerome and Raoul Lufbery watched the grease-blackened mechanics work on the engine of Lufbery's Nieuport. One of the enlisted men turned to Lufbery and shook his head.

"It's a magneto," he said. "We won't have her ready for you until tomorrow."

Lufbery shrugged as though it made little difference. I'll take Campbell's Nieuport," he said.

"GHQ says the Fokkers are out in force to the west," Jerome told him. "They've won local control of the air over the Marne."

"The Huns must be stopped." Lufbery slapped his riding crop against his trousers. "France is tired. England is disillusioned. This offensive is the German beast's last lunge for victory. Before the Americans arrive in force."

Jerome nodded. He watched Lufbery leave the hangar and climb into a plane sitting on the field. After a few minutes Jerome walked to his Spad, intending to make a short flight to familiarize himself with the plane and to practice firing his machine guns at targets set up on the ground to the east of the aerodrome.

His Spad climbed slowly toward wind-swept cumulus clouds. After ten minutes he was at 2,000 feet and saw, perhaps five miles to the north, a lone Nieuport at the same altitude. Lufbery's plane. Lufbery continued to climb until he was just below the clouds. Suddenly Jerome spotted another plane ahead of the Nieuport, a two-seater.

A German Albatros.

Jerome pointed his Spad's nose north and started to climb toward Lufbery. After five minutes he had halved the distance between their two planes. Lufbery, either not seeing his Spad or disdaining to wait for help, attacked the German and the two planes disappeared behind the clouds. When they reappeared the Nieuport was climbing away from the slower two-seater as the German gunner in the rear cockpit fired his Spandau at the American.

Lufbery hovered above the German. To Jerome, it looked as though he was trying to clear his gun. Lufbery circled over the other plane. He must have cleared the Vickers, Jerome told himself, for he was again diving to attack the Albatros from the rear.

A cloud drifted between Jerome and the other two planes. After a moment of hesitation, he plunged the Spad into the cloud, intent on helping Lufbery. The mist closed around him, beading his goggles and dampening his face. He could see nothing except his plane and the swirling moisture of the cloud. Flying at full speed, he shot from the cloud.

Lufbery was climbing toward the Albatros from the rear, firing as he came, the German gunner doggedly returning the fire. Suddenly Lufbery's Nieuport burst into flames. He flew on past the Albatros on a straight course and then his plane tilted down as smoke streamed behind him.

Jerome dove under the Albatros and climbed into the other plane's blind spot. As the Albatros zigzagged, he saw the winking of Spandau machine gun fire from its rear. He held off and held off. Finally he pulled the trigger of his Vickers. Tracers fired at the rate of 800 rounds a minute bracketed the German plane. The

Albatros wobbled and veered away. Jerome fired again.

The Albatros climbed unsteadily and Jerome banked to the right. Bullets slammed into the fabric on the bottom of his lower wing. The firing stopped. When he glanced back, the Albatros had vanished in, the clouds.

Jerome banked and looked below him. The Nieuport, still burning, was heading toward the earth at a forty-five degree angle. When the stricken plane was less than five hundred feet above the ground, Lufbery stood up in the cockpit with flames dancing around him. Below his plane a small stream wound through farmland.

Lufbery jumped from a height of two hundred feet. His plane, Jerome guessed, was traveling at a speed of a hundred miles an hour. Lufbery plunged to the earth and his plane crashed in flames a few hundred yards beyond.

After glancing around him and seeing no Germans, Jerome circled low above the stream. Below him he saw a small house and the burning plane but there was no sign of Raoul Lufbery. Again Jerome looked above him. There was still no sign of the Albatros. Tears came to his eyes and he lifted his goggles onto his helmet and wiped his face with his sleeve.

He landed at once and drove a staff car north to the site of the crash. When he arrived he found that two French women had carried Lufbery into a peasant's house and laid him on the floor. He was dead and had been dead when the women found his battered body in the garden near the small stream. Had he been trying to dive into the water on the thousand to one chance he could survive the fall? Jerome didn't know.

He turned away and drove slowly back to the aerodrome. Lufbery was dead. The death seemed an omen; he sensed impending disaster. The Fokkers would sweep the Spads, Nieuports and Camels from the sky, the Germans would drive across the Marne and take Paris, the French government would fall and a new government would sue for peace.

He remembered flying in the cloud without being afraid, without having time to be afraid. His concern for Lufbery had overridden his fear. He nodded grimly to himself. If he had to die, at least he'd be able to die as a man.

There's a long, long trail awinding,
Into the land of my dreams.
Where the nightingale is singing
And the pale moon beams.

The waiter showed Francis and Eileen the uncooked duck. It was small with a rounded breast.

When Francis nodded, the waiter carved the breast in small red slices and laid them on a platter. He placed what remained of the duck in a press and turned a wheel and they heard the bones crunch.

"I can't get over how much you've changed," Eileen told Francis as soon as the waiter returned to the kitchen.

"And you. You're more beautiful than ever. I particularly like your dress." She wore a floor-length pale blue gown with a high neck and long sleeves. He noticed for the first time that her black hair was prematurely tinged with gray.

"I've gained five pounds in the last three months," she said. "I've never worked harder in my life yet I've put on weight."

They sipped their wine.

"You look older," she said. There were lines around his eyes and mouth that she was sure hadn't been there before. He smiled less often, she noticed, and when he did the smile was more sardonic and world-weary than she remembered. He looked more mature, she thought, less like the handsome youth she'd known.

"I am older. Two years older. I feel like I've lived fifteen years since I saw you last."

"The uniform becomes you."

He was dressed in the muted o live of the Air Service with his flared trousers tucked in the tops of high leather boots. The strap of his Sam Browne belt crossed the front of his tunic and over his left pocket he wore the silver wings of the Air Service.

"I've felt like I'm an imposter in this uniform since your brother grounded me."

"Jerome must have had a good reason."

"He thought he did. Frankly, Jerome's surprised me. I didn't think he'd last a week as the 7th's CO and here it is almost three and he's still hanging in there."

"We Kurmans aren't as soft as you might think. We're like bulldogs once we set our minds to something."

The waiter brought the steaming duck from the kitchen on a silver tray. He set it on the table between them and poured a hin wine sauce over the browned meat.

"It's delicious," Eileen said as she started to eat. "The asparagus tips are good, too."

"I had two confirmed kills the day he grounded me," Francis said. He ate quickly, as though the food was of little importance.

" 'Kills.' How I hate that word."

"Victories then. Call them whatever you want. They're still kills."

"When will it end? The killing."

Francis shrugged. "Next year. The year after. Never. The war may go on and on and on."

"At least I'm thankful you're safe. That you aren't flying."

He paused with his fork halfway to his mouth. "Do you think I had myself grounded on purpose?" he demanded.

"I didn't say that. I merely said I was glad you were safe."

"I'm not about to let Jerome Kurman tell me how to fight the Huns. Not him or anyone else."

"Why are we quarreling? We don't see each other for two years and when we do we fight."

"I'm not fighting. You're the one who as much as called me a coward." He put his fork down and drew in a deep breath. Reaching across the table, he covered her hand with his. "I'm sorry," he said. "It *is* good to see you, Eileen."

She smiled through tears. "It's good to see you, too, Francis."

Later, they walked through the French village in the direction of the hospital. The streets were muddy and the ditches smelled of sewage but te breeze was warm with the promise of spring.

"Let's get away from here," he said, taking her hand. "Away from people. They spoil whatever they touch."

He led her along a lane and then on a path through an orchard to the top of a low hill. As they looked down at the village and the hills beyond, a red Very light flared in the sky to the north.

"That means there's a pilot missing," Francis said. "They're showing him where the field is in case he'd lost instead of down somewhere.'

Another light glowed in the sky. Around them the night was quiet except for the steady chirping of insects. For a moment the war seemed far away.

"How's Billy?" she asked.

"Just great. He likes Boston. He's in the ninth grade now."

"I didn't want to tell you in a letter," Eileen said, "but after you sailed for France I found I was carrying your baby. I lost it. I wanted to have your baby, Francis. In the worst way."

He stared down at her. "I don't know what to say," he told her.

"Don't say anything. Put your arms around me."

He opened his arms to her and she laid her head against his chest. Eileen was dry-eyed now. She didn't think she would ever be able to cry again.

"Was it a boy or girl?" he asked.

"They told me it was too early to tell, but I know it was a boy. I wanted it to be a boy."

When she heard him sigh she thought her heart would break.

At the hospital, after kissing him quickly and slipping inside, she stood with her back to the door listen-

ing to him walk away. She heard the cry of a soldier
in pain from the floor above. So much suffering, she
thought, so much death. Yet death was a part of life.
Everyone and everything was born to die. Her father.
The baby. Her brothers, Curt and Martin.

Love.

19

JEROME threw the sheaf of medical reports on his desk and walked to the window where he stood looking out at the storm pummeling the aerodrome. Lightning flashed, thunder rolled, and wind drove water against the pane to blur his view of the muddy field and the rain-darkened hangars.

Francis was half blind and yet he'd told no one. What fantastic *chutzpah*! He'd flown in combat in France for two years without anyone suspecting the truth. Jerome felt a grudging admiration for the man. What a marvelous flyer to be able to hide his handicap from experienced pilots flying with him day after day.

There was a quick rap-rap-rap behind him and he turned to find Lieutenant Mackey standing in the open doorway with rain dripping from his oilskin.

When Jerome nodded the other man crossed the office and saluted.

"The field's a Goddamned lake," Mackey said.

"Take off your coat, lieutenant," Jerome told him, "and sit down."

"No, sir," Mackey said. "What I have to say will only take a minute."

Puzzled, Jerome stood behind his desk with his finger tapping the medical reports.

"The morale of the squadron has improved tremendously since you arrived, Lieutenant Kurman," Mackey said. "That's straight. You know I'm not the kind to brown-nose."

"I've thought things were going better. It's hard to be sure about something you want badly. So I'm glad to hear you say it, lieutenant."

"Your talks with the mechanics did a world of good," Mackey said. "Our engines are in the best shape I've ever seen them. I guess all of us realize how important the grease monkeys are but we're apt to forget to tell them often enough. Not only the mechanics, the armorers, too, and all the other enlisted men on the base."

"They say the pilots get all the glory and the men all the shit. I don't think they resent the glory because they know the flyers risk their lives every time they go up. They just don't appreciate the shit."

Mackey nodded. "That's not the only reason I came to see you," he said.

Jerome waited.

"It's Kincaid, sir. In my opinion he should be reinstated to active duty."

"Now just wait one . . ."

"I know what you're going to say. That I recommended sitting Kincaid down. That I was the one who didn't want him to fly with my patrol. True enough. But that was more than three weeks ago. The Huns are putting everything they have into the air. Richthofen's dead but the Black Falcon's taken his place. We've lost two men and four aircraft in the last five days."

"I'm aware of the statistics, lieutenant."

"LaDou and Campbell aren't statistics, sir. They were damn good pilots."

Jerome's hand clenched into a fist as he controlled the impulse to lash back at Mackey. He stared at the other man and said softly, "I know that, lieutenant. I don't need you to tell me."

"My apologies, sir," Mackey said. "I was out of line, totally out of line. I'm apt to speak without thinking. The habit cost me two teeth once in Toronto."

"You recommend that I reinstate Kincaid. Is that what you came here to tell me?"

"Don't close your mind to what I'm saying because of me, because of the way I fouled it up. The squadron needs Kincaid. It's not just because he's the best we've got, though he is. It's more than that. There's something about him that makes the men want to do their best. They'd gladly follow the crazy bastard to hell and back if he asked them to."

"Are you suggesting that Francis Kincaid should be squadron commander?"

As soon as he'd spoken, Jerome regretted his words. Mackey had suggested no such thing. To make the question of reinstatement a duel between himself and Francis was a mistake. Someday he'd learn how to command, he told himself. It might take years, but he'd learn.

"No, sir," Mackey said flatly, "not at all. He'd be a total disaster as commander, we both know that. The pilots would run all over him. I can see I'm making a holy mess out of what I came to say. We need Kincaid. That's the long and short of it."

"Francis Kincaid will fly," Jerome said, "when he accepts the fact that, whether he likes it or not, there's a commander at the 7th Aero Squadron, whether he likes him or not, and that he's to follow that commander's orders. This has to be a team effort, lieutenant, now more than ever, not a collection of flying prima donnas who are only interested in improving their kill records."

"Thanks for taking the time to hear me out, sir." When Jerome nodded, Mackey saluted and left. A few moments later Jerome saw him slogging across the airfield in the pelting rain.

Am I wrong about Francis? Jerome asked himself. Am I letting personal feelings cloud my judgment?

Once he had thought he hated Francis but now he knew he didn't. In a strange, perverse way he liked the man. Perhaps more than liked him. Mackey was right when he said the squadron needed Francis. He, Jerome, knew it better than anyone. But he'd be damned if he'd be a puppet that jerked every time Francis pulled the strings.

He heard someone clear his throat behind him and turned from the window. Sergeant Ingram crossed the office with a message in his hand.

"We're all behind you," Ingram said. Jerome remembered wondering if Ingram was Jewish. He wasn't, he'd discovered; the sergeant was an Episcopalian. When Jerome said nothing, Ingram added, "About Lieutenant Kincaid."

Jerome nodded and held out his hand for the message.

"From GHQ," the sergeant told him.

As Jerome read the decoded orders, he smiled. The colonel was beginning to give the 7th more than the crud of routine patrols. The squadron was slowly gaining respectability. Recognition.

"Frank Luke's flying with us tomorrow," Jerome told Ingram.

Both men looked to the window. Thunder rolled in the distance and rain still fell steadily but the sky to the west had brightened.

"Tomorrow," Jerome said, "the 7th goes after those damn Hun balloons."

His alarm clock wakened Jerome at three the next morning. Sunrise would be at 0535 and the planes would leave the aerodrome at 0500. He telephoned the hangar to verify that the Spads and Nieuports would be ready and then joined the pilots scheduled for the mission.

They sat in the lounge, eyes heavy with sleep, drinking coffee. William Mackey stared morosely into his cup. Henry Gaspard shuffled and dealt a hand of solitaire while Sumner Parsons listened to Hal Hoffman spin a tale of a border skirmish along the Rio Grande.

Frank Luke came into the room with Alex Banning, a friend from before the war when they'd both worked in the Arizona copper mines.

"You sure you want me to talk to them?" Frank Luke asked Jerome.

"Whenever you're ready. You know more about shooting down balloons than the rest of us put together."

"I'm not much at talking," Luke said. He walked to the front of the room and sat uneasily on the edge of a table.

"When I first got to France," Luke told them, "and I saw them big Hun balloons just sitting up there in the sky like birds on a wire and somebody told me they was worth three times as much as an airplane, I thought it would make good sense to knock a few down. And be easy, to boot." He ran his hand over his blond hair. "I found it makes good sense but it ain't that easy."

The pilots nodded in agreement. Jerome remembered the unsuccessful attack on a balloon he and Mackey had made a few weeks before.

"What with all the Archies around the balloons," Luke said, "at first I wanted to fly in close, fire off a few rounds, and then get the hell out. I found that ain't the way to shoot down balloons. You got to go after them as careful as you'd go after a spiny cactus. Or a Fokker. And if they don't go down you got to go after them again. You just got to learn to ignore them Archies."

"And pray," Gaspard said.

"And pray like hell," Luke agreed with a slow smile. "It's been my experience that the best time of day to go after them is at dawn or in the evening just before dark when the balloons are being raised up or pulled down. The damn gunners can't see you then as well as they can during the day. That's why we're up so damn early this morning."

"Will all our rounds be incendiaries?" Hoffman asked.

"Every last one," Luke said. "Even when you hit them damn balloons with the incendiaries they don't always burn. Sometimes the bullets go through the whole bag without the gas catching fire. A little patch and they're as good as new."

Jerome walked to the front of the room and sat on the table beside Luke.

"The doughboys go over the top at eight hundred hours," he said. "These balloons are the Hun's eyes and it's up to us to blind him." He remembered Francis' medical report and went on quickly. "Except for Lieutenant Luke we'll work in teams with two pilots for each balloon. With Luke himself it's the other way around. He'll have two balloons all to his lonesome. You've all seen the photos of the balloon locations and you all had a chance for a personal look-see after the storm yesterday. Any questions?"

The pilots shook their heads and, talking and joking, walked from the lounge to the airfield. When they separated to go to their planes, Jerome said, "Good luck, men."

They waved to him and to each other. The pilots not assigned to the mission watched from near the hangars as the airmen revved up their engines and then waited while flares were lit along the length of the field. They took off with water spraying from their wheels and climbed into the dark sky as the flares blinked out below them.

Jerome and Mackey were partners so Jerome flew behind and slightly above the other pilot's Nieuport. As they had agreed, they climbed to 10,000 feet and crossed deep into German territory so they could attack their balloon from the least expected direction.

Clouds clustered on the western horizon but overhead it was clear. Though the sun had not yet risen, the sky above Jerome was turning slowly from black to gray to a pale blue as the new day swept toward France from the east. He breathed deeply of the cool damp air of early morning. It was his favorite time of day.

The Spad's 235 horses roared throatily and the wind sang in the wires. Jerome was flying a good plane against a despised enemy on an important mission accompanied by men he liked and admired. He had never been happier, he knew, and he wondered if he would ever be this happy again. Perhaps not. Probably not. The thought didn't trouble him. He considered the idea, shrugged and put it from him, content to enjoy the moment.

The past seemed to fall away from him like a discarded cocoon. All his life he had tried to fit the role others seemed to give him, to be a peacemaker, to solve problems through compromise. He'd acted that way with his father, his brothers, with Eileen. And with Francis Kincaid. He had worried and vacillated and sidestepped and what had it all gained him? Precious little.

Could he change? He didn't know, not for sure. But he did know he wasn't the same man he'd been two years before or even a month before. Colonel Mitchell had thrust him into the crucible of the 7th Aero Squadron by naming him acting CO, Francis Kincaid had applied the heat and now he, Jerome, was emerging a different man. Whether his new self was better or worse than the old, he didn't know.

What unmitigated crap, he told himself.

Mackey was wagging his wings. Below and ahead of them their *drachon*, their balloon, was slowly rising from the ground on the end of a tether attached to the rear of a truck. The balloon had reached an altitude of a thousand feet.

Jerome followed Mackey down and circled above the balloon watching for Fokkers. He saw none. Mackey dived in below the balloon, his green-brown Nieuport a pale shadow against the darkness of the ground. Jerome waited for the German Archies to open fire but they didn't. Mackey climbed toward the balloon, his guns winking flame, the incendiaries streaking into the fabric.

Jerome turned, dived, pulling out below a thousand feet. Mackey had swept past the apparently undamaged balloon and was now banking to the right. Jerome climbed to the attack. The Archies opened up when he was still five hundred yards from the balloon and shells exploded in yellow bursts ahead and beside him.

He flew on, climbing at a slight angle. A burst of anti-aircraft fire rocked the Spad. He ignored it, intent on the balloon. Another shell exploded directly in front of him and he saw the burst through his whirling propeller. Nothing the Germans threw at him could touch him, he thought. He was invincible.

At a hundred yards, he opened fire. His bullets slammed into the balloon's fabric, round following round. Nothing. Still firing, he pulled back on the stick and zoomed past. Looking behind him he saw a flutter of white below the balloon. He smiled with satisfaction. The German observer had taken to his parachute.

With a whoosh the balloon ignited. Flames from the burning hydrogen hissed as they leaped into the sky. The Spad glowed in the sudden light and Jerome felt the sear of heat from the flames on the side of his face.

Exhilarated, he watched the remnants of the balloon plunge earthward with black smoke rising from the burning folds. Jerome shook his clenched fist in the air. When he looked up he saw Mackey's Nieuport slightly ahead of him. The other pilot waved from his cockpit and Jerome waved back.

They flew east toward their secondary target, another balloon, with the sun rising above the horizon ahead of them. All at once another sun appeared, a great ball of yellow flame, and Jerome nodded. A second balloon brought down. Gaspard wouldn't need any help from them.

The 7th Aero Squadron didn't have to take a back seat to anybody. That cocky ex-racing car driver at the 94th, Eddie Rickenbacker, was always boasting that his squadron was the best in the business. We'll give them a run for their money, Jerome promised himself.

Below and to the south guns flashed as the American artillery barrage began. Only five minutes had passed, Jerome realized, since their attack on the first balloon. Another flare of fire glowed off to the right. A third balloon down, probably one of Frank Luke's.

Their mission over, Jerome followed Mackey toward the lines, heading for home. He was elated. I may not be as good a pilot as Francis, he thought, not as daring. I don't have Francis' *sang-froid*, but there ies something I can contribute to the squadron that he can't.

Unlike Francis, who seemed to act on instinct, Jerome knew he had to be constantly thinking about what he was doing while in the air. He had to learn the ins and outs of aerial combat, the maneuvers, the aerobatics, the tricks, step by step. As he learned, though, he could do something Francis seemed unable or unwilling to do, he could pass his knowledge to the new pilots joining the squadron. If he helped them survive he'd benefit not only the men under his command but the Air Service as well.

Tac-tac-tac.

He jerked erect. The sound of machine guns came again. Glancing behind him while at the same time pulling back on the stick and shoving his rudder to the left, he saw a Fokker triplane less than a hundred yards off his right wing.

As his Spad climbed, Jerome smiled grimly to himself. He was a fine one to teach others. He'd let his elation at the squadron's success in the attack on the balloons cloud his judgment. His lack of concentration had let the Fokker approach unnoticed.

Jerome brought his Spad up and over. He had a sudden hunch that the Hun would reverse course, so instead of completing a *retournment* to fly in the same direction as before, he brought his plane out of its dive going the opposite way to put himself on the Fokker's tail.

The Fokker was nowhere to be seen. Looking behind him, Jerome saw the other plane flying away from him. So much for hunches. He rose in a climbing turn and saw the German doing the same.

They were three hundred yards apart flying directly at one another. At a hundred yards, Jerome opened fire. The German fired at the same instant and tracers and incendiaries streaked across the dark sky making it appear as though the planes were joined by four shortening ropes of fire.

I'll be damned if I'll shy away, Jerome told himself. The planes rushed at one another. He braced himself for the crash. His Spad, hit by Spandau fire, lurched violently. The Fokker rose at the last minute and he saw round after round from his Vickers lace the other plane's belly.

The Fokker burst into flames and fell over on one wing. As Jerome swept beneath him, the Fokker fell into a spin and he saw the dark figure of the pilot trying to push himself from the cockpit. Jerome glanced around to see if there were other German planes in the vicinity. A lone aircraft dived from his right. He began to climb, the Spad unsteady, when he realized it was a Nieuport. Mackey coming to his assistance. He saw no other planes.

Looking down again he saw a spurt of flame rise from the ground behind him. The Fokker crashing? In the darkness and with the continual flash of the artillery he couldn't be sure. There was no sign of a parachute.

He was trembling. No, it was his Spad. The engine was shaking. He eased the throttle down and the vibration lessened but didn't stop. Oil pressure O.K., fuel O.K., no sign of fire. Had the motor been hit when the planes roared directly at one another?

Jerome felt dizzy. He closed his eyes for a moment, clenching his hands into fists. The right side of his head ached. Opening his eyes he put his gloved hand to his head. The glove came away stained red. He'd been grazed and hadn't known it.

The Spad was well under a thousand feet and still vibrating. If the engnie failed he'd be able to glide only a few hundred yards. He prayed. Still vibrating, the engine refused to quit. Jerome turned right toward the emergency field east of Commercy. There. In the dim light of dawn, he eased his Spad over the tree-tops and landed with a jolting bounce.

The plane slowed to a stop and the propeller ticked over a few final times. He stared in amazement. One blade of the propeller was shattered, had been cut in half by the Hun's bullets. No wonder the engine had vibrated, he'd been lucky to get down at all.

Jerome unbuckled his harness and began to pull himself from the cockpit. His dizziness returned tenfold and he stood holding to the sides of the cockpit. His head throbbed. Drawing a deep breath, he swung himself from the plane and dropped to stand on the ground.

Two soldiers were running to him. He took a step toward them and blackness closed in and the dark muddy earth rushed up to meet him.

20

JEROME opened his eyes, blinking in the light. The dull throb in his head was like the distant pounding of guns. Putting his hand behind his ear he felt three strips of adhesive holding a small bandage in place. He winced when he probed the wound with his finger.

Looking around him, he saw a shaded window to the left of his hospital bed. Across from him and to his right were other beds in which men sat, reading or idly staring about, lay back, sweat glistening on their faces.

A nurse walked toward him between the two rows of beds. Blonde and blue-eyed, she was one of the most beautiful women Jerome had ever seen. He stared at her. He was still staring when she stopped beside his bed to take his pulse.

"How are you today, lieutenant?" she asked.

"Great," he lied.

"The doctor will be in the ward around noon," she said. "He thinks you only had a mild concussion but he wants to keep you here until then to make sure."

"What's your name?" he asked.

She looked at him with a smile in eyes that were the deep blue of an October sky. A saucy cap sat on the back of her bobbed blonde hair. She was a fair-skinned, diminutive girl, her figure concealed by the straight lines of the nurse's uniform that fell below her knees.

"My name's Lois Hyde, lieutenant," she said. "Miss Hyde. Lift up your head." When he did as she asked, she plumped his pillow. He continued to stare at her.

"I'm sure you'll be able to go back to your squadron as soon as the doctor sees you," she said.

Returning to the 7th Aero Squadron had suddenly become the farthest thing from his mind.

"Where are you from, Miss Hyde?" he asked. "In the States, I mean."

"Ontonagon, Michigan. You've probably never heard of it."

"You're right, I haven't. Tell me about Ontonagon."

"There's not much to tell. It's a small town in Michigan's Upper Peninsula. On Lake Superior."

A booming voice interrupted them.

"Well, well, well, what have we here?"

Reluctantly, Jerome looked from Lois Hyde to the foot of his bed where Sumner Parsons stood grinning at him. Behind Parsons were Bill Mackey, Henry Gaspard, and, surprisingly, Francis.

"Here we drive all the way from the oerodrome," Parsons said, "expecting to find you on your death bed and instead you're being nursed by the prettiest little gal this side of Tulsa."

Lois nodded to the pilots as she passed them. She walked between the rows of beds, smiling and talking to the patients. Francis, Jerome noticed, watched her for several moments before he looked back.

"We shot down all five of the balloons," Mackey said. "Frank Luke said it was one of the best missions he'd ever been on. And everyone got back to the field in good shape."

"Except me," Jerome said. "That Fokker you saw shattered my prop."

"I saw the prop," Gaspard told him. "They put on a new one and I flew your plane back to the aerodrome. It's as good as new. We nailed your old prop on the wall of the lounge."

"When you come back to the squadron," Parsons said, "I'll take your picture standing in front of it. It'll be something to show your grandchildren when they ask you about what you did in the great war. The war to end wars."

"Are you okay?" Francis spoke for the first time.

"I should be out of here this afternoon according to the nurse." Jerome glanced to the far end of the ward, hoping to get another glimpse of Lois Hyde, but she was gone.

"From what I've seen of the nurses," Mackey said, "it might be worth a little concussion to have a chance to get better acquainted."

"Your sister's a nurse, isn't she?" Gaspard asked. Jerome saw Francis frown.

"Yes," Jerome said. "At the hospital near Toul. This is the Red Cross hospital outside Commercy, isn't it?"

"Right," Parsons told him.

"How did the land attack on the Germans go?" Jerome asked.

"The A.E.F. is advancing all along the front. The squadron's been flying support missions since yesterday morning. We were just back from patrol when we drove over here."

"And have to go up again this afternoon," Mackey said. "We'll drive over tomorrow if you're not back."

Each man went to the bed in turn, gripping Jerome's shoulder or shaking his hand. All except Francis, who nodded. The pilots left, waving, Gaspard telling him to ask his nurse if she had a sister, and for a few minutes he heard them laughing in the hall outside the ward.

Footsteps approached from the other direction and he turned to see Lois Hyde walking rapidly toward him, looking neither right nor left. When she reached his bed he started to speak but she walked past without a glance and left the ward.

So much for the start of my great love affair, Jerome thought ruefully. He swept the covers aside and swung his feet over the edge of the bed and sat for a moment staring at the shaded window. Tentatively, he put one foot on the wooden floor and then the other. Holding to the bed, he stood.

Though he felt a slight dizziness, a vague whirling sensation, he was able to take his hand from the bed and stand. He walked a few steps, testing his balance. The dizziness receded. Jerome walked back and forth beside his bed. Though still weak, he felt better.

He went to the window, reached down and pulled up the shade. He was on the second floor of the hospital. Below and to his left was a staff car with Mackey in the driver's seat, Parsons beside him and Gaspard in the rear playing with a small brown terrier. Where was Francis?

Looking to his right, to the steps leading from the side of the hospital, he saw him, concealed from the men in the car by high bushes. Francis was talking to Lois Hyde. Even though she stood two steps above him he still looked down at her.

She smiled as she talked. Not the same way she had smiled at him. He couldn't put his finger on what the difference was at first but it was there. Her smile to him, Jerome decided, had been a nurse's smile. Her smile now was a woman's.

He had the impression that they had known one another for a considerable time. As he watched, Francis, grinning, put his forefinger beneath Lois' chin and raised her face to his. She was no longer smiling. Her lips were parted, her eyes seemed to gleam in the sunlight.

Francis kissed her. A long kiss, their bodies apart, only their lips touching. Francis was the first to draw back. Lois leaned to him for a moment before she, too, drew away. Francis was talking, gesturing. Jerome couldn't hear what he said. Lois nodded as she listened, said a few words and nodded again, still looking intently at him.

Francis turned and walked along the flagstone path to the car and climbed into the back. The dog abandoned Gaspard to lick his face. Only when the engine roared to life and the car sped around the circle at the side of the hospital did Lois step from behind the concealing bushes. She walked to the roadway where she stood looking after the car until it disappeared.

Jerome slowly pulled down the shade and returned to bed. When he heard her footsteps approaching from the hall he closed his eyes and feigned sleep. She walked past his bed and was gone.

As soon as Jerome returned to the aerodrome that afternoon, he went to the officers' lounge. Since most of the pilots were on patrol, he found only Alfred Enright in the room. Enright looked up from the piano, greeted Jerome with a wave and played a chorus of the Michigan fight song.

Jerome opened the cabinet behind the bar and took out a bottle of Old Crow. He poured himself a shot and drank it down. Putting the bottle back on the shelf, he raised his hand in a cocky salute to Enright and left the lounge.

He found Francis leaving the hangar where his Nieuport 28, now assigned to another pilot, was stored.

"I was looking for you," Jerome said.

"Oh?" Francis raised his eyebrows. His hands were stained with grease and there was a black smudge on his blond hair.

Jerome balled his hand and swung. His fist struck Francis on the jaw and he staggered back.

"What the hell?" Francis said.

Jerome clenched his other fist and swung at the taller man. Francis warded off the blow with his forearm.

Francis shook his head. "I'm not about to fight

our wounded hero," he said. "Look me up in a few days and I'll beat the shit out of you."

"You've only got one eye," Jerome said. "Doesn't that make us even?"

"I figured you'd pry into that once you got the chance." Francis unbuttoned his tunic, took it off and laid it over a sawhorse beside the hangar. Jerome removed his jacket and tossed it from him onto the muddy ground. They put up their fists like professional pugilists.

"This is asinine," Francis said.

Jerome heard the drone of the returning patrol. Glancing over Francis' head he saw five black specks coming in from the north. When Francis half-turned to follow his gaze, Jerome hit him as hard as he could on the chest.

Francis staggered back and, slipping on the wet grass, fell with a plop to the muddy field. He looked up at Jerome in surprise and anger.

"Why, you bastard," he said.

He pushed himself from the ground and charged, bull-like. Jerome retreated. When he was a few feet from Jerome, Francis stopped and flicked out with his right hand. Jerome raised his arm to shield his face and Francis' left drove in under his guard and buried itself in his stomach.

Jerome grunted and his head jerked forward. Francis hit him on the chin with all his strength. Jerome sat down. The field, the hangars, Francis' face, all whirled around him. His headache of the morning returned tenfold. He wouldn't get up, he'd stay where he was even though the water was slowly soaking through the seat of his trousers.

"God damn you," he muttered. He rose to his knees, staggered to his feet.

Francis hit him again, the blow glancing off his nose. Blood spurted. Jerome counterpunched wildly. Francis jabbed two lefts to his stomach and Jerome grunted, bent over and dropped to his knees.

"Had enough?" Francis asked.

Jerome shook his head. Looking up, he saw Francis' blond hair and blue eyes through a blur as he tasted the blood streaming down his face from his nose. Jerome drew in a long breath and, lurching to his feet, charged head down, slamming into Francis' midsection.

Taken by surprise, Francis backpedaled. Jerome flailed at him with his fists, stepped back and butted up with the top of his head. He felt a stab of pain as his head struck Francis under the chin. Francis seemed to lift from the ground and then sit down. Jerome scooped a glob of mud from the ground and hurled it at the other man, the mud striking Francis' mouth. Francis wiped some away with his hand and spit the rest out.

Jerome heard the whine of landing planes.

Francis pushed himself slowly to his feet. He attacked cautiously, jabbing and then counterpunching as Jerome swung wildly at him, Jerome's blows landing harmlessly on Francis' forearms. Francis weaved and bobbed in front of him, his fists lashing out, his knuckles red with the blood from Jerome's nose.

Jerome heard a shout. Looking up, he saw Mackey running from his plane with the rest of the pilots behind him, calling to them to stop. Catching Mackey's eye, Jerome shook his head just as Francis' fist shot out,

a blow straight from the shoulder that caught Jerome
on the side of the face.

He grunted and pitched forward to the ground,
his face in the mud. When he drew in his breath, he
choked on water and his own blood. He pushed himself to his hands and knees. He had no strength left.
His arms were lead, his head throbbed and he had to
close his eyes to try to ward off the blackness threat-
ening to engulf him.

By God, Jerome thought, *I won't let him lick me.*
He stood, his hands hanging heavy at his sides, his
left eye puffed shut. Through his good eye he saw
Francis advance on him, saw Mackey and the others
behind Francis, watching, making no move to inter-
fere.

Jerome lunged. His arms were so heavy. He
swung woodenly. A hand clasped his wrist and he felt
himself being pulled forward. He closed his eyes, waiting for the final blow to fall. Someone was holding him
up, clasping him in his arms, supporting him. He tried
to push himself away. Why wouldn't Mackey let him
go? Let him fight?

He opened his one good eye and saw that it
wasn't Mackey who held him, it was Francis. Francis
was smiling. *I'll wipe that smile off his Goddamned
smug face*, Jerome told himself. He tried to wrench
himself free but couldn't.

Francis was talking under his breath. So the
others wouldn't hear? What was he saying? Jerome
couldn't make out what he was telling him.

"What?" he mumbled through swollen lips.

"You win." Francis' lips were close to Jerome's
ear. "Do you hear me, you crazy bastard? You win."

"What?" Jerome asked again. "Win what?"

"I'll do it your way," Francis said. "No more lone wolf tactics. I'll fly the way you want me to. I won't like it worth a damn, but I'll do it."

Jerome nodded. "Good," he said. Why did he feel like crying? He drew back and looked up at Francis' smiling face. Francis was smeared with grease, mud and blood but seemed untouched.

"I'm not much of a fighter," Jerome said.

"You're one hell of a fighter," Francis told him. "Maybe you don't do too well in the preliminaries but you manage to win the big ones."

Jerome tried to brush the mud from his pants.

"You'd do better if you wait till it dries," Bill Mackey said.

Jerome looked across the field at the planes and then overhead at the clear blue sky.

"What do you say we go up?" he asked Francis.

"You're not in much shape for flying," Francis told him. "Not with that eye."

"If you can fly with one eye," he said so only Francis could hear him, "then so can I. I'll put some ice on it. Are you game?"

"Why not?"

"You, Bill?" Jerome turned to Mackey.

"I'll fly point," Mackey said.

"The hell you will," Jerome told him. "I'm the commander of this squadron. It's high time I was its leader, too. I'll fly point."

"What did they dose you with at that hospital?" Francis asked. "I'll order some of the same."

Remembering Lois, picturing Francis kissing her, Jerome was silent. After a moment he picked up his jacket and said, "Let's go," and he and the other two pilots crossed the field to the hangar.

A half hour later they climbed slowly into the limitless sky with the horizon a huge expanding circle on all sides of them. The day was bright and clear with a soft summer breeze from the east. Jerome smiled as he listened to the thrum of his Spad, felt the plane's steady vibration, smiled as he looked behind and above to see Francis' and Bill's planes following him toward the front.

Only the day before he had thought, as he flew on the sortie against the balloons, that he had never been happier and probably never would be as happy again. He'd been wrong. He was happier today. You're turning into a Goddamned romantic, Kurman, he told himself.

As they neared the lines flying at slightly more than 5,000 feet, Jerome saw the steady flashing of German artillery in the north and the occasional response of the American guns beneath him. There were no other planes in the sky as far as he could tell.

He wagged his wings and swooped low over No-Man's-Land to fly beneath the trajectories of the German shells. Below him he saw Hun soldiers looking up from their trenches. He pointed the nose of his Spad down and raked the trenches with round after round of machine gun fire. Some Germans fell, others scrambled out of sight.

To his right a group of helmeted Germans in front of a dugout raised their rifles to fire at his low-flying plane. Jerome swerved in their direction and, before they had a chance to aim, raked them with rounds from both of his Vickers. He smiled when he saw the

Huns lower their guns and try to crowd through the entrance to the dugout with his tracers streaking among them.

Looking back, he saw Mackey and Francis following him, their guns winking fire as they strafed the German lines. After a few more runs, Jerome climbed with the other two planes of his patrol behind him and returned to fly over the trenches once more. The Germans, who had been returning to their posts, scrambled for safety at the sound of his Spad.

He swung left behind the German lines and, a mile to the rear, saw a battery of 77's firing at a rapid rate. As he neared, the gunners went on with their work, hurrying to and fro as they picked up and passed forward the fifteen-pound shells. The guns of the battery fired again and again at the rate of at least a round a second.

He lowered the nose of his plane and, pressing the triggers of both Vickers guns, fired into the first of the German artillery pieces. Men fell, others ran, the guns were silenced. Jerome banked and came about, firing at each of the groups of artillerymen in turn until all were lying dead or wounded on the ground or had dispersed into their dugouts.

Again he circled the battery and swept low overhead. He saw a German truck a short distance away and nosed down. When he pulled his triggers, the Vickers guns failed to fire. At first he thought they had jammed but then he realized he was out of ammunition.

He climbed and circled until Mackey and Francis came to fly beside him. Wagging his wings, he turned and led the patrol south over the lines and back to the aerodrome. When Jerome climbed from his Spad he waited beside the plane for Mackey and Francis. The two pilots joined him and, arm-in-arm, they crossed the field.

Sergeant Ingram was waiting beside the hangar. Jerome left the two pilots and walked over to him. The sergeant glanced at Jerome's swollen face but made no comment. By now the whole aerodrome must have heard about his fight with Francis.

"Sir," Ingram said, "there's a Captain Munson waiting for you in the orderly room." The sergeant had a strange look on his face, Jerome thought, one he couldn't read. All Ingram said, though, was, "It's good to have Lieutenant Kincaid flying with the squadron again."

"Now that Francis is back," Jerome said as they walked to the headquarters building, "the 7th will be the best squadron in the Air Service, bar none."

Captain Robert Munson, young, blond and be-medaled, followed Jerome into his office and sat across the desk from him.

"I've been sent from GHQ," Munson said, "to take over as the CO of the 7th. These are my orders." He laid an envelope on the desk.

Jerome, stunned, said nothing.

"Colonel Mitchell talked to me yesterday," Munson went on. "He appreciates the work you've done here while you've been the acting CO and intends to make those feelings known. He's giving you the option of staying with the 7th as a flight leader or transferring to another outfit."

"I understand, captain," Jerome said. "I realized all along that my assignment here was temporary."

"From all I've heard," Munson said, "the 7th's rounding into a good outfit."

"Do you have a preference, captain, whether I stay with the squadron or transfer?" Jerome asked.

"I'd be glad to have you serve in my command. On the other hand, I'd understand if you choose to leave. I don't have to have your answer today. Take time to think it over, lieutenant."

"I don't have to, sir. I'd like to stay with the 7th."

"Very good. I'll review the squadron's operations with you. At your convenience."

Jerome stood and saluted and, after Munson returned the salute, walked past him out of the office. Ingram was waiting in the orderly room.

"That's the Army for you," Ingram said. "All fucked up, as usual."

21

"FRANCIS," Eileen said, "you're the most persuasive man I've ever met. If someone had told me yesterday that I'd be going with you to Paris for two days I wouldn't have believed them."

They were rumbling west in a sleepy night coach. The windows were curtained in wartime black, giving Eileen the sensation of traveling through a perpetual tunnel.

"Paris is a world apart," Francis told her. "What happens there doesn't count. We're not held responsible for anything we do in Paris."

"I think I've heard that idea somewhere before." Eileen smiled slightly. "I don't believe it for a moment. Whatever we do, wherever we do it, we still have to live with ourselves afterwards."

"Maybe that's the difference between the Kurmans and the Kincaids. You Kurmans are doomed to live with your pasts while we Kincaids can forget ours and get on with the business at hand."

"Francis, you're just talking to hear yourself. You don't believe a word you're saying."

"But I do, in a way. I'm trying to understand what makes people the way they are, Eileen. I'm thinking out loud."

"You have changed. I never knew you to want to really understand anything. Except maybe how to make an airplane fly better."

"I think you've told me that before," Francis said. "You say I've changed so much. What was I like before?" He grinned. "Maybe you shouldn't tell me."

"Before? Besides being the most persuasive man I knew, I thought you were the most egotistical. You never seemed to think of anyone except yourself. What's in it for Francis Kincaid? That's the question you always seemed to ask yourself first. Or else you didn't think ahead at all. You just did whatever you damn well felt like doing."

"Were the Kurmans any better? With their grandiose plans for the store, for the business, their passion for making money. Ambition's the curse of the Kurmans. After all, where did it ever get them?"

They were silent for a time, remembering. The shrill whistle sounded, the train slowed and rattled over switches, then speeded up again.

"Two weeks ago I drove to Martin's grave."

Eileen's voice was so low that Francis had to lean toward her to hear. He glanced at the other passengers in the coach, two old French women, a British corporal, his head nodding, a white-bearded patriarch with both hands clasped on the head of his cane. They paid no attention to the two Americans.

"There was a white picket fence around the plot," Eileen said. "The grass had been cut and there was a stone marker on the grave with Martin's name and rank and the dates."

"The pilots in the Lafayette *Escadrille* gave the stone," Francis said.

"There were flowers on the grave, Francis. Fresh flowers. Chrysanthemums. I found the cemetery caretaker and asked him about the flowers. He told me the florist from the village had been there that morning, that he came every week. So I went into town and asked at the florist's shop. Do you know what he told me?"

Francis shook his head.

"I had a hard time understanding him. When I did make out what he was saying all he'd tell me was that it was a lady from Paris. He wouldn't tell me her name. 'A cousin of the brave American aviator,' he said. 'She has paid me to leave the flowers once a week.'"

"A romantic notion."

"I didn't believe the florist. For one thing, we don't have a cousin in Paris. You may, Francis, you're half French, but Martin didn't." She frowned. "Did he know any women in Paris?" she asked.

"He wasn't in France very long," Francis said slowly, remembering Andrea, remembering Denise. He wondered what had become of Denise. The last he had seen her, over a year ago in a cafe near the Ritz, she was with an English major.

"I hope Martin had a girl in France," Eileen said.

"A wonderful, fun-loving girl. I hope he and she were happy together. Martin was so young to die. I hope he was happy at the last."

"He did mention a girl," Francis said, "and she did live in Paris though I think she came from the provinces. Her name was Andrea. I don't think I knew her last name. If I did, I've forgotten it."

"When I saw Martin's grave, I cried. For my brother. For all the boys who've died. I don't cry often but I did that day. This terrible, terrible war."

"The tide's finally turning," Francis said. "The Allies are on the offensive all along the front and they've got the Huns on the run. Do you know what I wish I could do before it ends?"

"I haven't the slightest idea."

"I wish President Wilson would come to France before it's all over so I could take him to at least a few of the battlefields and walk with him through some of the carnage. Not fly, walk. Let him see a battle with the 75's and the 77's exploding and the soldiers going over the top into the face of the machine gun fire. Let him see the dead men hanging on the barbed wire.

"I wish I could take him behind the lines and let him see the debris of war. I'd show him the wasteland that used to be France. The carcasses of what were once magnificent horses. The rubble of what were once beautiful villages. The mangled bodies of what were once men. I'd have him ride with me in an ambulance with its terrible cargo, let him see the walking wounded hobbling toward the rear. We'd visit the first aid posts and the field hospitals and I'd show him all the butchery that goes on in those pestholes. Necessary butchery but butchery all the same."

Eileen looked at him in surprised silence.

"If Woodrow Wilson came with me and saw what I've seen, I think he'd feel the way most of the soldiers here feel. British, French and American, it makes no difference. They know we'll have a lasting peace only after the Huns are completely and absolutely defeated. Do you remember what they used to call old U.S. Grant? Unconditional Surrender Grant. America needs a man like him today. The Huns have to be made to pay for all the misery they've caused."

"Yet hate only begets more hate."

"Compromise and forgiveness will beget us another war. Wait and see."

"You have changed, Francis. You're not the young man I used to hear all those stories about. The lothario who drank champagne at all the Washington parties."

"God, that seems so long ago. Was that me? Was it really me? The Rough Riders, the Smithsonian, the Roosevelts, my brother Jules. They were in another life. Another existence. The war ended all that. They were before the war. From now on we'll remember everything as being either before the war or after the war."

"Before the war," Eileen repeated slowly. She put her head back and closed her eyes. "Listening to the train," she said, "I can almost believe we'll soon be arriving in Boston. Or in New York. And they'll all be on the platform waiting for me. My family. Jerome holding Benny in his arms. And Curt and Martin. And my father." Her voice caught and she sighed.

Francis took her hand in his.

"I'm not usually this morbid," she said, opening her eyes. "I was usually the life of the party when I was younger. That's what they used to say, 'Here comes Eileen Kurman, the life of the party.'"

"Don't," Francis said.

"I didn't mean to spoil your leave."

"You could never do that. Just being with you is all I want. You've changed, too, Eileen, you're more beautiful than ever."

"That's not really very important to me anymore. It was once but not now."

"It is to me because that's you, Eileen. Do you know what I like most about you, though? I can always talk to you. Say what I really think instead of what I think you want to hear. I don't have to try to impress you. It's like you're a part of myself. You know how the censor cuts secrets out of our letters? I don't have to cut anything out of what I say to you."

"That's one of the nicest compliments anyone's ever paid me." She rested her head on his arm for a moment and he breathed in the scent of lilies-of-the-valley.

"We've all changed," she said. "I used to think I was entitled to the world with a red ribbon tied around it. I was Eileen Kurman, daughter of Leon Kurman, and so I deserved the best there was. I deserved perfection. If I didn't find it right away, I kept looking. Know something, Francis? I've stopped looking for what isn't there. Now I take what I can get."

"I don't know if that's a compliment or not." He grinned. "I think I should feel insulted."

"I wasn't talking about you, Francis. Not exactly."

The train slowed and, amid the hiss of steam, came

to a stop. The passengers looked about them with dull early-morning eyes.

"Paris," Francis said.

They left the train. Inside the station, officers and soldiers waited in a long line in front of a ticket window. To one side of the window a French gendarme in a blue cape and wearing a sword was checking their orders.

Shouting above the confused bustle of the street outside, Francis hailed a horse-drawn cab and they rattled over cobblestones to the Continental Hotel.

"Separate rooms?" he asked her.

"Separate rooms," she said.

He bowed slightly and, as soon as they were registered, they climbed the stairs carrying their own bags to the rooms on the second floor.

"Do you want to rest awhile?" he asked.

She shook her head. "We've only the two days," she said. "I don't want to sleep a minute while we're in Paris."

"I tried that once." He remembered drinking champagne as he and Martin returned to the aerodrome, remembered the look on Thenault's face when he roused the captain in the middle of the night. That was one of the troubles with getting older. There were so many echoes.

"The result was a disaster," he told her.

"Well, I don't want to take a nap now at any rate," Eileen said. "Show me Paris, Francis. There's so much I want to see and do. I don't know where I'll find the time."

"There's never enough time. Shall we hire a cab or would you rather walk?"

"I'm tired of riding, I'd like to walk."

They crossed the Pont-Royal in the dim blue light of early morning with the mist rising from the Seine. Beneath the bridge, the dark slow-moving river flowed silently through the sleeping city. From where they stood they saw other bridges with purple shadows gathered under their stone arches. To the east, dark and magnificent against the pink sky, were the towers of Notre Dame.

They passed the Louvre and the statue marking the spot where, or so it was said, Joan of Arc had been wounded near the walls of Paris in another war centuries before when the English occupied the city.

In the rue Saint-Honore, women were pushing up the iron shutters in front of their shop windows. Water flowed from a hydrant into the gutter and men used brooms to sweep it onto the sidewalk. Overhead, the upper stories of the houses were golden in the light of the rising sun.

They walked into a square where old women were unloading wagons from the farms and building great pyramids of beets, radishes and lettuce on their market stalls. Old men and women, cooks and house-wives, walked among the stalls filling their string bags with vegetables.

At the corner a flower lady held up a bouquet of carnations to Eileen, some of the flowers white, others a delicate pink. Francis bought two, one of each color, and pinned them on the front of her cape.

"From the gardens near Nice," he told her.

They stopped to eat in a cafe, a small crowded neighborhood restaurant, the windows facing the street opaque with steam, the men and women laughing and calling greetings to one another.

There was an explosion, a dull thump, a few streets away. The cafe quieted.

"The Boche," Francis said. "Their long range guns can still reach Paris."

The talk began again, more subdued than before, as though the war, like an unwelcome stranger, had joined them for breakfast.

After they ate, they walked along the boulevards and through the parks. Later, Francis hired a cab and they drove to the Eiffel Tower.

"When we were boys," Francis told her, "Henry, Jules and I, we loved to build wooden models of the Tower. I remember one that must have been six feet high. Henry was so proud of that tower. I wonder whatever became of it."

They rode to Versailles, strolled in the gardens, picnicked on the grass. It was late afternoon when they returned to the city where, after paying their driver, they walked slowly back to their hotel. They paused on a bridge and leaned against the stone wall.

Francis took his silver cigarette case from his tunic pocket and they smoked as they stared down at the water. A tug churned upriver and the late afternoon sun glinted from the mounds of white sand on its two barges.

"Someday," Eileen said, "after the war, we'll come back to Paris, you and I, and we'll stand here on this bridge just as we're doing now." She paused. "I wonder what we'll be like then. What we'll be doing. If we only had a crystal ball so we could see into the future."

She leaned forward on the wall and looked down, saw the darkening sky reflected in the river, saw her own pale face framed by her black hair. She looked in vain for Francis' reflection beside her own.

She turned and found him standing a few feet away watching a funeral procession led by a hearse drawn by two black horses. The hearse was black with black curtains. Not real curtains, she realized as she looked closer, but wood carved to resemble curtains. Men in black, women in long mourning dresses, two French soldiers wearing black armbands, walked behind the hearse in somber silence. A woman sobbed, raising a handkerchief to her veiled face.

"I always used to think funerals were barbaric," Francis said, "but I've changed my mind. The dead should be remembered. Honored."

"We've had enough of death," Eileen said, drawing him away. "Let's do something lively tonight. Go dancing. Go where there's music and singing."

"The theater?"

"Great. I'll have to change first, though."

At the end of the first act they strolled to the restaurant located off the foyer. Tobacco smoke drifted above the tables. On a dais a Negro band played jazz, the drummer throwing his sticks in the air and catching them. The song ended, the lights dimmed, and a spotlight followed a short thin black man as he stepped forward, the light reflecting from his curly black hair.

Peg o' my heart, I love you,
Honest I do . . .

Francis lit two cigarettes, reached over and put one in Eileen's mouth, and they sat smoking and sipping champagne.

"It was you, wasn't it?" she asked.

"I don't know what you're talking about."

"It wasn't a lady from Paris at all. You were the one who arranged to have the flowers put on Martin's grave."

"I thought it would be what you'd want. If you had been there. Maybe what he'd want."

She covered his hand with hers. "Thank you, Francis," she said.

Later, they walked to the hotel along streets glistening after a sudden shower, holding hands like young lovers.

"Eileen o' my heart," Francis sang softly. She pressed his hand.

At the door to her room he took her in his arms and they kissed. She led him inside and, slowly, not looking at one another, they undressed and slid into the bed from opposite sides. As though they were husband and wife, Eileen thought.

He kissed her, telling her he loved her, telling her there was no one else like her and never had been. Their bodies joined slowly, with tenderness, deliciously, she thought, her breasts against his chest, their lips open, their tongues twined.

Her passion rose with his, receded only to rise once more, mounted again and again, each time to greater heights than she had thought possible, until at last they pulsed together in final ecstasy.

Francis' head nestled in her hair and, after a time, his steady breathing told her he slept. She closed her eyes, dozing and coming awake, dozing again.

She heard a cry in the night. She sat up.

At first she didn't know where she was. The hospital? An injured man calling for her? Again she heard the cries of Johanson, the dying soldier who cried out in the foggy night.

Then she remembered. Francis. She reached out and turned on the light beside the bed. Awake, he was lying beside her staring up at the ceiling.

"Are you all right?" she asked.

"I think so." He tried to smile. "Yes," he said, "I'm all right."

A German shell exploded somewhere in the Paris night.

"I had the strangest dream," Francis said.

"Do you want to tell me?"

"Yes, in a minute. I have to try to remember exactly how it went first." He sat up in the bed beside her, his chest bare, frowning as he folded his arms around his raised knees.

"I was sailing on a ship," he said slowly. "It was a packet. I even remember the name. The *Eagle*. I was with my brothers, Jules and Henry, and we were talking in French though we were in America. We were landing and I was excited and afraid at the same time. I saw two old people on the dock, a man and a woman. The man had red hair and carried a furled umbrella. It was my grandfather. I jumped up and down on the deck of the packet, calling and waving to him."

When he didn't go on, she asked, "Was that all?"

"No. All at once I wasn't on the ship any longer. You know how disconnected dreams are. I was flying. Not in one of the French fighters but in a Kurkin from before the war. Flying by myself. The sky ahead of me was dark. More than dark, it was black, with lightning flashing and thunder rumbling. I flew into the storm, expecting to find turbulence. Instead it was peaceful and calm. I flew out of the clouds and headed into the sun. I was climbing toward the sun. I thought to myself, 'The war's over. There'll be no more fighting.' I had no control over the plane but that didn't seem to matter. As I flew into the sun I kept getting hotter and hotter. I cried out. Because of the heat. And that's all there as to the dream."

"I never was any good at figuring out the meaning of dreams."

"They don't mean much of anything," Francis said. "I was thinking about my brothers earlier today, didn't I mention them to you? We saw the tug on the Seine, that must have reminded me of the boat. And my brothers and I were coming from Europe when we sailed to Fall River on the *Eagle*. Of course I think about flying all the time. The dream didn't mean a thing."

She reached to put out the light.

"Don't," he said quickly. When she looked at him, he added, "I want to be able to look at you."

She turned to him, sliding down into the bed beside him. She took Francis into her arms and held him to her and, after a time, they made love in the dark of a Paris night.

Soon after, Francis fell asleep. Eileen, though, remained awake with her arms around him, holding him, protecting him, until she saw the dawn streak the sky over the buildings across the street. Only then was she able to sleep.

22

WHEN Francis returned to the aerodrome he found the squadron preparing to fly its planes to a new base near Rembercourt, a town southeast of the Argonne Forest.

"Enright cashed in his chips yesterday," Gaspard told him. "As best we can tell from what's left of his Spad, a Fokker hit an oil line and his engine froze at 16,000 feet. He tried to glide down but the Fokker kept on his tail and brought him down in flames. The buggers are still playing nasty."

"We'll miss him," Francis said.

"Captain Munson's asked headquarters to send the squadron a new piano player. We thought maybe, while we're waiting, you might . . ."

"Sure, be glad to. I'm not much good, though. I just play by ear."

The day after the 7th Aero Squadron arrived at Rembercourt, Captain Munson called a meeting of all pilots. Jerome walked beside Francis on the way to the lounge.

"Tough luck about Enfield," Francis said. "He was a cheerful son-of-a-bitch."

Jerome nodded. "I almost caught it myself the day before yesterday. I pulled a classic beginner's trick. Probably because I *am* a beginner at this. I flew up behind a Pfalz in his dead zone and was ready to put him away when somehow I put the Spad in his slipstream. My damn plane shook so hard I couldn't aim for love nor money. By the time I came around he was gone. I'll never pull that boner again."

"You're learning," Francis said.

"When do you stop learning?"

"When you're dead, not before. Every time I go up I find out something new about the Nieuport or the Huns. Or about me."

Jerome raised his eyebrows as though surprised to hear Francis admit he was still learning.

"One thing I've found out these last few years," Francis said, "is that I don't know it all. I used to think I did back at Plymouth and then when I was flying in Mexico with Foulois and Pershing. Not any longer. The more I go up the more ignorant I realize I am." He grinned. "Don't get me wrong. That doesn't mean I don't know more about flying than most of the pilots in this squadron."

Jerome listened to the drone of planes in the distance. All at once he stopped and looked at Francis.

"It's funny," he said. "I never thought I'd hear my-self say it, but when the war is over, I'm going to miss it. Not just the flying, the fighting, too. Is there something wrong with me?"

Francis shook his head. "Most of us will miss combat even if we won't admit it. I know I will. Fighting gets into your blood. We're trained to fight, we're here to fight. God, the peacetime air service is going to be hell."

"I don't know what I'll do after the war."

"More than likely you'll work for my brother Henry at Kurkin. Making airplanes."

"I don't know, Francis. After this, Kurkin's going to seem pretty tame."

"What I have in mind for after the war," Francis said, "is putting together a new barnstorming group. We'll do stunt flying at fairs and air shows, maybe make a few bucks to pay expenses by taking the natives for fifteen minute spins over the old home town. See beautiful Plymouth from the air. Maybe I'll test-fly new planes on the side."

"Sounds great to me."

"I'd like to have you with me. We could call ourselves Kincaid and Kurman, *Aviateurs Extraordinaire*. Interested? Think about it, Jerry. We'll have one hell of a time—and I'm sure your brother Curt would have approved. We won't have any trouble finding pilots, either, they'll come a dime a dozen after the war."

"Kincaid and Kurman," Jerome repeated as they went into the lounge where most of the squadron pilots were waiting for Captain Munson.

". . . life flashes in front of you," Sumner Parsons was saying. "At least that's what they tell me."

"I went into a spin last month south of Commercy," Banning said. "In a new Spad. Couldn't pull her out, no matter what I did. When I saw the ground coming up at me like the fist of God, I told myself. 'This is it.' I sure as hell didn't see my whole life flash in front of me then." He smiled as though embarrassed. "I thought about my mother. And I was just scared. Oh, God, not now, I remember thinking."

"Whenever it looks like my number's up," Hoffman said, "I try to make a deal."

"A deal?" Jerome asked.

"Sure, a deal with God. If you get me out of this one, I tell Him, you'll hear no more swearing and see no more drinking by Harold E. Hoffman. Once I promised to give up smoking for three months."

"You're leaving one thing out," Gaspard said.

"Yeah, I know. Gambling. I've offered to give that up, too."

"Not gambling. I didn't mean gambling." Gaspard smiled. "What I had in mind begins with an 'f.' And it's not flying."

Hoffman shook his head. "I never promise more than I think I can deliver."

"Ten-hut."

The pilots came to attention as Captain Munson entered the lounge.

"Stand at ease." The captain walked to the end of the room where he stood in front of the shattered prop from Jerome's Spad.

"Our biggest operation of the war begins at dawn tomorrow," Munson said. The pilots leaned forward.

"As you know," the captain went on, "the German spring offensive was stopped at the Marne. Now it's our turn. The British, the French and the Americans will attack all along the front at daybreak tomorrow, the twenty-sixth. The immediate American objective is to clear the Huns from the Argonne with Sedan our ultimate goal. There's not much time left. It's late September so the rains will start in earnest soon and end major operations for the rest of 1918. The Huns have to be forced to surrender in the next four to six weeks or we'll see another year of war."

At Munson's nod, Sergeant Ingram unrolled a large map and tacked it to the wall.

"We're located here a few miles east of Rembercourt." Munson used a riding crop as a pointer. "The 7th Squadron's section of the front extends across the Argonne from Varennes in the east to Ville-s-Tourbe in the west. The Huns will put everything they have in the air. It's all or nothing for them. We have one job: take and keep control of the air over our sector. If we don't, the Argonne offensive is in trouble before it gets started."

"Are you expecting the German tactics to be the same as we've been seeing the last couple of months?" Francis asked.

"Pretty much. Fifteen or more Fokkers in a flight. They'll be protecting their reconnaissance planes. The Germans will be sending Halberstadt photo aircraft over our rear at high altitudes and other observation planes over our front lines at under 2,000 feet. We'll have to be ready for both."

The entire squadron was up before four the next morning. The airfield was electric with excitement, tense with anticipation. Three squadrons, the 7th, 94th and 95th were coordinating operations as they prepared to send more than fifty fighters into the air.

Francis, impatient, walked around his Nieuport

as he listened to planes rev up, taxi into position and take off. He joked with his mechanics. At last Captain Munson climbed into his Spad and Francis and the other squadron pilots lowered themselves into their cockpits, adjusting goggles and harnesses and going through the pre-flight routine.

"Contact!"

The Nieuport's engine roared to life, stuttered, caught again. The mechanic ran around the wing and, waving his hand back and forth, shouted up at Francis.

"Needs more work," Francis heard him say.

Francis shook his head and pointed down at the chocks. The mechanic hesitated a moment before he grabbed the oily rope and pulled the chocks from in front of the wheels. Francis let his motor run up. It sounded good enough, he told himself. Yet he had to admit he heard a miss under the roar.

He let the engine idle, waited, was waved forward behind Gaspard, waited again as Gaspard taxied and rose into the air. A wave from the groundman sent Francis speeding between the gasoline flares. His tail came up and the Nieuport lifted from the field. She sounds okay now, he thought.

They formed in a flight of nine and climbed behind Captain Munson to 15,000 feet before leveling off. Below them the ground was still dark but the eastern horizon glowed pale yellow with the promise of dawn. The day was crisp with a high film of clouds.

Munson waggled his wings. Looking ahead, Francis saw at least fifteen two-seater Halberstadt biplanes climbing above them. He searched the skies for a Fokker screen but saw none. He looked again, trying to pierce the high cloud cover where, he was sure, the protecting fighter planes must be laying in wait. Still he saw no German aircraft except the flight of Halberstadts.

The Germans opened fire at the extreme range of 400 yards. Munson climbed toward them leading his flight of Spads and Nieuports. As Francis watched, a single Halberstadt dropped beneath the other German planes.

A Spad, Parsons' plane he thought, took the bait and charged after the German. As he neared the enemy plane, three Halberstadts swooped down behind him. Parsons didn't waver.

Francis peeled from the formation, intending to harass the Germans from behind to give Parsons time to get clear. As he climbed toward the three Halberstadts he saw a Spad off his right wing. Jerome. Francis smiled. Kurman might make a combat flyer yet.

The three Halberstadts fired at Parsons, the photographer-gunners swinging their Parabellum machine guns on their swivel mounts, as Francis and Jerome, in faster planes, slowly overtook them. At a hundred yards, Francis triggered his guns and saw his tracers arc wide of the mark. At the same time flame spurted from the fuel tank of Parsons' Spad and an ominous cloud of black smoke trailed behind the plane.

Again Francis fired and again he was wide. He closed on the tail of the tag-end Halberstadt as the German rear gunner swung his Parabellum on its *tournelle* and fired. At fifty yards, Francis returned the fire with both Vickers. His tracers raked the fuselage of the enemy plane and the German gunner fell limply against the side of his cockpit.

Francis closed on the Halberstadt. The German pilot pointed his nose up as Francis, on his tail, sent round after round pouring into his plane. The Halberstadt seemed to hang in midair. Francis thought he saw the pilot slump back. The plane dived, hurtling past him at a steep angle and, as he watched, one of its wings tore loose and fluttered above the plummeting German aircraft.

Francis looked around him. He could no longer see Parsons' crippled Spad. Another Halberstadt angled away from the flight, trailing smoke. Glancing above the German, he saw Jerome's Spad. Jerome wigwagged his wings. He's getting to be a cocky bastard, Francis thought.

Tat-tat-tat. Machine gun fire from his right rear, his blind side. Instinctively, Francis lifted the nose of his Nieuport, climbed, then dived. The slower Halberstadt loomed in front of him. He pressed the triggers of both Vickers. Tracers streaked into the German. His guns jammed. Both of them at once. Francis swore.

Climbing as he banked to his right, he worked the cocking lever to unjam the guns, yanking with both hands while letting the Nieuport fly itself. He cleared the jam and fired a few rounds into Germany to test the guns. Okay. Again he looked around him.

Over his head the American and German planes had scattered in a swirling, vicious dogfight. To the south, light from the rising sun silhouetted a second flight of Spads. Still no Fokkers. Where were those damn Fokkers?

Francis climbed toward what was left of the pack of Halberstadts, now some thousand feet above him and a mile to the west. As he reached their altitude and began climbing to attack out of the sun, he saw the Fokkers.

Seven of them, all painted the garish red of the Flying Circus, dived from the cloud cover at the approaching flight of American Spads. Francis glanced behind him and saw a lone Spad. Jerome. He waved his hand and pointed his plane at the attacking Fokkers. Jerome answered with a wigwag of his wings.

The Fokkers, intent on intercepting the Americans, either hadn't seen him or chose to ignore him. Francis smiled grimly and dived with the sun at his back. As he neared the Germans, he held his fire, swooping down at them at an angle and from the side. At fifty yards he opened fire, his tracers finding their mark on the fuselage of the first of the German planes and then on the second.

Jerome roared in behind him, firing as he came. Francis pulled back on his stick and climbed up and away from the Fokkers with Jerome forty yards behind him. An enemy plane dropped on one wing and plunged in a death dive.

The crack of machine gun fire startled him. Looking over his right shoulder, he spotted a single Fokker behind and beneath him. The plane had the black insignia of a falcon on its fuselage. Francis grunted with satisfaction. He'd been waiting to settle his score with the Black Falcon. Now was as good a time as any.

He put his nose down. No longer hearing the bursts from the German's guns, he dived, pulled back, and rose in a rolling inside loop. At first he couldn't find the German. There he was, on Jerome's tail. His twin Spandaus winked flame.

Francis climbed after the Fokker. He should, he knew, try to get behind him but he didn't have time if he was going to help Jerome. No matter how Jerome maneuvered his Spad, twisting and turning, climbing and diving, he couldn't shake the relentlessly pursuing German.

Francis' Nieuport sputtered as he lost power. Damn. The engine roared back to life and he breathed easier as he fired his Vickers'. Round after round streamed into the Fokker and beat a deadly tattoo along the rear of his fuselage. The enemy plane climbed and Francis saw Jerome slip onto one wing and drop away from the pursuing German.

Francis climbed, turning, with the Black Falcon climbing a short distance away. Beyond the Fokker he saw two planes with Maltese Cross markings plunge earthward, mortally hurt. The second American flight had arrived and planes battled across the sky in a jumbled chaos. A Halberstadt limped past him toward home as its pilot struggled with the controls. The rear cockpit appeared empty.

Francis swung his nose at the Halberstadt and fired a short burst. He closed on the enemy and fired again. The pilot turned to stare at him. As Francis roared closer the other pilot didn't move and Francis realized that his stare was the stare of death. All at once the other plane nosed over and disappeared below him.

Tac-tac-tac. The Falcon's machine gun chattered behind him. He climbed to his right, turning, the torque of his rotary engines speeding his maneuver. He heard the thud of the Falcon's bullets on his lower wing. Tac-tac-tac. The bastard was still on his tail. He dived and, as his plane plummeted, another burning Fokker fell alongside him and, as he pulled from the dive, the smoke enveloped his Nieuport for a moment, choking him.

The Spandau fire from the Black Falcon wasn't repeated. Francis zoomed from his dive and glanced around. The Fokkers and Halberstadts were fleeing to the north into German territory, every pilot on his own. Francis joined the pursuit, flying behind and below the other Americans. After ten minutes, Captain Munson signaled with his wings to regroup. Francis joined the Spads and Nieuports as they followed Munson back toward the American lines.

No, damn it, the Black Falcon wasn't going to escape again.

Francis climbed, diving and turning to follow the Fokker. His pursuit made no headway as the enemy plane stayed a good mile ahead. When his Nieuport sputtered warningly, Francis cursed, reluctantly deciding to give up the chase and return to the aerodrome.

The Fokker climbed and turned, heading at him. Francis felt the hair rise on the back of his neck. The German had seen him and was accepting his challenge. Francis opened his throttle and plunged ahead, the two planes on a collision course. Nearer and nearer the German came, the Fokker looming large in front of him. At two hundred yards the Black Falcon opened fire. Francis waited until the distance between them was halved before he pressed his triggers.

Bullets streaked past him and he heard the dull thuds of hits. His engine coughed, caught again. Was the Fokker pilot lifting himself from his cockpit? Did he intend to leap from his plane at the last moment, parachuting to safety while letting his Fokker ram him?

Francis grunted as a blow struck his left leg with the force of a sledge. He felt along his flying suit. When he held up his glove it was wet with blood. Damn. He pulled back on the stick and nosed his plane upward. Bullets slammed into the Nieuport.

Flame spurted in front of him. The Nieuport was on fire. He glanced behind him and saw the Black Falcon looking at him, his hand raised. Another plane appeared as if from nowhere, guns winking fire, spurting lead. Jerome. By God, Kurman *would* make a fighter pilot by the time he was through.

A ball of fire engulfed the front of the Black Falcon's Fokker. The German pilot pulled himself up and leaped from the cockpit, his hand reaching for the cord to release his parachute.

"Good luck, you son-of-a-bitch," Francis muttered aloud.

He nosed the Nieuport into a dive. His leg didn't hurt. Shock, he supposed. Flames darted around him, whipped by the wind. His only chance was a dive so steep, so swift, that the flames would have no oxygen to give them life. A hundred-to-one shot.

The Nieuport streaked toward the earth. The dive steepened. Down, down, down. He saw the darkness of a forest below him. The flames lessened but burned nearer to the cockpit. The heat stifled and seared him. Refusing to panic, he unfastened his harness. He heard a tearing sound to his left. A shred of fabric whipped away in the wind. The upper wing groaned, the wires sang shrill warnings. He held the plane in its dive.

Far below a German staff car appeared from beneath the trees, disappeared, appeared once more. The flames weren't going out. Another shred from the wing flapped beside his cockpit. Again the car below him disappeared into the trees and appeared again.

He remembered another day, long ago, four years ago, when he flew the Kurkin back to the field at Plymouth and saw, below him, the long trail of dust from the Mercer Raceabout. Eileen's car. Eileen driving to the field to meet him.

Eileen. He pictured her pale skin, her black hair, murmured her name. What had gone wrong? There should have been more for them, for him and Eileen. Something more and better. He'd only done what he had to do. And yet, somehow, it should have been different. From the beginning.

Francis pulled back on the stick. The Nieuport struggled to come out of the dive, faltered, the upper left wing ripping away. He saw trees, a road, the staff car, two uniformed Germans in the car staring up at him, waving their arms. He aimed the plane at them. They leaped from the car and ran to avoid the death plunge of the doomed Nieuport.

23

THE day was quiet. The stillness seemed unnatural, Jerome thought. There was no roar of guns. The squadron's planes, the Nieuports and the Spads, were arrayed on the airfield, row upon silent row.

A bell tolled in the distance, the sound rising and falling on the chill November air. Another bell pealed from the opposite direction and then another and still another. Joyous bells sending their message of peace across the French countryside.

Near one of the hangars men frolicked like children. They coated each other with mud, rolled on the wet ground, built a human pyramid, slipping and sliding as they climbed on top of one another, finally falling into the mud, shouting and laughing.

"The war's over," Parsons said as he hurried past

Jerome. "By God, we've lived through the war."

We've lived through the war, Jerome repeated to himself. At least some of us have, the lucky ones. Francis hadn't. Frank Luke hadn't. The nemesis of German balloons had crashed behind the German lines and been shot to death in a cemetery while trying to escape an enemy patrol.

"Lieutenant Kurman?"

Jerome turned to find a lieutenant wearing the wings of the Air Service looking expectantly at him. He didn't recognize him. The officer was older than most new pilots, perhaps thirty. His hair was blond and he smiled easily.

"I'm Kurman."

"Mike Ritchey." The two men shook hands. "The reason I looked you up," Ritchey said, "is that they told me at squadron that you were a friend of Francis Kincaid. His best friend, they said."

"We'd known each other for a long time. Since before the war."

"I heard what happened to him," Ritchey said. "I wanted to tell you how much I admired him. Even though I only met him once."

"Francis was like that. You weren't apt to forget him. You might not always agree with him or like what he did but you never forgot him."

"Francis Kincaid was the reason I asked to be assigned to the 7th," Ritchey said. "I wanted to fly with him. To fight alongside him. Now he's dead and the fighting's over. I guess I'll have to wait for the next war."

"Where did you meet Francis?"

"In Mexico. I was a sergeant on Pershing's staff on his expedition against Pancho Villa. Francis Kincaid flew one of those old Kurkins with Captain Foulois's squadron. He took me up for my first flight. I guess you could say he changed my life 'cause the next week I put in for flight training. Finally got my transfer to the Air Service. And here I am. Too late."

"It's good to have you with us, Ritchey."

"I was lucky to wangle an assignment to an outfit like the 7th," Ritchey said. "I had to stretch the truth a little to swing it. Captain Munson was looking for a piano player and I said I played. I'm not really much good. I play by ear."

They heard someone picking out a one-finger melody on the piano in the officers' lounge.

Ritchey grinned. "I think maybe I can do better than that." He nodded to Jerome. "*Au revoir,*" he said as he turned to walk to the lounge.

"See you."

Jerome crossed the field in front of the open hangars. They were empty and silent. Avoiding puddles, he walked along the rows of planes. When he reached his Spad, he stopped and looked up at the bullet-shaped fuselage, the heavily strutted wings, and the swept-back tail. After a moment's hesitation he climbed onto the lower wing and into the cockpit. Somehow the twin black Vickers in front of him no longer seemed menacing. The propeller tilted at a forty-five degree angle.

He wondered what kind of a pilot Ritchey would make. The man reminded him of Francis. Probably because of his blond hair and smile; he didn't look like Francis.

The week before the Armistice, Jerome had visited Francis' grave in a great cemetery where white crosses marched row on row over the hills and into the valleys. He found wilted flowers on top of the raw earth. Twelve carnations, six white and six pink.

Eileen. He wondered what she'd do now that the war was over. No matter what happens, he thought, Eileen will be all right. Somehow she survived.

He thought of Francis' son, Bill. He'd talk to Bill when he got home, tell him of his father's bravery, his daring, his spirit. More than anyone he'd ever known, Francis had taken each day as it came and lived it to the full.

What would he do now that the war was over? Jerome wondered. Go back to Kurkin Flight Research? The war had brought so many improvements to aircraft. More powerful engines. Packard's V-12 Liberty generated 400 horsepower. Better construction. Wood and cloth had given way to plywood and then to metal tubing covered with cloth and aluminum. The Germans, with the Junkers JI, had built the world's first all-metal airplane.

He frowned. Kurkin, despite the changes, would be pretty tame after France. "Kincaid and Kurman, *Aviateurs Extraordinaire*," he murmured. That had been a dream but he believed in dreams.

Jerome looked along the line of tied-down Spads, their noses lifted expectantly to the sky. It was a good day for flying with a light breeze sending white clouds scudding from the west. When he glanced at the sun, the light dazzled him and he closed his eyes.

"Contact!"

"Contact!"

"Contact!"

All down the line of Spads he heard the shout. The planes roared into life, the pilots ran up their powerful engines, idled, waiting. One by one they taxied along the field and, one by one, they sped past the hangars, water sprayed from their wheels, their tails came up and they lifted into the sky.

Jerome watched from the field as they formed in a V. Lufbery flew point with the others behind and above him. Frank Luke, his brother Martin, Hugh Ross, Paul Campbell, Raoul LaDou, Alfred Enright.

The drone of the Spads and Nieuports lessened as they climbed away from the aerodrome, heading north. One plane, a Nieuport, peeled from the formation to fly alone. Francis Kincaid. The Nieuport climbed into the east and for a moment the biplane was silhouetted against the disc of the sun. Then the light dazzled Jerome's eyes and when he looked again the plane was gone.

He blinked. The field was silent. The hangars stood open and empty. The planes were still aligned on the field, row on row. In the distance, the bells tolled.

Jerome climbed from his Spad, dropped to the ground and walked across the field to the officers' lounge. When he pushed open the door and went inside he found Mike Ritchey at the piano with the other pilots clustered around him. They were shouting a final chorus of "Hinky-Dinky-Parley-Voo."

Parsons and Hoffman made room for him. Parsons poured champagne, the wine overflowing onto the piano.

Bill Mackey raised his glass. "To the end of the war."

"To what's going to be the best damn party we ever had," Parsons said.

Jerome raised his glass and the others looked at him. "To those who couldn't come," he said.

They drank, putting their empty glasses on top of the piano. Ritchey picked out a melody with one hand and, putting their arms around one anothers' shoulders, they sang:

> Should auld acquaintance be forgot
> And never brought to mind?
> Should auld acquaintance be forgot,
> And auld lang syne!
> For auld lang syne, my dear,
> For auld lang syne.
> We'll take a cup of kindness yet,
> For auld lang syne!

ABOUT THE AUTHOR....

Jane and John Toombs are award-winning authors of twenty published books—westerns, historical sagas. Regencies, gothics, and romance novels.. John and his wife, Jane Toombs, edited each other's works and often wrote with one another.

BIRDS OF WAR, a story of American pilots flying for the French in the First World War, is an action-packed look at this war and the Yanks who became Flying Aces as they fought for their belief in freedom.

THE NIGHTINGALE MAN, written by both John and Jane, is a spy story set during World War I, with plenty of action in the air and on the ground, featuring double agents and a romance beset by the fortunes of war.